Dear Reader:

It is my pleasure to present *Love's Damage* by Timothy Michael Carson, an intricate tale about love, friendship, and overcoming the pain in relationships. Sometimes in life, we all have desperate moments. We panic when we think the person of our dreams is a flight risk and we do everything within our power to convince them that we are their true soul mate. But here is the thing; everything that looks good is not good for us and oftentimes the best solution is to simply let go.

Carson is phenomenal when it comes to developing his characters to the point where they seemingly leap off the pages. In *Love's Damage*, he once again earns his worthiness as a writer to be reckoned with. There are many situations in this novel that you, the reader, will undoubtedly be able to relate to and others that are so extreme that they will keep you on the edge of your seat. A lot of things can go right in the game of love, but a lot of things can also go wrong. Carson explores them all in this exciting story.

As always, thanks for the support shown to the Strebor Books family. We appreciate the love. For more information on our titles, please visit www.zanestore.com and you can find me on my personal website: www.eroticanoir.com. You can also join my online social network at www.planetzane.org.

Blessings,

Zane

Zane
Publisher
Strebor Books International
www.simonandschuster.com/streborbooks

Also by Timothy Michael Carson

When The Truth Lies

ZANE PRESENTS

LOVE'S DAMAGE

A NOVEL

Timothy Michael Carson

SBI

STREBOR BOOKS
NEW YORK LONDON TORONTO SYDNEY

Strebor Books
P.O. Box 6505
Largo, MD 20792
http://www.streborbooks.com

ISBN 978-1-59309-309-9
ISBN 978-1-4391-8850-7 (ebook)
LCCN 2010925106

First Strebor Books trade paperback edition August 2011

Cover design: www.mariondesigns.com
Cover photograph: © Keith Saunders/Marion Designs

10 9 8 7 6 5 4 3 2 1

Manufactured in the United States of America

ACKNOWLEDGMENTS

Never in my wildest dreams did I think that I'd be writing acknowledgments for a second novel. The fact that I am, is purely an attestation for everyone that has a dream and a passion. You should never give up! Do whatever it takes to acquire success and follow your heart.

I would like to thank everyone who supported my literary debut, *When the Truth Lies* (2010). The emails and the Facebook messages encourage me to continue doing what I love doing, which is writing.

In addition to supporting my writing by purchasing a copy of my books, I am truly appreciative to everyone that has told a friend, hosted one of my books at a book club meeting, attended a book signing, or came to a meet the author event. I know this is cliché, but without you—the readers, my stories wouldn't be told.

While writing *Love's Damage*, I found a new strength in my literary voice and a newfound confidence. Shaking the fear of underdelivering and zealously trying to acquire public acceptance, I now simply write for the pure enjoyment of entertaining. I write from my heart because it is a passion, and because I feel it is HIS ultimate plan for me to do so. If I can touch a heart, bring a smile to someone's face, or give someone the opportunity to temporarily escape from reality, then this is just an added benefit.

I send my gratitude to Zane, my publisher, and her sister, Charmaine Parker. Thank you both for giving me another opportunity to tell my story.

I would like to thank the staff at Atria Books and Simon & Schuster for standing behind *WTTL* and *Love's Damage*.

To all my Facebook family and friends, thank you for being my virtual street team and for getting the word out.

To Tyran Weldon, of Ty Xavier Photography, thank you for another set of great photos.

Lorenzo Turner, of NZO Designs, thanks for the website updates, and for designing all my promotional items.

Keith Saunders, of Marion Designs, I love the cover. Kudos for taking the vision I portrayed to you and successfully designing a cover that illustrated it.

Although *Love's Damage* is a fictionalized story, it is truly a testament to all lovers, regardless of their sexual orientation and ethnicity, that there is a downside to love. Love, something that is thought to bring about euphoric memories, also has the capability to be detrimental to the unsuspecting heart. When uttering the four-letter word—LOVE—make sure that you are really committed to that person and relationship. Don't be the one to keep the cycle of hurt, pain and damage going. Be the one to break the cycle.

So I leave you with the following: Be careful when allowing someone to validate your state of happiness by luring you with a superficial utterance of "I love you." If you don't, you are giving that individual the power to take away that state of happiness, thus leaving you as another victim of love's damage.

With Love—

Timothy Michael Carson

And think not you can direct the course of love.
For love, if it finds you worthy, directs your course.

—Kahlil Gibran
The Prophet

LOVE'S DAMAGE

By Timothy Michael Carson

Can't function or think straight
It's as if my everyday routine is in total disarray
I never knew I'd feel this way
Always heard it sung about in songs
Wouldn't think I'd find myself so far gone
At first I tried to deny it
Then I wanted to fight it
Always told myself that romance was for the birds
Helplessly, I found myself falling for that four-letter word

The first time you uttered you were in love,
I found myself high like I was drunk from a buzz
You promised me forever,
That you and I would now be a "we" and an "us"
Had me thinking that I was more than enough
If I only knew of the damage that would ensue
I wouldn't be sitting around dazed and confused
You were successful in making me the fool
Why did you have to utter that four-letter word?

I'm trying to understand what was true
It's as if you don't know how to play by love's rules
Told me you never really loved me
Only gave me a ring to appease me
Yet, you come around to sporadically lay-up with me
Emotionally mistreating me
Yet, I keep telling myself that you still need me
You look me straight in the eye
Saying that there is still a chance for you and I

Imagine my dismay
When I found out that day
That some random trick is carrying your seed
The very seed you promised to me
You promised her *my* forever
That you'd shield her from the rainy weather
You now belong to her,
And she to you
But what about me?

I'm told that I'm jaded
My picturesque life faded
I'm losing myself
My heart's in distress
I'm a total mess
To all lovers be warned
Choosing to play with the heart is tragic,
And in the end, you'll endure the wrath
of Love's Damage.

PROLOGUE

"Anjel, he burned you again?! How many times are you going to let him get away with this before you say enough is enough?" Shawna questioned me. She had an incredulous look on her face and I couldn't tell if she was disgusted with me, or if she simply thought that I was pathetic for allowing this to continue.

I don't know why I even bothered to tell her anything. She never took my side, and why should she? This was the second time that Mason had given me a STD. We were supposed to be faithful and committed to one another, yet here I was again having to make a trip to my doctor to get an antibiotic. I cringed at the thought of getting another shot in the ass. That has to be the most excruciating pain in the world. I didn't have kids, but in my head, I'm sure that the shot of penicillin ranked somewhere up there with childbirth.

"Look at her acting like she didn't hear you?" Kenton teased.

The two of them were my best friends in crime, and we always seemed to help one another out when it came down to love problems.

"I heard you. I was just thinking about the last time and how much it hurt, getting that shot in the ass. I still remember the way the nurse looked at me like I was some slutty whore. They never believe you when you tell them that you're in a committed relationship."

"And why should they?" Shawna countered.

"Come on, Shawna; why are you giving Anjel such a hard time?

It isn't going to do any good. He talked his way out of it the first time and I'm certain that he'll manage to do it again." Kenton put in his take on my situation.

"Wow, is this what friendship is really all about?" I interjected in jest. We all laughed. There was nothing like being ribbed by your friends whenever you were going through a rough patch.

"So, Kenton, what's going on with you?" It was time to change the subject.

"Shift the attention off of you and onto someone else," he voiced. "But since you asked, things are okay. There are problems in the bedroom, but they'll pass."

I almost spat out my sweet tea. "Problems in the bedroom?" I gagged.

"Yeah. Trevor hasn't been able to keep it up lately whenever it's time to do the do. I think it's stress related, and hopefully it'll pass…soon."

"You've been telling us about Trevor for months, but we've yet to meet him. When are you going to make that happen?" I had posed this question before and Kenton still hadn't brought his friend around. This really wasn't like him. Usually, he couldn't wait to introduce us to one of his new love interests.

"It wouldn't be such a problem if he wasn't so damn scared of acknowledging that he likes men."

"Oh no! Tell me you aren't dating a closeted DL brother?" Shawna's eyebrows were raised and she had a look of revulsion on her face.

"What is the term that you dub guys on the low?" I asked Shawna.

"Dick loving!" Both Kenton and Shawna simultaneously yelled out.

I was so embarrassed. People from the neighboring tables were gawking at us. It was like the two of them didn't realize that not everyone enjoyed crude language while enjoying a nice meal. I mouthed, "I'm sorry," to one of the women staring at us.

"Can you two keep it down?"

"Let the bitch look," Shawna's foul mouth spat. She said it loud enough for the woman to hear. "So enough about you two. Let's talk about me."

Kenton. "Okay, lil' cuz, what's good with you?"

Shawna. "I'm going to kick Ryan to the curb."

Shawna had been going through it with Ryan for over two years. He seemed to take her for granted and never happened to be available whenever she needed him to be. On top of that, he had four kids with two different baby mamas. The worst thing was that the brother was no older than twenty-five.

Shawna was definitely doing herself an injustice by dealing with him. But it wasn't my place, or anyone else's, to tell someone who they should and shouldn't date.

"So what did Ryan do now?" Kenton asked. His lack of interest was evident.

"I think he got some bitch pregnant."

"You think, or you know?" I asked.

Shawna. "You never know until a paternity test is done, but I'm almost certain. I've dealt with his cheating and his baby mamas for too damn long. I'm done!"

"Sounds like we all have some shit on our plates." I let out a deep sigh. I was doing my best to mask my frustration.

"That's an understatement," Kenton added. "Let's hope that we all can manage to make it through the tough times and work things out with our partners."

We looked at one another. Our thoughts were all the same. There was no certainty in our relationships; only time would tell if we would be able to weather the rough times, that accompanied love, intact.

CHAPTER 1
Anjel

"Now I lay me down to sleep, I pray the Lord my soul to keep...fuck that!" I sarcastically muttered to the emptiness of the room. Sprawled across my king-sized poster bed, slightly inebriated from the half-bottle of Rioja wine I had downed earlier when I had arrived home, I was preparing to call it a night.

It was another evening filled with disappointment. After being cajoled by my sorors to begin dating again, I decided to finally get out of the house and hit the social scene. I allowed one of my closest friends, Shawna, to introduce me to an associate of one of her male companions. Needless to say, it had been nothing but a waste of time. Next time, I'd stick to my strict rule of "no blind dates!"

When it came to dating, I was very old school. I still believed in chivalry. Meaning, I wanted a brother to come to my front door to pick me up and open my car door. At the end of the night, he'd walk me to my doorstep and wait for my signal on whether or not I wanted to grant him a goodnight kiss. Well, apparently my evening date, Kelvin, didn't know the rules of dating. Except for initially coming to my door, he failed to do any of the other chivalrous acts.

Arriving twenty-minutes late without a courtesy call, I should've known right off the bat what the evening was going to entail. Instead of ringing my doorbell, he loudly banged on my door like he was the damn police. His only salutation was a weak "w'sup" and "you ready?" Going against my better judgment, I pushed all caution to the side and put forth the energy to see the date through to the end. That was another mistake.

As he drove to the restaurant, I prayed for dear life that we'd make it there safely. It was obvious that he had no knowledge of what a stop sign or a red light meant. It was a struggle hearing myself think; his inconsiderate ass had the audacity to blast his gangsta rap music at full volume. He made no effort of making small talk or building a rapport.

At the restaurant, he ordered an appetizer for himself, along with three drinks and two entrees. I was dumbfounded trying to figure out where he was going to put it all. He must have seen the bewilderment etched across my face; he explained that one of the meals was for later. As we waited for our food, I listened to this thirty-something grown-ass man rattle off his interests. These included playing with his Sony PlayStation, hanging in the streets with his boys, partying, and pursuing his rap career. The only questions he asked about me centered on my current financial status.

Before I realized it, I had rolled my eyes and sucked my teeth when he inquired about my salary. According to him, I had "to be balling to live in such a *phat-ass* crib." Of course, I maintained my cool and played it off by jokingly telling him that it was a little too soon to be discussing our finances. Yellow flags were waving left and right, but I chose to ignore them. I was almost certain his next question would be somewhere along the lines of how long I waited before allowing my man to move in. Now, that would've sent me over the top; especially since I wouldn't allow any man to move into my place. To me, the man was the provider; plus, I wasn't a supporter of a man moving into his woman's place. There are exceptions to every rule. For instance, my place might happen to be bigger or in a better neighborhood. In my eyes, a man was expected to be standing on his own two feet where co-habitation shouldn't be a concern.

I'm going to kill Shawna, I vowed to myself. I don't know why I let her young twenty-three-year-old ass try and set me up on a date. It was obvious that we had different tastes when it came to men.

Forty-five minutes after our plates had been placed on the table, our waitress *finally* came to see if we wanted dessert, or if we were ready for the check. I quickly declined dessert, but his greedy ass opted for an Apple Pie à la Mode. I was forced to tolerate him for another twenty minutes as he devoured his dessert. Luckily, when the waitress brought it out of the kitchen, she had also placed the check on the table.

When Kelvin finished, he picked up the bill to view the damage. "Whew, this bill is high!" he declared. Closing the bill holder, he pushed it over to me, asking if I had it. He went on to explain that he had to pay rent, his car note, and cell phone bill.

Before I could catch myself, I dropped my guard and lost my cool. "Are you fucking kidding me? I sat here eating a salad and drinking lemonade while you woofed down a damn twenty-ounce steak, a loaded baked potato, a side salad, and an extra serving of broccoli. Let's not forget the three beers, the extra entrée, and the dessert that you just *had* to have. Now you're asking me to foot the bill when I've been forced to sit here and watch that tire of a stomach of yours expand throughout the night? It's a wonder you can see your dick when you look down without having to suck in your stomach," I angrily ranted.

The waitress tapping me on the shoulder stopped my venting. I didn't realize that my voice had escalated and the other patrons' eyes were all on me. It wasn't my intention to disrupt their evening. Quickly grabbing my purse and opening my wallet, I handed the waitress enough money to cover my meal and a tip. As I stood up, Kelvin had the nerve to make a tired comment about wanting an "independent bitch."

I didn't even take the time out to address his statement. I was elated that the evening was over. Exiting the restaurant, I breathed a sigh of relief as I trekked down the sidewalk away from Ruby Tuesday and headed toward the nearest hotel to get a taxi.

Now as I lie in bed, I started to review the night's events, causing my blood to boil all over again. Trying to close my eyes, I couldn't fall asleep. I was deeply disturbed about how tonight had gone down. During the day, whenever I was bored, I'd venture online to visit Bossip.com, one of my favorite weblogs. As entertaining as the stories were, the stories in their "Sex & Relationships" topics would have me shaking my head at some of the foolishness that people would write in about.

Entertainment aside, it was very disheartening when men were running around singing, rapping, and claiming to want an independent woman having her own. True, I was in fact one of these "independent" women, but me having my own didn't eradicate the responsibilities of a man. I wasn't selfish like some women who ran around screaming, "Why spend mines, when I can spend yours?" But I did expect for a man to take the time out to court me. Treat me to a nice dinner. Ask if I'm doing okay financially. Inquire about the last time I got an oil change, had the pressure in my tires checked, or had a car tune-up.

I remember back in 1999 when so many men were upset when R&B girl group TLC came out with their song "No Scrubs," and in the same year Destiny's Child came out with "Bills, Bills, Bills." Men didn't understand where these ladies were coming from. TLC wasn't male-bashing. They were simply saying that they wanted a man who wasn't living off of what someone else had. In short, they didn't want a man who rode on the coattails of others. And Destiny's Child wasn't asking for their men to pay their bills; they were asking for them to pay the bills that they accumulated and contributed to.

I don't know what happened to today's men, but somewhere down the line, some of them had obviously lost touch with what being a man was about. Being a man was deeper than having the physical anatomy between your legs. In conjunction with the dick, being a man came with certain responsibilities and a state of mind. This is what separated the boys from the men.

The liquor had begun to take effect on my body. Closing my eyes, a pillow in my arms, I finally fell into an alcohol-induced slumber. Tomorrow would be a different day, but with the same ol' shit.

CHAPTER 2
Kenton

The tears fell from my eyes as I sobbed uncontrollably. I couldn't believe that I had allowed this to happen to me *again*. Each time, I promised myself that I wouldn't fall victim to its alluring power. But like a crack fiend, I desperately needed another hit. My attempts to go cold turkey and quit had all ended up being short-lived. Like dirty water going down the drain, I was sucked in once again. Unable to prevent it, I found myself once again in love.

"Man up, Kenton!" I chastised myself as I wiped the tears from my eyes with the back of my hand.

It all happened so quickly. I would find myself wrapped up once again in another relationship. For months, I would give and give. As each day passed, I would lose a little bit more of myself. I would become blinded by its hidden agenda. Then BOOM! I was once again crying myself to sleep. I never understood why love had it in for me. Reining me in, I would allow it to overtake me and block out any rational thinking. When it was done with me, I would be released from its hold.

I had given that muthafucka everything that he desired. There wasn't anything that I wouldn't have done. I had even allowed him to degrade me by passing me around to his friends. He claimed that watching others fuck me was the only way he could keep an erection. I didn't understand how his attraction for me had changed so quickly after a few months. When we had first met nearly a year-and-a- half earlier, he couldn't keep his hands off of me. My silly ass thought that it was my duty to play the role of a freak. I was a firm believer in the motto: "What you won't do, someone else gladly will."

In the beginning things were great. After we were done sexing, I'd be left panting, but extremely satisfied. My favorite time with him happened at the club. As the deejay spun the latest Beyoncé jam, I pretended to give Trevor a lap dance. What everyone failed to realize was that I was actually grinding on Trevor's dick. He had cajoled me into cutting a hole in the crotch of my favorite skinny jeans and to lube up before we hit the club. Earlier in the evening, as the two of us grinded to song after song on the dance floor, my anxiety escalated. I didn't know what he had in store for me, or where it was going to go down and my curiosity was getting the best of me. I had previously shared with him how I had always wanted to do it in a public bathroom, or in the stairwell of a staircase. I was certain that he was going to help to fulfill one of these fantasies.

Imagine my dismay when he pulled me to the side and asked me to sit on his lap. "Babe, sit down on my dick," he seductively whispered in my ear. I could smell the liquor on his breath. I looked back at him to see if he was joking. Looking into his glassy, hazel eyes confirmed that he was indeed serious. I noticed his exposed erection protruding through his zipper. I wondered if anyone else noticed his massive protrusion. It was sheathed in a black condom; it was the color of black licorice. The opaqueness, brought about by the lack of light in the club, helped to camouflage it.

I grinded along to the beat of the song and as my hips gyrated in sync with the music, I lowered myself lower and lower. When he was completely inside of me, I leaned back on his exposed, sweat-drenched chest. His natural scent intermixed with his perspiration sent me to an all-time high. His pheromones were simply intoxicating. It was only our third official date, and I was fucking him in a room full of people.

I don't know what had overcome me. My lack of caution probably had a little to do with the blunt I had smoked earlier, and the three Long Islands I had thrown back over the course of the evening. For the first time, someone had gotten me to release the locked-away freak that I kept hidden. I continued grinding and bobbing while sitting in his lap, allowing him to invade my inner walls inch-by-inch until he became one with me. I knew that he was about to reach his zenith when he pulled me closer, gripping each of my butt cheeks. He grunted something unintelligible and pressed his chest to my back, which resulted in him penetrating my body deeper. I felt the condom's tip fill, and I relished in the fact that I had done something so uninhibited.

Our sex life had been active since that day. He fulfilled both my bathroom and staircase fantasies. He even added to that list. We did it on the balcony of his apartment, in the closet of a house party, and in the dressing room at Macy's department store. So I was truly stunned when we were six months into our relationship and he couldn't keep an erection during our sexual encounters. This is when I allowed him to invite guys that he had met online and a few of his friends to participate in our sex life. When a stranger was present, he always managed to remain hard. I'd be lying if I said that I wasn't bothered that I could no longer please my man without the aid of another.

I always thought this was just a temporary fix, but as the months passed, it seemed that threesomes were a regular part of our sex life. I never could understand how he could get off on seeing me with someone else. During these rendezvous, he would barely touch me. The extent of his affection would extend as far as telling me to "man up and take it like a man." Whenever he penetrated the other person, I would be filled with bouts of jealousy, but I kept my feelings to myself. The last thing I wanted was for him to become upset with me. What can I say? He had me sprung.

On numerous occasions, I tried to initiate things in the bedroom when it was just the two of us; but he would always tell me that he wasn't in the mood, or he'd give me some other lame-ass excuse. In our relationship, he was the top, which meant that he was the one to do the penetrating. I suggested that we try having a more versatile relationship where we both did the penetrating, but he quickly shot that notion down. We went from having sex an average of three times a week to almost once a month. Looking back now, I should have listened when I was told that he was more than likely getting his elsewhere. It should have been evident to me that I was no longer of any interest to him. Even with this revelation, I still refused to let go and continued to convince myself that if I held on, this would all come to pass. Unfortunately, I would never think this way again.

One afternoon, I decided to come home early from an out-of-town business trip. To be honest, I didn't feel like being bothered. I wanted to curl up in my bed and sleep the day away. I was slipping into a massive state of depression and didn't know how to pull myself out of this funk. I should've walked away from Trevor, but I couldn't. I had isolated myself from my friends and family; I breathed him, day in and day out. For the last eight months, he was the only thing that I knew.

Even today, I remember the details of that day so vividly. I entered my house, dropping my messenger bag on the floor at the door, and headed to the kitchen to get a glass of juice. Heading upstairs to my bedroom, I heard the shower running. I had given Trevor a key to my place for emergency purposes. At this time of the day, he should have still been at the office. Placing the glass of juice down on the nightstand, I kicked off my shoes, and proceeded to disrobe. My desire to ignite a fire in our passionless romance wasn't completely dead.

Completely in the nude, I crept to the bathroom door, which he had left slightly ajar. Slowly opening the door, I began to enter, but stumbled back, flummoxed by what I was witnessing. Trevor was pinned against the shower wall, being penetrated by some burly stranger. My heart sank into my chest as my ass hit the floor. The commotion that my fall created caused both of them to divert their attention toward me. My eyes met Trevor's through the steamy glass doors, and I battled to keep the tears from falling from my eyes. I wouldn't give him the satisfaction of knowing that he'd gotten the best of me.

Without uttering any words, I hastily scrambled to my bedroom and began to get dressed. I could hear the two of them muttering amongst themselves in the bathroom, but I was totally incoherent and their whispered words were foreign to me. I rushed downstairs and out of the house—my house. I don't recall much after that. But when I returned after the sun had set, my house was empty. There was no trace of Trevor. He had taken all of his clothes and belongings that he had haphazardly left throughout the course of our relationship. On the nightstand in the master bedroom, he had left the spare key. There was no explanation, no "I'm sorry," or any indication that he wanted to work things out. It was over. We were over.

I spent the next few days in seclusion with only my tears to comfort me. I vowed to never give my heart to another with the same intensity and openness that I had allotted Trevor. That was nine months ago, and I sometimes still found myself having a pity party as my heart remembered the pain that it was subjected to.

To help keep my mind off of Trevor, my homegirl, Anjel, bought me a Boxer puppy. I named her Kai. Keeping up with her and trying to train her certainly did help to distract me. But it was nights like this, when I was lying alone in bed, that thoughts of him crept into my mind. I said a silent prayer to the Man above, and closed my eyes. I was certain that it was going to be a restless evening. The coldness didn't help matters—everyone wanted someone to hold when it is cold. But like I'd done since my relationship's demise, I endured the loneliness.

CHAPTER 3
Shawna

I was on point in my fitted blue jeans and turquoise halter top. I was on the short and petite side, and they both accentuated my body frame and my cocoa brown complexion. To give me a little height and my booty that much needed lift, I was sporting my favorite pair of five-inch, open-toe pumps. It was nearing the end of winter, but I still had to look cute. Plus, once inside, I was sure that I'd do enough physical activity to remain warm. My upper body was kept warm with a light black, mid-waist leather jacket, which I had unzipped.

Stepping into the club, I was alone. I had decided to roll out solo that evening. I was at the club for a purpose and didn't need anyone cock-blocking or disrupting my flow. Making my way through the crowded dance floor, I waved at those whom I recognized and threw a smile at some of the men gawking over their girlfriends' shoulders, trying to catch my eye. I wasn't in the mood for any drama. I was simply interested in having a little fun, breaking a sweat, and leaving with someone who could offer me a little exercise in the bedroom.

There was no shame in my game. I never pretended to be someone or something that I wasn't. I was twenty-three years old and had a huge sex drive. At the moment, I wasn't the settling-down type. In the past, whenever I had tried, I tended to grow tired or bored. So I always exercised all of my options. Some people—females mainly—would classify me as a hoe or something just as derogatory. But call it what you want, I knew what I liked and there was nothing and no one that was going to change that. Plus, I made sure to always practice safe sex. So for me, the sky was the limit.

Two years ago I was this naïve little girl that thought love was flawless, and I dreamt of the perfect man that would sweep me off of my feet. Haphazardly, I fell in love with Ryan, who was the epitome of what I thought the perfect man ought to be.

In the beginning, he would do the typical. He would wine and dine me. He'd constantly tell me how beautiful I was, which always caused me to blush. Occasionally, he'd have a floral arrangement delivered to my door. He was very attentive to all of my needs. But as time passed, I fell helplessly in love with him. Looking back now, it shouldn't have been a surprise when he changed for the worse. It was as if he knew that I was madly in love with him and smitten by his charm.

Apparently when Ryan realized that I was emotionally dependent on him, his demeanor changed altogether; and although he was never physically abusive, he was extremely emotionally and verbally abusive. He made it a daily habit to tell me what my flaws were and to tell me what I should do to change so that I was more in line with his ex-girlfriends. No matter how hard I tried to please him, nothing really seemed to matter.

Like any woman in love, I overlooked his downfalls and concentrated on the stronger characteristics. As hard as it was, I learned to tolerate and worked with his two baby mamas and even played babysitter to his four kids whenever they came to visit and he wanted to go out with his boys. I bit my tongue whenever I suspected that he was still messing around with both of them and convinced myself that he'd never betray me in such a manner.

It took me two years to break away from him, and another year to get him completely out of my system and to regain my self-confidence. Now I was more determined than ever to not allow another man that type of power over me. Just like men were capable of fucking without becoming emotionally involved and leaving, so was I. In fact, it was my new sexual practice. I didn't need anyone spending the night, and I didn't want to see anyone's face when I awoke the next morning. To emphasize this point, when someone asked to stay over, I'd tell them to go into the refrigerator and to count the number of eggs. The number of eggs would indicate how many people would be staying over for breakfast.

The thought of some stranger snoring in my ear and their morning breath hitting me in the face caused me to scowl. Pushing the thoughts of my past with Ryan aside, I turned my focus back on the present moment. As I stepped to the bar, my favorite bartender, Soraya, smiled at me as she handed me a pomegranate mojito. This was my favorite drink of the moment. I liked Soraya, but she *liked* me and made sure to let me know this with every chance that she could. I had nothing against lesbians. Growing up, I had a few associates who swung that way, but this young tenderoni was strictly into the type of dick that came attached to a man and was made of flesh and muscle. Not to say that I'd never consider letting a woman lick the kitty. I was never one to cancel what the future might have in store for me.

Taking my drink in my hand, I turned toward the dance floor to scan for my prey of the evening. The deejay was playing a song by one of these young Tampa rappers that had all the chicken heads popping their pussies and trying to back it up. I despised today's hip-hop music. When did it become a trend for a man to sing about a woman having her own so that he didn't have to worry about stepping up to the plate as a man should? Where was the chivalry in rapping about how many women you sexed?

And who really gave a damn about someone rhyming about how much money they dropped at a strip club? Hell, if you let some of the women that these rappers call themselves smashing tell it, most of them would reveal that most rappers used this type of bragging as a way of overcompensating for the skills that they lacked in the bedroom.

This was something that my girl, Anjel, and I shared. To us, a man was a provider. Not to say that he should be dipping into his pockets to financially support a woman, but when it came to courting and dating, he should initiate and make the effort to illustrate that he was the man in the relationship.

I can't necessarily blame men for this new lazy mentality. In actuality, it was these so-called independent women running around screaming they didn't need a man and that they could do it all on their own that had given birth to this type of thinking. It was those women who were allowing deadbeat men to lie up around the house and smoke weed all day; and if homeboy did work, it was doing some meaningless job. Of course, let's not forget to mention that those brothers, in those women's eyes, weren't real men if they weren't fucking everything that threw her legs up in the air. All the time, they were treating their so-called loves of their lives with every type of disrespect humanly possible. Sometimes I had to shake my damn head at the standards that women held men to. Sad thing about it was that I used to be one of those women.

I sipped on my mojito, trying to erase some of the anger that I was feeling. When I looked up, I was staring into the eyes of one the sexiest brothers that I had ever seen. His skin was the color of dark chocolate, he was well over six-feet tall, and he had the brightest smile that shined through the obscurity of the club. Seeing that he had my attention, he made his way over to me.

"How are you doing tonight?" he asked in a foreign accent.

Blushing, I couldn't help but to smile. I couldn't recall a time when I had met a man that had me speechless. Finding my voice, I managed to stammer, "I'm doing fine. And yourself?"

"Mmm, now that I'm standing in your presence, I couldn't be better. I'm Farai, and you are?"

"I'm Shawna. Farai, huh? That's definitely a unique name, and I hear an accent. Where are you from?"

"I'm from the African country of Kenya. It is said that my name means 'rejoice.'"

As I took him in from head to toe, I couldn't help but to think about how I was going to be the one rejoicing when I got him behind closed doors. We engaged in small talk while I sipped on my drink. I was mesmerized by his encapsulating smile. It radiated through his perfect white teeth.

I had a fantasy about what it would be like to get it in with an African brother, and maybe it was the slight buzz I was feeling or just my horniness, but I thought that there was no time like the present to make that fantasy a reality.

I set the little bit of what was left of my drink on the bar and took Farai's hand. Gently leading him toward the dance floor, I wanted to see if rhythm was truly an innate African trait. Twisting my hips to the beat as I led him to the middle of the dance floor, I was certain that his eyes were on my protruding bouncing ass.

When we reached a spot a few feet from the DJ's booth, I went into full swing as I seductively began gyrating against Farai's body. Much to my delight, he got into the groove as well. Holding me from behind, he grinded against me until his manhood was resting between my buttocks. We danced to some of the latest jams—hip-hop, R&B, and reggae before deciding to take a break.

Leaning up against the wall, I looked up into Farai's eyes and he returned my gaze. We both knew what was on each other's mind. He was undressing me with his eyes and I was doing the same to him. From what I could feel on the dance floor, Farai was packing the type of piece that required a girl to do some pussy exercises.

As I was catching my breath, Farai flashed me his signature smile before leaning down to whisper into my ear. "Would you like to get out of here and go back to my place?"

I came here on a mission and in almost an hour, it was almost complete. I allowed Farai to take charge and lead me out of the club. I was growing moist with the anticipation of what was about to go down.

CHAPTER 4
Anjel

"Anjel, you are so damn picky!" Alexandria exclaimed while rolling her eyes.

I had just given her a recap of my blind date with Kelvin. "You think I'm picky? Hell, I can't help it that I have standards. I'm not trying to lay up with any and everything," I protested.

"I'm not saying that you have to. All Shawna was trying to do was to get you back in the game. Kelvin was nothing but some practice. Shit, you could've even used him to clear out some of them cobwebs that are growing inside of that pussy of yours."

"Okay, you have jokes, I see. I don't need a man to help clean out any 'cobwebs.' That's what my battery-operated boyfriend is for."

"You need to leave that thing alone. With the abundance of dick out there, you don't need anything that requires batteries."

"Why not? It gets the job done and I'm never left unsatisfied," I countered.

For a minute, silence filled the room as I focused my attention on the fireplace's mantle. I fixated my eyes on the original painting that was mounted on the wall in the center. It was a constant reminder of a life that I no longer lived. It was one that I yearned for. The artist's use of earth tones brought the abstract painting alive. I sometimes would be enthralled in the spirals of browns, the blocks of oranges, and hues of reds.

"You're thinking about him, aren't you?" Alexandria inquired.

As one of my closest confidantes, she knew that whenever I went into a silent spell, I was more than likely reminiscing about

Mason. "You'd think that after all this time, it'd get easier. But every inch of this townhouse reminds me of him. All the decorum brings back memories of him. Everywhere I turn, I'm constantly reminded of him."

"Have you considered selling the townhouse? Being bottled up in here isn't exactly helping you to move on."

"I've thought about it, but honestly, a part of me is still hoping that we'll work things out and get back together. I keep telling myself that he needs this time to get out and explore his options. You know, like that Mariah Carey song 'Butterfly' or Maxwell's 'Pretty Wings.'"

"Anjel, have you taken into account that this might not happen? I mean, he might have truly moved on and is happy with her?"

"He's not with her anymore," I nonchalantly revealed.

"What? How do you know this? You've spoken to him?"

I hesitated before I answered Alexandria's questions. I wasn't proud of what I had done, and I wasn't sure that I wanted her going off and running her mouth to our circle of friends.

"Well?" she inquired. Her left eyebrow was raised and you could see the furrows in her forehead. Her lips were in a straight line.

"I went by his place the other night. I waited in the shadows until he got home. When he arrived, he had some Asian chick with him."

"What the fuck? Are you stalking him now?"

"I wasn't stalking him. I was feeling nostalgic and I needed to see him. I needed to see if he was really happy with…that trick," I angrily spat out. "When I saw him with this new girl, I realized that he wasn't. He's merely being a man and playing the field."

I reached forward and grabbed my glass of sparkling Moscato wine off of the coffee table. I took a small sip, allowing the bubbles to tickle my palate and the sweetness to run down my throat. My light-headedness and my gift of gab could be attributed to the wine. I was sipping on my third glass while Alexandria was still nursing her first.

"Anjel, you might want to consider slowing down a little with the wine. The sun hasn't even set and you're almost off your rockers."

"I can hold my own!" I exclaimed as I drew my right foot up and rested it under my left leg. Looking down, I took notice of my French-pedicured toes. I had treated myself that morning to a manicure, pedicure, and full body massage at my favorite spa, which was nestled in the suburbs of Orlando in the upscale Celebration area. I was feeling relaxed and refreshed.

"Anjel, I want to ask you something, and I don't want you to think that I'm being a pessimist."

Usually when someone made a comment like that, they were indeed going to do the very thing that they didn't want to do. So I braced myself for the negativity that Alexandria was about to bring my way. "Speak your mind," I uttered.

"Why would you even consider taking Mason back after what he's done to you? If what he did to you is defined as love, then I don't want to ever be in love."

I smiled to myself at Alexandria's inquisitive question and at her naivety. She was a few years younger than me and had yet to find true love. Looking her up and down, I took her in. She was so oblivious to the beauty that she possessed. She was a book-worm that spent the majority of her time working to complete her master's degree in early childhood education.

Whenever the girls and I managed to convince her to get out and run the streets, we'd have to put in the additional effort to transform her from the nerdy, frumpy-looking girl to the beautiful woman that she truly was. She had a nice, thick frame with curves to die for. I was always envious of her small waist. Oftentimes, I found that thick women lacked curves, had a nonexistent waistline, and were plain out slovenly. Alexandria changed my misguided perception of that. She was, in fact, the complete antithesis.

"Alexandria, no one ever said that love was going to be picture-perfect. A relationship isn't only filled with happy times. Along with the good comes the bad. There's no better way for me to put it, other than to say that love hurts to different degrees."

"I hear you. That's why I keep my focus on my studies. I don't have the time or the energy to nurse a broken heart. I've seen what men put women through and I don't think I'd want to subject myself to that type of heartache."

"And when you get an itch, what do you do?"

"I never said that I didn't get my freak on from time to time. I know you and the girls like to think that I'm some goody two-shoes, but I'm a discreet freak. I have a few guys on reserve that I can call on when I need a little loving. I don't get caught up in love. I don't get caught up in feelings. Like Shawna says: 'If there aren't two eggs in the refrigerator, then you're not staying for breakfast.' So far this hasn't failed me yet."

I burst out in laughter. I was seeing a different side of my girl. A side she had done a great job of keeping undercover.

"Damn, look at the time! As always, it was good seeing you, Anjel. Keep me in mind the next time that you want to hang out. I'm sure I can pry myself away from my studies to run the streets."

"I'll do that." I rose up from the sofa and walked Alexandria to the door. I waited until she was seated in her car before heading back into the house. I was going to continue my pity party with the comfort of a chilling bottle of wine.

CHAPTER 5
Kenton

I drove erratically to get to my destination. I wasn't in the best of spirits, having been awakened at 4 a.m. by my cousin, Shawna. She interrupted my peaceful slumber, pleading for me to come and pick her up from the south side of town. Apparently she had met this guy at the club and decided to retire for the evening at his home. Somewhere in the mix of things, he had gotten a little out-of-pocket, not knowing who he was dealing with.

Although Shawna was a mere 5'4" and petite, she was from the streets of Chicago. Back in our hometown she had a reputation, and anyone who possessed any type of sense knew not to test her. She had a temper worse than 2005's Hurricane Katrina, which battered and nearly demolished New Orleans.

I pulled into the gas station where I'd been instructed to meet her and watched as she sashayed over to the passenger's side. Her long, artificial ponytail swung from side-to-side with each step she took. She looked good in her fitted jeans, which accentuated her curvaceous assets, and her breasts protruded through the restraints of her halter top and unzipped leather jacket. She looked taller, but this was credited to her black five-inch-heel stilettos. If height wasn't an issue, she would've definitely been a shoo-in for a high-fashion model.

She climbed into the car and crossed her arms at her chest. Her Armani perfume instantly perforated the air. I glanced over in her direction. Her bottom lip was poked out and she was staring out of the window. She appeared to be in a trance. This was my cue to inquire about what had happened. Not wanting to disappoint, I took her bait.

"So explain to me why I had to get out of my bed in the middle of the morning and drive forty minutes to meet you here," I demanded with feigned annoyance. Prepping myself, I realized that whatever her response, it was going to be definitely off 'da chain.

Silence followed my question and Shawna looked as if she wasn't going to answer. Moments after the silence settled, she blurted out, "I can't stand these weak-ass men living here in Florida. Their country asses make me so goddamn sick! And for the implants, if they've been in Orlando for six months or more, they're country too. If I had the slightest inclination to 'bump pocketbooks' with a woman, I'd definitely jump at the opportunity."

I couldn't suppress the snicker that erupted from my mouth at the mention of Shawna engaging in any type of intimacy involving a woman. She lived by the motto: "strictly dickly." Her bottom dresser drawer was full of dildos in different shapes, sizes, lengths, and widths. She was truly a woman who enjoyed variety and at twenty-three years old, I didn't blame her.

"Okay, so what happened?" I questioned again, anxious for her to divulge what had her pissed off.

"Check this out. I met this African dude named Farai in the club and we're getting our groove on. He was sweet-talking me, talking about his name means 'rejoice' and shit. On the dance floor, he seriously had some major skills. We throw back a few drinks and he invites me over to his place to unwind and chill out. I'm thinking 'cool.' My goal tonight was to get some good dick, and brother was from the Motherland and was packing. Well, let's just say when we got back to his place, everything wasn't 'cool.'"

I listened intently to Shawna, simultaneously trying to keep my eyes on the road, as she described her encounter with her mystery man.

"We started watching a movie and before long, he started touching on me, I started touching on him, and everything was good. He was fine as hell. So now we're getting all into it and he placed my hand between his legs to feel his erection. I liked what I felt and decided I needed to do a closer inspection.

"So I unzip his zipper, he reclines back, and I go to work, doing what I do best. When I turned my head up, this muthafucka had his cell phone in his hand recording me giving him brain. So I grabbed the phone and threw it against the wall."

I burst out in laughter and tried my best to keep control of the car. This was all too funny. Shawna had no problem playing the role of the freak, but she was a closet freak. She didn't put her business out in the streets like that so I could only fathom her dismay when she saw that homeboy was recording her servicing him.

Shawna continued her narrative. "Not a second after the phone bounced off the wall, dude was all up in my face. He was calling me all kinds of 'bitches' and 'hoes.' I told him to ease up on disrespecting me. Well, he stayed up in my face and continued pointing his finger as the spittle from his mouth made contact with my face. Cuz, I really tried. I tried counting to three. I tried praying. Hell, I even asked, 'What would Jesus do?'"

"Shawna, please tell me that you didn't do what I think your hot-tempered ass did," I pleaded.

"You damn straight I did what you're thinking. I laid that muthafucka out. He fucked with the wrong one. I don't disrespect anyone and I expect the same in return. When he hit the floor howling, I took that as my queue to bounce. That's when you came in the picture."

I wasn't sure if I was expected to laugh or not. I was generally concerned about Shawna. She had helped me through some tough times; especially when I was hitting rock bottom after Trevor. She helped me to pull myself back together. I glanced over her way, and noticed that she was reclined back in the passenger seat with her eyes closed. She was about to fall asleep and my observation was affirmed when her light snoring filled the car.

Turning up the radio, I hummed out of key to the Brian McKnight song playing on my satellite radio. I didn't have the energy to drive her back to the club so she could get her car and then head back to my side of town. So entering the freeway, I pressed the accelerator of my Lexus SUV until we were cruising at 80 mph. Tonight, Shawna's feisty ass would retire in my guest bedroom.

Kai's hyper ass would be probably waiting at the door when I arrived. She'd be ecstatic to be in the company of some estrogen and as rough as Shawna seemed, she was still very much a lady.

CHAPTER 6
Shawna

Standing in front of the easel floor mirror situated in one corner of my bedroom, I scoped out my physique. Tonight was girl's night out, and I was dressed to catch the attention of any and everyone that wasn't blind. Satisfied with the fit of my crimson-colored, mid-thigh, satin, DKNY draped mini-dress and accentuating four-inch Manolo Blahnik pumps, I was certain I'd create a buzz at tonight's concert.

After my run-in with Farai earlier in the week, I needed a weekend of pure relaxation. I didn't want, or need, the drama that men seemed to bring with them. I was in a funk. I hadn't had a good sexual release in a minute and my attitude was beginning to reflect it. As much as I enjoyed sex, I was beginning to grow tired of the monotony of club-hopping and meeting up with random guys. I was actually yearning for a little consistency—not to be mistaken for a relationship.

This evening was to be an intimate pre-Valentine's Day affair for the single and sexy. My favorite performer, Uniyah, was scheduled to perform, as well as her label mate, up-and-coming male crooner, Tyvon. The evening would be perfect if I walked away with a solidified date with one of the few heterosexual bachelors that Orlando had.

Finishing my outfit with some minor accessories—earrings, bracelets, and my favorite silver necklace, I took a spin in the mirror to ensure that I was looking good. Glancing at the wall clock, I needed to get my ass downstairs. That evening, I was rolling with my homegirl, Noeshi. Her blasian ass better not try and show me up. I had to put in some extra work with my "male sponsor" to get him to cop this outfit for me.

Some might call what I did "tricking," but I never forced a man to pay for my time or for my body. I simply set the expectation that if they expected quality, then they'd have to step up above the rest. This simply meant wining and dining me, occasionally treating me with lavish gifts, and understanding that every time we got together it wouldn't be to have sex. My male sponsor, Kyler, understood this. More importantly, he understood my desire not to be totally committed to a man that was already committed to someone else. Even though he wasn't married, he was damn near it. He'd been engaged for fourteen months. His fiancée and her feelings weren't my concern. Kyler's finances could support the both of us.

The major drawbacks with living a life like that were the many nights of sleeping alone, the uncommitted romance, and the lack of consistency. All-in-all, these could wear a woman down. In my past, I was never one to be promiscuous. I'd had little bouts here and there, but then I was longing for a true love. Now, I had a hard time trusting. My cousin didn't ease things. It was because of Kenton that I now had to question every man that I decided to show an interest in three times over. I was totally taken aback by some of the men he'd dated. Many of them could easily fool the best of us, myself included. Nowadays, gaydars were outdated and were just as credible as a lie detector test in a court of law.

Exiting the lobby of my apartment building, I stood at the curb looking at a slightly perturbed Noeshi. I don't know why she didn't ring my cell phone to let me know that she was waiting. Looking though the car's window shield, I felt my envy rising. I loved how her Asian genes were reflected in her facial features;

especially her eyes. Don't get me wrong, I definitely loved my own African-American features, but her Black and Asian heritage deemed her as "exotic" in the Black community. I, on the other hand, was merely another beautiful woman among many. But I carried what I had well and, apparently, it was appreciated by many.

Climbing into the passenger side of Noeshi's BMW 350i, I looked my girl up and down and she did the same.

"You're looking good, gurl!" Noeshi exclaimed.

She poked out her lips and rolled her neck for emphasis. This signified our transition into our routine "chicken head" mode. Whenever we got together, the two of us took hoochie and ghetto to another level. We would trip out as if we were in high school. No matter what was on my mind, whenever I got with my girl, it all dissipated and got placed on the back burner.

"You ready to do this?" I inquired while checking my makeup in the car's passenger vanity mirror. There was no way in hell that I was going to show up and not have my face together.

"And you know this! Shaunté and Keri are going to meet us there."

"That's w'sup. I'm definitely not in the mood to deal with Keri when the evening is over and she walks away with no numbers and no play."

"That ain't right, Shawna. It ain't her fault that she was raised to walk around with her nose tooted in the air and to look down on others. Let her tell it, there isn't one good man out here deserving enough to even get a whiff of her snatch."

"Shit, if she continues playing hard to get, then her ass won't get got. I wonder how long it's been since she's been laid. Her pussy's probably so dry it'd take a whole bottle of K-Y Jelly to moisten it up."

We both continued to snap jokes back and forth about the

other half of our troop. I'm sure they were doing the same. It was our style. We snapped jokes about one another, but ultimately, when it came down to it, we loved one another dearly. There was no one and nobody that would ever come between us!

As we neared the downtown vicinity, traffic began to thicken. Not wanting to be late, Noeshi, utilizing her car's navigation system, decided to venture off the interstate and use the side roads. I hated Noeshi's erratic driving when she was in a hurry, so I turned up the volume on her XM radio to divert my attention. Setting the tuner on a station that boasted to play smooth R&B jams, I nestled into the leather bucket seats and allowed the voice of Maxwell's sensual falsetto to soothe me.

I was determined that tonight I was going to make a solid love connection that would eradicate this dry spell I was in. All the fine and single bachelors should've been warned. This single diva was still on a mission, and it was one in which I was determined to come out victorious. With my eyes closed, I slipped into a world of unconsciousness and began fantasizing about all the attention I was sure to garner that evening. I wasn't conceited in the least; I was confident. I recognized my strong attributes, and I understood my weaker ones. I made sure to emphasize the stronger ones so that their weaker counterparts wouldn't be noticeable.

Noeshi made a twenty-five-minute drive in less than fifteen. As we neared the valet parking, I reached into my Michael Kors clutch for an Altoid breath mint. I didn't want to be up in a good-looking brother's face with bad breath. As the male valet attendant opened my door for me to step out, I immediately transitioned into diva mode. Lights, camera, action! It was now show time!

CHAPTER 7
Anjel

It had been three weeks since I'd been intimate with Mason. I'd sworn that the night after the club when he came over would be the last, but we had somehow ended up back in bed twice since then. I don't know why I kept doing this to myself.

Now I was sitting behind closed doors looking into the worn face of a moderately handsome, middle-aged Jamaican man. He was positioned across from me; his legs were crossed as he balanced a writing tablet in his lap. To his right was a laptop that was powered up and within his reach. His glasses were perched on the tip of his nose, and as he peeked over the brim of the frames, his gaze rested upon me.

The room was cold, causing me to shiver and my teeth to chatter. Some soft jazz played in the background and a scented candle burned. The candle had a scent of cinnamon. The décor of the room was bland. A painting, obviously bought at some department store, hung on the wall across from me. The walls were painted an unflattering sage green. It was obvious that the paint job wasn't a professional one. The printed hunter green drapery was outdated and clashed with the walls.

"So Anjel, how are you dealing with getting over your ex?" Dr. Lynn, the certified licensed counselor I had been seeing for the last month, inquired. His accent was thick. It was as if he had just come from the Caribbean. Sometimes I had to strain to hear him, or ask him to repeat himself to catch what he was asking. This was my second visit; probably the last. He didn't really offer any advice. He simply listened and asked me question after question. I didn't see the benefit of wasting my money on a therapy session where I left as perplexed as I was when I came in.

I hated being so open with a stranger. I didn't need him to judge me or to tell me how stupid I was for allowing Mason to break down my defenses and to play me for stupid. Mason always had the ability to say what I needed to hear in order to have his way with me. Our last encounter had been no different. His false promises about reconciling our relationship and setting a wedding date had instantly caused my clothes to fall to the floor.

There was no denying that I missed him being inside of me. I'd never had anyone make love to me the way that he did. Our love-making was always intense, like the volatility of a bad storm. My body was like the thunder to his lightning strikes. My thighs clamped around him as he made my body tremble. I knew where to touch him, where to kiss him, and how to match his thrusts. When it came to pleasing me, he knew the same.

With him, the sky was the limit. There wasn't anything that I wouldn't do for him. He brought the freak in me out of the dark and into the light. I thought I was everything that he'd ever need, and he promised me that I was.

So imagine my dismay seven months ago when he came home after a business trip, and out of the blue, he informed me that he didn't think that he had ever been in love with me. He shattered my already fragile heart when he told me that our six-month engagement was a mistake. As I looked into his eyes that evening, I saw a void. His voice lacked affection. It was as if he were some-one else. At that very moment, I understood what Tamia was talking about when she sang about a stranger being inside her house. Naïve, I thought that he was having a bad day, and like most men, needed someone to dump on. I had no problem being his doormat. Lord knows there were plenty of times when he served as mine; especially when I didn't get my way.

But that night was different from all the other times. There was no love in his eyes. There was no warmth in his voice. He'd uttered that phrase nonchalantly like he had come to this realization a long time ago, and now he thought he'd share his revelation with me. He'd taken all the time he needed to fall out of love, and now he was forcing me to do it in one night.

That night I rushed out of the house, determined not to give him the satisfaction of seeing me cry. Erratically driving away from the home we shared, I convinced myself that I must've been disillusioned. There was no way that he meant what he had said. I had no place to go. Due to the embarrassment, I couldn't turn to my friends. During the three years we were involved, I had devoted my undying attention to him. He was the center of my world. I always thought of us to be like an axis—he was the y-axis and I was the x-axis. At zero, we connected and were dependent on the other. How fucking stupid was I to allow him to have such a pivotal role in my life?

I drove around most of that night before pulling into a parking lot of a motel to rest my eyes. I was tired of crying. I was tired of beating myself up about what I did or didn't do. I foolishly convinced myself to give him some time so he could see what it was like not having me by his side at night. I fought every urge to return home. For once, I wanted him to stay up and worry about my whereabouts.

I stayed holed up in that rundown motel room for three nights. On the fourth day, I convinced myself that it was time to return home. I fought back the tears that were filling my tear ducts. Going into the bathroom, I showered, brushed my unkempt hair, and put on the outfit I had originally worn when I checked in.

After calling down to the front desk to inform them that I was checking out, I got into my car and headed to the mall for a day of pampering and a complete makeover. When I arrived home, I wanted Mason to see what he was considering giving up. I could be difficult at times, but what woman wasn't? In actuality, he wasn't guiltless of throwing tantrums when things didn't go the way he wanted them to.

I spent the majority of the day in the mall getting my hair done, a manicure and pedicure, a facial, and getting a wardrobe overhaul. As I pulled up to our townhouse, which was nestled west of Orlando in the quaint area of Winter Garden, my legs wobbled unsteadily as I forced myself to walk through the front door. My mind told me that I wasn't seeing what I thought I did. He had not been up these last few days wondering about my state of being or whereabouts. He had used my time away to pack up all of his things, and some of things we had purchased together, and had vacated the premises. His clothes, his office, the living room furniture, most of the electronics, and all the paintings were gone, except one. Hanging up above the fireplace's mantle was the first painting that we had bought together. We'd spent countless evenings in front of the fireplace with the dancing flames bouncing off of the walls. Many nights were spent having intellectual conversations as we admired the circles of browns, the orange cubes, and brushstrokes of reds.

I wouldn't share these personal details with Dr. Lynn. Maybe as time passed and I felt more comfortable with him, this would change, but at the present moment, I'd keep this to myself. Sitting in the chair across from Dr. Lynn, I listened to the rain pelting against his office window. I reclined in the chair with my legs chicly crossed. I had never really revealed to anyone the details of the failure of my relationship with Mason. Today would be no different. So I faked the funk and pretended that I was making great strides in getting over Mason and that I was on a speedy road to recovery. When my fifty minutes were up, I would schedule another appointment for the following month and hurriedly make my exit. I had no intentions of making the appointment.

As Dr. Lynn scribbled away on his white tablet, I excused myself to go to the restroom. Hovering above the toilet, I remembered that night like it had happened moments ago. There wasn't a single day when I didn't relive it. I was reminded of it in my dreams. It was in my forethoughts while trying to concentrate at work. It plagued my nights as I lay in my king-sized bed. My nights were lonely. Like Alicia Keys declared in her song, "This Bed," my king-size sheets required more than a queen. They needed their king. I needed my king.

I tried everything to forget that night. Never a drinker, I found myself enjoying two to three glasses of wine a night along with sleeping pills to help me get a few undisturbed hours of rest. I was even guilty of taking a few tokes from a joint—definitely something I hadn't done since my freshman year of college.

It's so easy for men to go astray and wander. As cliché as it is, they are like dogs. You let them off their leashes and they go running around the neighborhood like they never had any training. So they lay up with any and everything. When they choose to return home, they bring the aftermaths of their indiscretions with them—fleas.

I'd been burned before. When in a relationship, I was truly committed to that individual and expected them to be totally committed to me. In long-term relationships, I didn't think anyone could say that they never had a slip-up in the heat of the moment, resulting in a night of unprotected, passionate sex. Falling victim to the power of the dick, in those spontaneous moments, my lover would be sliding inside me from the back sweating out my hairdo.

My estranged fiancé was no different. I'd had to endure two bouts of chlamydia because of his indiscretions. Each time, I'd forgiven him, remembering that the tramps he laid up with were things of the moment. He came home to me. I was the one that he loved. But apparently one of those tramps had also realized his growing potential and had successfully gotten his nose wide open. She was the reason why he had decided to leave and throw everything we had away.

In my first meeting with Dr. Lynn, I recounted limited parts of this to him and he listened intently. The entire story was something that not even my girlfriends knew about. I remember Dr. Lynn rapidly scrawling notes as he listened to me recount that horrible evening. I'm sure he was mentally calculating how much money he was going to rake in on trying to fix me.

Finishing in the bathroom, I noticed that my time was up. I hurriedly made an appointment with Dr. Lynn's receptionist and climbed into my car. I was glad the rain had momentarily let up. When I finally pulled up to my townhouse, I had come to the conclusion that I was going to recoup the love that I had lost at any cost. I wasn't crazy in the least. From prior experience, I realized that you couldn't make someone love you. I also realized that sometimes our loved ones required a reminder of the love that awaited them at home.

I wasn't concerned, in the least, about failing. Pouring myself a glass of Pinot Noir, I sat in front of the fireplace and concocted how I was going to win back my soul mate and make it so that he'd never think about leaving again.

CHAPTER 8
Kenton

As I lay sprawled across my bed, I watched as my "piece" of the night washed up in the bathroom. Since the deterioration of my relationship with Trevor, I had vowed to never again give my heart away. I was only twenty-seven years old and more damaged than a canned good that had been dropped numerous times on a grocery store's linoleum floor. I would never again play the victim to love's games or feel its wrath.

"Can you get me a towel?" I heard an alto voice call from the master bathroom.

I rose from the bed and headed to the linen closet. Pulling out an old towel that I reserved primarily for my sexcapades, I entered the bathroom and handed my visitor the extremely worn towel. Admiring him from the back as he wiped off my scent, I couldn't help but wonder what was so special about him.

Normally, I was known to love'em and leave'em. Not a minute after I climaxed, I would be on my feet and pulling their clothes together. There would be no kissing, no cuddling, and the conversation that was shared would be at a minimum. Spending the night was definitely out of the question. Only one person occupied my bed and that was me. On occasion, I'd allow Kai to climb up and sleep at the foot of the bed. She was all the companionship that I needed at the moment.

It had been almost a year since that traumatic night when I had walked in on Trevor getting fucked by some other dude in my house. I was still angry, but wasn't sure at what. Part of it had to do with him disrespecting me by cheating with someone in the house I paid the mortgage on; another part of me was hurt that he had allowed someone to do the one thing that he had denied me access to do—penetrate him. Many nights I had pleaded, attempted to coax, and downright begged for him to share that part of himself with me, but he would always turn me down.

After our split, I soon began to realize how it was so easy for tops—guys who did the penetrating—to simply walk away from failed relationships. It didn't require much emotional or mental attachment to get your dick hard and invade someone else's body. Bottoms—guys who got penetrated—had to endure another person doing something that was truly invasive. Many, me included, would have to be mentally and emotionally attached to a person to allow such an encroaching procedure to occur. Don't get me wrong, there were several bottoms that could just be as mentally and emotionally detached as a top. There will always be exceptions to the rules.

Every guy I had been intimate with since Trevor, and there were many, had been my bottom. I don't think I could ever trust another with my heart again, and I definitely wouldn't allow another to get me emotionally involved. So what was it about this guy, Marcel? This was the fourth time he and I had been intimate within the last month.

"So are you going to put me out as usual?" he questioned as he headed over to me. I tried my best not to get caught up in his seductive grin, or his deep, almond-shaped eyes. I was truly a sucker for a guy with pretty eyes and, not wanting to go against my own rules, I nodded my head in the affirmative.

"They fucked you up that much?" he continued while simultaneously wrapping his arms around me. Standing face to face, Marcel rested his head on my chest. He was almost four-and-a-half inches shorter than me, standing 5'7". I was originally attracted to him physically when I happened to come across his picture on a gay Internet chat site. Something about his skin complexion, enhanced by his toned body, had caught me and kept me mesmerized.

There was no romantic story about how we met. I hit him up online that evening and within minutes, he responded. After a few notes, he had directions to my house. We both understood what our meeting was about. This wasn't a love connection. It was nothing more than a booty call. This was allegedly a one-night stand; yet it had already turned into a four-night stand.

"What are you talking about?" I casually countered. I did my best not to make eye contact with him. There was definitely legitimacy in the old truism: "the eyes are windows to one's soul."

"Let me spend the night? I realize that you have an early morning, but that doesn't matter to me."

"C'mon; you know how I feel about people spending the night."

"Well, I don't think I can do this any longer. When we originally met, it was only presumed to be about the physical, but honestly, I wasn't really trying to fuck that night. I wanted some companionship. When we met, I looked deep into your eyes and when you touched me, I couldn't help but to give myself to you. We've had sex four times since that night. Believe me when I say that having you stick that damn boa up in me isn't the easiest thing to do."

"Look, this was only about the physical and nothing more. Why are you trying to make it more than what it is?"

Gently grabbing my chin and pulling my face down so that we were making eye contact, he looked me in the eyes. Standing on the tips of his toes, he pulled my head even further down until his lips were inches from my ear. "Don't punish me because they hurt you. I'm not trying to hurt you, and if you'll let down your guard, you'll see that."

I don't know what overcame me, but our lips connected and we shared our first kiss. His tongue danced wildly as it darted in and out of my mouth. Feverishly, I kissed him back, allowing myself to once again to feel for another. We spent the remainder of the evening exploring each other. The only difference was that I was no longer detached. I allowed Marcel to lead me to the bed.

Lying on my back, I allowed his lips to kiss me from head to toe. He moved from my lips down to my neck. Moving down to my areolas, he gently nipped each one with his teeth before aggressively suckling them. Moving down to my belly button, his tongue imitated the same actions it had done when it was in my mouth. He surpassed my groin and kissed my thighs. When he reached my toes, he gently kissed the soles before he French-kissed each of my toes. Being ticklish, this was an overly sensitive part of my body. I had to restrain myself from kicking him in the face. The feeling was indescribable. No one had ever explored that part of my body before.

Sensing that I couldn't take anymore, Marcel made his journey back up to my engorged manhood. I was surprised at my massive erection, seeing that I had ejaculated no more than thirty minutes ago. I allowed Marcel to give me lip service until I felt my toes twitching. My breathing became labored, and I became light-headed. Marcel pulled away just in time to see my seed erupting from my penis and splattering onto my chest.

Wickedly, he smiled down at me as he made his way back over to me. Softly, he whispered, "So, can I stay the evening now?"

Pulling him up toward me, I kissed him before nodding my head in confirmation. After cleaning me up, he nestled inside my arms and we spooned. As we started to slip into a peaceful sleep, a whimper came from the other side of the bedroom door. I got out of the bed and opened the door so Kai could come in and claim her space at the foot of the bed. Now that we were all in bed nestled together, the three of us quickly drifted to sleep with the light snoring of Kai interrupting the evening's silence.

CHAPTER 9
Shawna

My three girls and I strutted into the event hall. The way we carried ourselves, the way we were dressed, and the strut in our walks told everyone that we were on a mission. Simply put, we were hot! We varied in shape, height, weight, and complexion. We all had different preferences when it came to men. The only common factor we shared about men was that they had to be about something. In short, they had to be on some grown man shit. We didn't have time for middle-aged dream chasers, wannabe thugs, and trifling boys that couldn't afford to take a woman out on a decent date. If a guy cringed when you ordered something off the menu that wasn't listed as a special, he was automatically dismissed.

We were setting the bar higher. If a man decided that our requirements were too high, then he could always opt to kick it with the girl around the way—the type that didn't mind going to Red Lobster, having a few dollars thrown her way to get a manicure, and more-than-likely had three or more babies daddies. Now if a man decided that he was ready to be with a grown woman, then he'd certainly be rewarded for his decision. None of my girls, myself included, were gold diggers. We understood how to treat a man. Don't get me wrong; not all of us were Rachel Ray in the kitchen, but we all could manage to do a little sumthin-sumthin. We were never afraid to reverse the tables and treat our man to an evening of pampering to let him know he was truly appreciated. We were college-educated and possessed professional careers. Many of us were well-off financially, or striving to be. Although I had a male sponsor, I still had my own finances to remain stable. My sponsor only added to my quality of life.

This was my biggest problem with women. Many thought that because they laid on their backs with their legs up in the air spread-eagle or, for the freakier ones, bent over the side of the bed, that it was their only responsibility to their men. I hated the saying: "you got to pay to lay." It demoralized the act of intimacy and reduced it to nothing more than two individuals fucking.

As we made our way to the center of the room where we had a reserved table, we garnered eyes from many onlookers. The room was filled with a very eclectic mix. The majority of the attendees were in their mid-twenties to late-thirties. I saw my ghetto fab sisters with their knockoff outfits and purses. You'd think we were at one of the Bronner Brothers' hair shows in Atlanta. Their hairstyle choices were so eccentric and over the top. Scanning the room, I couldn't help noticing the perpetrating brothers that deemed baggy jeans, boots, and polo shirts as appropriate attire for an elegant evening affair. Entwined within this mix were your sisters who recognized that, for an event such as this, you needed to visit your beautician and wear an outfit that was flattering to your physique. The brothers who actually were about business were looking very debonair. I smiled as I took in the fresh haircuts and shaven heads, alluring mixtures of colognes, and those who decided to dress to impress.

That was my weakness—a man that knew how to dress. As we took our seats, we were instantly approached by two overly confident brothers. Both were sporting the improper attire that I previously described; in addition, one had a full grill in his mouth and both reeked of weed. What made them actually think that we'd be interested in them baffled me.

"How are you doing, ladies?" one of them managed to slur. His breath was laced with the smell of alcohol. If my senses were correct, he had been drinking Hennessy.

"We're fine," we nonchalantly chanted in unison.

"You mind if we join you ladies for a few?"

Not wanting to be rude, we obliged and the fellows joined us. After ten minutes of small talk, none of us were interested in pursuing anything with either of them. They both were in their late-twenties with pipe dreams of becoming the next Jay-Z. Neither of them had any type of backup plan, means to support themselves, or a partner if their rapping careers didn't take off. One lived with his mother in the south suburbs of the city and the other rented a room in a rooming house off of South Orange Blossom Trail. When it came to children, both fell into society's stereotype of straight black men. Between the two of them, they shared a total of five children and none of the children had the same mother.

One kid was okay, but several kids with more than one baby mama to deal with was out of the question in my book. I'd had my share of dealing with baby mamas and didn't want to venture down that road anytime soon. We all were in our mid-twenties and not trying to be burdened down with the headache of having a relationship that was boggled down with the interference of another woman. As the brothers continued to dig themselves deeper and deeper into a hole, one-by-one we excused ourselves to go grab a drink and to mingle.

After being gone for twenty minutes, the brothers finally took the hint and decided to vacate our table and to try their luck elsewhere. After they departed, we all regrouped at the table. This evening wasn't going to be a complete bust. Shaunté had managed to catch the eye of one guy who had asked her to dinner later in the week. Noeshi also had obtained a pocketful of business cards. She never gave hers out and always informed the guys that she'd take theirs and call them. When she got back to the table, she took out all of the business cards and began writing her own descriptions and notes on the back. This would help her to choose who she'd actually call. That left Keri and me without any takers. Keri had an excuse. She was turning her nose up at many of the men in the room. She had a thing for the Latino men. She rarely dated black men, and if she did, he more than likely had some type of exotic lineage.

Frustrated, I headed to the bathroom. Upon exiting, I accidentally bumped into one of the most suave-looking men that I ever had the opportunity to lay eyes upon. His looks were breathtaking, his eyes were beguiling, and his aura made my legs feel like rubber. If Trinidadian-born model Keston Karter had a twin, this guy was certainly him. I blushed from the embarrassment as I apologized profusely for being so clumsy.

With a flash of a smile, he replied, "It's no problem. It actually works in my favor."

He could tell that his comment went above my head as I wore a look of bewilderment on my face. So he elaborated. "Let's just say, I was waiting for you to step away from the lioness' den so I could get a moment of your time."

The lioness' den that he was referring to was my group of friends. "We aren't that intimidating," I jokingly countered.

"You are for a shy guy like me. I'm Antoine, and you are?"

"I'm Shawna." I extended my hand toward his; he gently grabbed it and brought it to his lips.

He chuckled. "Wow! I realize that was super corny."

"I thought it was a sweet gesture. There are so few true gentlemen left out here for us women."

"How nice of you to try and put me at-ease. Would you like to join me for a drink?"

I obliged and we headed over to grab a glass of wine and retire to a vacant table. Antoine's conversation was invigorating. He was definitely a well-traveled individual. He was a military brat and had traveled all over the world. He was originally born on a military base in Germany, had graduated from a prominent historically black university in D.C., and had spent two years working and living in England. He'd been a Florida resident for ten years because he loved the hustle and bustle of Orlando. I found it astonishing that he was only thirty-three years old.

"So how about you, Shawna?"

"What about me?" I timidly responded.

"Why don't you tell me a little more about yourself? Are you married? Have kids? Where are you from? You know, the typical things that people share with strangers."

I gave Antoine a brief rundown of my simple and boring life. I was originally from Chicago, but for the last five years had resided in Florida. I was the oldest of five and hailed from a middle-class family. My traveling experience was only domestic and definitely limited. I was still in college, trying to acquire a bachelor's degree in business. It was my dream to have my own business like my cousin, Kent, and my homegirl, Anjel. I was in my final year at Central University and was determined to graduate on time. It had been a rough and expensive journey and it'd be a lie if I said I wasn't glad that it was about to come to an end.

Antoine and I engaged each other in small talk as we traded stories from our past. In the background, I could hear Treyvon's sensual, countertenor vocals singing along to a pre-recorded track. We seemed to have a lot in common. We were tennis fanatics, enjoyed all genres of music, loved sushi, and had a desire to travel the lands of Asia. Asian culture intrigued me more than any other culture outside of my own. There was no denying that the two of us shared a connection and just when we both found our comfort zone, the lights to the ballroom dimmed and the band took their seats. Playing a familiar tune that currently was dominating the radio airwaves and had managed to set a new record on several of *Billboard*'s charts, the room erupted in applause as R&B songstress, Uniyah, sashayed to the stage and serenaded us with her sultry voice.

Antoine held out his hand and I placed mine inside of his as he pulled me to the front of the stage. This all seemed like a fantasy, one that I hoped would materialize into reality. I was so tired of being sick and tired. Over the years, I had grown fatigued of enduring the ups and downs of dating. Things were getting so bad that I was contemplating celibacy. Keyword was "contemplating." Putting my anxieties aside, I relaxed as Antoine stood behind me and we swayed to the music, totally mesmerized by Uniyah's voice. My knees almost buckled when Antoine's soft tenor voice began softly singing the song's lyrics in my ear. Life couldn't be this good; especially after all of my life's disappointments. I was determined not to rush into anything serious, but only time would tell where this would lead!

CHAPTER 10
Anjel

My head was spinning as the sunlight seeped into my bedroom through the bay windows. Two days had passed since I met with Dr. Lynn. Whenever the two of us met, I'd slip into a major depression that I'd attempt to self-medicate with an alcoholic elixir. Revisiting all of my past failed relationships always sent me into a downward spiral. I was fortunate that I was self-employed and didn't have to worry about punching anyone's time clock.

I was privileged to not have to wake up at the crack of dawn, fight the horrific Orlando traffic, or have to endure a pesky boss that had a chip on their shoulder. I made my own hours and chose my own assignments. The only thing I had to be concerned about was meeting my deadlines and not being censored by my editor, who also doubled as my business partner.

That was the only benefit I loved about being a freelance journalist and columnist that specialized in issues surrounding the black community. I could choose to work whenever I decided, but my drinking binges were causing my funds to get low because I wasn't doing much working. Soon I'd have to take on a few assignments in the next few days to replenish my bank accounts. Not that I was truly hurting. Over the years, I had invested in some property that I rented out to college students. The majority of them paid me in advance using their financial aid checks. Plus, I had done a great job of stacking my cash when I was with Mason. He was such a man. He had to always be the one to foot the bill and provide for the household. We'd only use my finances on our trips abroad.

A memory of our first anniversary crept into my mind. We had flown to Costa Rica and stayed for a week. It was one of my favorite vacationing spots due to the early morning sunrises, the year-round tropical weather, and the plethora of black and white sand beaches. I enjoyed the exotic fruit and the foliage of the Latin country.

Whenever I went to another country, I always made it a point to sample their food. Costa Rica was no different. I loved the breakfast tamales, which consisted mainly of corn, pork, seasoned rice, potatoes, and various spices all cooked and then wrapped up in a plantain leaf. Their signature dish was Gallo Pinto—fried rice and black beans. They seemed to eat rice and beans in variations at all meals.

That year Mason and I explored as much of the country as we could and spent the nights making love. I remember our first night. The hotel was having a party and the majority of the guests were in the ballrooms and restaurants. With the moon above us, Mason and I snuck away to the farthest part of the beach away from the hotel. On the secluded beach, we engaged in primal lovemaking. This was the first time that our lovemaking wasn't preceded with foreplay or teasing. With his beach shorts at his waist, my sarong hiked up over my ass, and the bottom of my skimpy bikini pulled to the side, Mason fucked me like it would be his last time inside of a woman.

We were ecstatic to be able to share moments like this with one another. My heart had been through so much over the years that I thanked God daily for His blessing. That night as we retired on the beach, with the ocean's saltwater lapping at our bodies, we made a promise to forever love and cherish the other—a promise I still expected him to uphold.

The country's air was refreshing and their mountainous countryside was simply breathtaking. We enjoyed snorkeling, kayaking, and deep-sea diving at my favorite beach, Flamingo Playa. Life in Costa Rica seemed so tranquil in comparison to life in the United States.

Pulling myself out of the bed, I let those memories fade from my forethoughts. I stood up and managed to make my way to the bathroom. It felt like I was floating in the air. I needed to beautify myself before I attempted to do something productive with my day. Besides being a freelance journalist, I had a budding online magazine that was beginning to take off. I had gotten derailed with my breakup, but I was determined to get back on track.

Looking into the mirror, I didn't recognize the woman that was staring back at me. Hair mangled and tangled, eyes bloodshot red, and a face that was swollen like a blowfish. I was allowing love to get the best of me. This wasn't like me. I was usually the strong one. I could end a relationship and within a few hours, be back on the prowl for a replacement. But Mason was different. He was supposed to be *the one*. It's like the singer Monica's song "One in a Lifetime." It was as if he was that one true love and if I didn't fight to reconcile with him, I'd never be able to replicate what the two of us shared with another.

No matter how hard I tried, or what I did, I couldn't seem to overcome my current dilemma. How was I going to make Mason realize what I already knew? How was I supposed to get him to see that what we shared was real? No matter what kind of tricks the next woman could do, she'd never be able to compete with what he and I had. I was not naïve enough to think that my pussy was the end to all, but my relationship with Mason went far beyond the physical. We had an in-depth emotional connection. Our chemistry was simply beyond words.

I'm not sure when, but at some point, he decided that he wasn't ready to make a lifetime commitment to me and make an honest woman out of me. Dogs often stray, but eventually they find their way home. In time Mason would do the same, but I wasn't prepared to idly sit by until he decided to pack his bags and come back home. Like most men, he'd need a little coaxing. What better way to do so than to evoke a sense of jealousy? No man wanted to think that their ex had moved on.

After brushing away the bile taste of morning breath and the remainder of my alcoholic dinner, I disrobed. Jumping in the shower, I allowed the tepid water to heat and release the tension in my aching muscles. Today was going to be a long one. I needed to get a makeover, sex-up my wardrobe, and join a gym. The next few weeks were going to be critical if I was going to win my man back.

Exiting the shower, I softly patted my body dry and wrapped a terrycloth towel around my shoulder-length hair. Standing in front of my vanity mirror, I admired my body as I applied body oil to my skin. I had an ass that any woman would kill for. I didn't need booty injections; it was all me. My legs were tight with no hints of cellulite. My C-cup breasts were ample enough for most men. They still held their shape and weren't sagging. I'd admit my stomach could have used a little tightening. I didn't have a spare tire or look like I was with child, but a few weeks of sit-ups were definitely needed.

Removing the towel from my hair, I gently ran a comb through it before adding some moisturizer to my scalp and allowing it to finish air-drying. I didn't want to do too much to it because that would come later with my makeover. Who knew? Maybe I'd get a golden mane like Beyoncé, go the short route like Toni Braxton, or get extensions so that I could replicate Sade's look.

Heading over to my walk-in closet, I picked out matching undergarments from my dresser. Squeezing into a snug pair of fitted jeans, a cotton blouse, and open-toed sandals, I grabbed my purse and headed out of the door. When I was seated behind the wheel of my convertible, I let the top down, put my shades on and zipped through the streets of Orlando. I was anxious to put my plan into motion and to get my man back.

CHAPTER 11
Kenton

I jumped into the driver's seat of my SUV. I needed to head back over to my crib before Marcel arrived. For a brief moment, I'd allowed him to enter my world. I'd let down my guard and had taken a liking to him being around. For the past two weeks, he and I had been going hot and heavy. After much coaxing, I finally relented and informed him that we could exclusively date. Truth is, I had only told him that to appease him. There was no way that I was going to enter into a one-on-one situation after only talking to someone for a few weeks.

I was sticking by a personal vow to not give myself totally to another. As much as I was beginning to adore Marcel, I did everything to ensure that I didn't fall in love. I decided after Trevor, that it was time for me to begin playing for keeps. It was finally my turn to switch things up. I was now playing the game to get mine.

I pulled out my cell phone to call Marcel. I needed to stall him so that I'd have time to get to the house and shower. I didn't want to be all hugged up with him and smelling like sex. I had to admit, even though I wasn't in love with Marcel, I was infatuated with him. I was beginning to develop some real feelings for him.

While attempting to control the wheel of my ride with my knees, I quickly navigated through my BlackBerry cell phone. While keeping my eyes partly on the road, I managed to compose a simple text message that read: *Running late from the gym. Meet me in 30 mins.* Satisfied with this message, I quickly hit the SEND button.

It's truly amazing, the type of man that I've evolved into over the last year. I went from being the hopeless romantic to a pure player. I didn't know how long I was going to play in this game called love, but one thing was for certain, and that was I wasn't giving my heart to another.

As I entered the freeway from the on ramp, I slowly inched through the standstill traffic. I truly hated Orlando for this one simple fact. No matter what the time of day was, there always seemed to be traffic somewhere. Glancing at the in-dash clock of my Lexus, it was evident that I wasn't going to be able to make it home within thirty minutes. Blasting the air conditioner, I was hoping that the freezing air would eliminate the stench of my sexual encounter.

The smell was evident; my Internet encounter of the afternoon and I had gone at it full force. What was even more intriguing is, in the middle of him giving me head, he asked if his roommate could join us. So of course, I said, "Yes." I was surprised when he came back into the room with a very attractive European woman. I hadn't been intimate with a woman in years, but I was still attracted to them. As a personal decision, I had chosen not to play on both sides of the field. But if she was down, then I was down.

I later learned that the European woman was French and her name was Antasia. I loved her unique accent. After each sentence, she would seductively lick her lips. Not the shy one, she quickly disrobed and dropped to her knees. Eyeing my penis, she looked up at me. Her big blue eyes met mine and she smiled in approval. Engulfing my shaft between her pouty lips, she placed one hand at its base as she moved her mouth up and down. When she reached the top, she would flicker her tongue at the head. Not wanting to be left out, my Internet piece joined in. Together the two of them went back and forth servicing my manhood with their mouths, tongues and hands. When it was apparent that I was ready to ride, I was thrown off-guard when it was actually Antasia who bent down on all fours and waited for me to enter her from behind. Without any hesitation, I quickly rolled a Magnum XL condom onto my dick and threw the golden wrapper to the floor. With ease, I penetrated Antasia from the back. She bucked like a bull, but I managed to hold fast to her buttocks.

My eyes started to roll to the back of my head as I moaned out in ecstasy as I reached my climax. Sensing this, my Internet hook-up, known as Down4Whateva, pulled Antasia away and quickly took her place. He opted to lie on his back with his feet reaching toward the ceiling. This was indeed one of my favorite positions. The slight interruption in switching partners allowed my climax to subside and I now had to work again to get back to that moment of sexual gratification. Down4Whateva expertly clenched his buttocks and somehow managed to throw it up at me at the right time. Stroking my ego, he told me how good I felt inside of him and how badly he needed to feel all of me. I was reaching my zone when I felt his muscles clenching my penis tightly, and then his own dick erupted with his seed shooting onto his stomach. Pulling out and ripping off the condom, I began rapidly stroking my dick. Within moments, I was climaxing. Afterward, resting across the bed, we tried to recoup and garner our strength. I was totally spent and felt like going home, showering, and climbing in bed for a nap. As I stood to get dressed, I noticed the time and made a hasty departure to get back on my side of town.

As I pulled into my driveway, I noticed that Marcel was already there. Still seated in his car, he patiently was waiting for me. As I exited my car, so did he. I looked deep into his brown eyes and saw the adoration that he felt for me. Whenever this thing we had concluded, I knew he'd be full of hurt. Hopefully he'd be able to bounce back and not hold it against the next guy. He was truly deserving of someone who could, and would, love him unconditionally. Unfortunately, that person wasn't me.

Following me into the house, we quickly embraced in a warm and genuine hug. Wrinkling his nose, he uttered, "Baby, we need to get you in the shower because you're wearing the stench of the gym."

Coyly laughing, I refuted, "You think all this sexiness comes naturally? I was trying to make it home so that I could have more time to spend with you, so I didn't shower at the gym." I silently wondered if my humor would mask the weakness of my lie. I so didn't want to hurt him, and I also wasn't prepared to let him go. He had some type of a hold on me and I didn't know how to shake it.

With him leading the way, we both headed upstairs to the master bath, where he would draw me a bath with Epsom salt to ease the soreness of my muscles; once I had relaxed, he would accompany me.

CHAPTER 12
Shawna

"How was your blind date with Kelvin?" I inquired of Anjel.

"I'm glad you mentioned that. I'm still waiting to see you so I can wring you by the neck!"

I knew why. I'd been avoiding her calls for almost a week. "Why, what happened?"

"Are you kidding me, Shawna? What would make you think that'd I'd be interested in a buster like Kelvin? To make matters worse, the motherfucker had the nerve to ask me if I would be picking up the check after he ordered most of the menu."

"I didn't set you up with him so that the two of you could get married. I wanted you to get back out in the game and find a distraction from that trifling ass ex of yours. Kelvin was to be nothing more but a little fun. I take it from your crabbiness that you didn't partake in the fun."

"Go to hell, Shawna. I'm not crabby. I'm just a little stressed."

"Hell, what do you expect when the only thing that is giving you love comes with batteries?"

"And it's doing a great job of handling my business."

Anjel and I traded a few more jokes back and forth. It was good to hear that she was in better spirits. This was a rare occasion. I'd been extremely worried about her after her breakup. She was like a big sister to me. In actuality, she was a big sister to me since we belonged to the same sorority. "So what do you have planned for tonight?"

"Probably sit my ass in front of the television watching *Project Runway* reruns on Bravo."

"You're beginning to act your age. I know you don't like to go out to the clubs, but why don't you amuse me and get up with the girls and me for a night out?"

"I'm not really in the mood—"

"I promise, if you come out with us tonight, I won't try to set you up for the next three months," I interjected.

"Now that's definitely hard to pass up on."

"So why try?"

"I'm not. I'll take you up on your offer, only if I get to pick out the venue."

"Bet. I'll be around your way about nine tonight, so make sure you do something with your hair."

"Ha, ha, ha! I took care of my hair earlier today. Don't worry about me. I'll be up on my game. Don't sleep on me because you're in your early twenties."

The last thing I wanted to do was to "sleep" on Anjel. She was a threat to any woman, regardless of their age. She had a physique that many women would die for. In her early thirties, she had a Coca-Cola-bottle shape. Her chocolate brown complexion complimented her big, dark-brown doe eyes. She had natural long eyelashes and the perfect set of dimples. An avid runner, she always boasted about her body fat being under 10 percent.

But it was her ass that caught most men's attention. She didn't have one of those Beyoncé-like butts. Hers was taut and rested atop of her athletic legs. Her 36C breasts earned her the most attention. She always wore something that was low-cut and exposed just enough of her cleavage to remain tasteful. If she was going out with us tonight, I'd definitely have to step my game up. As soon as I got off of the phone with her, I'd make a call to my sponsor. It'd been awhile since I treated myself to something nice.

"So Shawna, who all will be coming?"

"Besides the two of us, Noeshi and Keri are coming."

"Keri, huh?"

"Play nice," I chastised. Anjel didn't really care for Keri; not only did she refuse to date black men, but she was constantly putting them down. Sometimes she'd slip up and infer that anyone who chose to date a black man was plain-out ignorant. The two of them had gotten into many heated arguments over this.

"I'm cool. Make sure you tell her not to come with all of that hatred and we'll all have a good time. I don't care what one's dating preference is; if they decide to date outside of their race, more power to them. Just don't try to make those who decide to date within their race feel inferior."

"Come on, Anjel; how many times are we going to have this discussion? Keri is still jaded after the last few relationships she's had with black men. We won't even talk about the lack of a relationship that she has with her father. Right now, she's doing what she feels is beneficial to her."

"Okay, okay. I digress. You already know how I feel on the subject. I wish she wouldn't allow the few bad men she's dated to close her mind to giving another black man a chance. She has to recognize that there could possibly be a problem in the type of men that she attracts and chooses. But let's move on."

"I agree. So tonight what venue are you considering?"

"I don't have to consider a place. I already know where we're going. We're going to Temptationz."

"Isn't that the spot off of Church Street?"

"That's it. You've been before?"

"Nah, but I hear it's a...different type of crowd."

"You mean the type of crowd where the men are employed and the women wear clothes? If so, then yes, it's a different type of crowd."

"So, why don't you want to go to our normal spot?"

"Honestly, I don't feel like being bothered by no lame-ass punks smiling all up in my face who are too damn cheap to buy a woman a drink. I'm in the mood to be around a more professional mix of people. People like us!"

"I guess you're right. I'm not trying to have some chicken head all up in my face, trying to fight me because her baby's daddy is checking for me. Hell, I really don't want anyone that has all of that baby mama drama."

"See, we're on the same page. So tonight, let's get our grown and sexy on and simply have a good time. Tell the girls to dress classy and not trashy. Believe me, the guys are far from being thirsty."

I quickly ended my call with Anjel. I loved her to death, but she had the gift of gab. Time was of the essence and I still had to make a call to Kyler. I was in need of a little more than the weekly allowance that he usually provided me with.

Pulling out my cell, I quickly texted Antoine. I hoped he'd be down for meeting me at Temptationz. I was very proud of myself. It had been a minute since I'd met a man and hadn't tried to bed him by the close of the first night. We had been talking on the phone for over a week since the pre-Valentine's Day gala. My excitement was piqued as I contemplated the evening and all of the fun that I was certain to have.

CHAPTER 13
Anjel

I pulled my convertible up to the front of Temptationz so I could have my car valet parked. The other girls were right behind us. Earlier I opted not to let the top down to prevent my hair from being in disarray when I made my entrance. It was a shame; the temperature was just right for speeding down the freeway with the top down. But Shawna would have a fit if one follicle of her hair was out of place. She could be a little too *extra* at times.

I had to admit that when she arrived to my place dressed in a mid-thigh, turquoise, satin, tiered dress, I was totally taken aback. Don't get me wrong, Shawna could always dress, but tonight she had stepped her game up drastically. I was certain that her dress alone had cost somewhere in the range of three-to-four hundred dollars. To top off her look, her hair was accentuated with bronze highlights and fell to her shoulders in free-flowing tresses. Her platinum Kate Spade t-strap sandals with four-inch heels finished her outfit. In all, Shawna had on a $700 outfit. I was glad that she had done a little research and had taken note that Temptationz was an upscale lounge.

I wasn't hating on my young soror, but I had to question where she was getting the funds to afford such a lavish outfit. She was still in college and she didn't really have a steady gig, so I was curious how she was capable of maintaining the lifestyle she had chosen to live. I'd warned her on many occasions not to trade her body for material things, but I was beginning to think that my advice had fallen on deaf ears.

As the valet attendant came to open my door, I allowed him to extend me his hand as I lifted myself out of the low-sitting coupe. I smoothed out my knee-length, silk, sleeveless maroon shimmer dress, grabbed my mini-clutch, and headed for the entrance. With the girls in tow, we were a sight to see.

As we made our way to the front of the growing line, we gave head nods, waves, and smiles to some of the familiar faces. When I got to the bouncer, I leaned into him and whispered into his ear. A smile came across his face and he ushered my girls and me into the club. I had chosen this locale for a reason. I noticed the heads that turned as we made our way to the VIP section. I wasn't concerned with turning their heads. I had come to turn one head in particular.

As we took our seats at a table that I had reserved for us, we placed our drink orders and scoped out the room. Alexandria was already seated and waiting for us. We tapped our feet and did a light bounce to the music blaring from the speakers. The atmosphere was very relaxing and upscale. Temptationz definitely wasn't your typical Southern booty-shaking club. The patrons all were professional, and I'm sure many of them could put it down on the dance floor with the best of them, but at the moment, they remained reserved. I'm sure this had to do with the fact that the majority of them had on outfits that cost as much as someone's rent.

"Damn, Anjel, I'm feeling your new hairdo," Alexandria commented.

I was glad that I had decided to invite her at the last minute. It was about time that she stopped being such a homebody and got out of the house. When she answered the phone, I was certain that she'd decline my invite and I was prepared to go to battle until she relented. "Are you serious? I was a little worried that I had cut it a little too short."

Keri. "No, she's right. You're working that asymmetrical bob."

"Excuse me, ladies," Shawna announced. Rising from the table, she headed over to a delectable brother who was beaming as she approached him. Since we arrived, she'd been preoccupied. Her focus was clearly not with us tonight.

Keri. "Ah, it looks like our little sister is smitten."

"And who is that?" I nonchalantly asked, trying to downplay my interest.

"That's Antoine," both Keri and Noeshi chimed in unison.

Alexandria. "Mmm, is that the one she met at that Valentine's thing?" Her voice showed a hint of jealousy.

Noeshi. "Girl, why are you trying to act like you haven't noticed that brother is fine? You haven't taken your eyes off of him since Shawna stepped over to him."

Alexandria."Shit, I'm not pretending. I was merely contemplating what I've been missing. Hopefully, he'll be the one to finally lock her ass down."

"Are we talking about the same person? The day she settles down with one man is the day I turn back to the brothers," Keri teased, slapping hands with everyone at the table.

I couldn't stop my smirk as I stared Keri up and down. "We all have our preferences, but don't turn your back on the masses because of a few bad selections. Remember, love is colorblind."

Keri. "I hear ya, and maybe with time, I'd be willing to travel down that road again."

We were interrupted by Shawna. She looked perturbed, like she had seen a ghost. Her eyes were wide and the color looked like it'd been drawn from her face. "We need to leave."

"What? We just got here," I protested.

"Trust me! We need to get out of here now." She was looking behind me. All of the ladies' eyes followed her gaze.

I positioned myself to see what it was that had caught their attention. Before I could turn around completely, Noeshi grabbed my arm, yanking my body back to the front of the table. "I agree with Shawna; let's get the hell up out of here."

"You all can go, but I'm staying." With that being said, I got up from the table, grabbed my mini-clutch, and excused myself to the restroom.

As I turned completely around, I noticed what had caught my girls' attention. My heartbeat quickened and I felt a shiver run over my body as I stared into the chestnut-colored eyes of Mason. My breath quickened as I took in his demeanor. There was no denying that we still had some unspoken chemistry.

I had to keep my composure. This was all part of my plan. The complete makeover I had undergone earlier wasn't purely for my own benefit. I had chosen this venue for a particular reason. I had the inside scoop as to his evening whereabouts. I knew that Mason would be in attendance, and I wanted him to see what it was that he was tossing to the wind.

It seemed like hours had passed before our eye contact was broken by his female companion. She was a sight to see. She looked to be in her early-to-mid-twenties and she was wearing a dress that looked like she had picked it up from a local bargain store; it appeared like she had allowed her cousin "Pookie" to do her hair in a makeshift garage salon. She was truly a downgrade from me. I was left to infer that she was nothing more than a piece of ass that had a great head game.

"Why should we leave? I can't stop living my life every time our paths cross." I did my best to feign like seeing him with his arms wrapped around someone other than me didn't bother me. Truth of the matter was that it bothered the hell out of me.

"Well, if you're cool, then we're cool," the ladies commented in roundabouts.

"Ladies, we're looking a little too cute to be sitting here. Let's get the hell up and hit the floor," I directed as I began strutting my stuff toward the dance floor. For the time being, my bladder would have to wait. As I headed to the dance floor, I was telling myself to remember the plan.

CHAPTER 14
Kenton

"Kenton, I don't understand why you want to play with fire," Roderick lectured. He and I had been friends since our college days in Atlanta.

"Look, Rod, the way I see it, I've tried to play by the so-called 'rules of love,' and each and every time I've gotten screwed. So now I'm all about me. Marcel is a great guy, but let's be honest; if you meet them on the Internet, chances are that's where you'll lose them."

"I totally disagree. I've been with Elle for close to four years and we're now engaged. Seems you've forgotten that she and I met on the Internet."

I knew he was going to bring up his relationship with his fiancée of three years. Sometimes that was the problem with having associates that were heterosexual. They sometimes didn't understand that things were different with same-gender-loving individuals, or in my case, "free-loving." With me, one's gender was of little importance. I would be satisfied as long as I was able to get mine. Plus, if things were so great between him and Elle, then I wished that he would explain why he had yet to set a date to actually jump the broom.

Regardless of our differences, I was very appreciative of my friendship with Roderick. Much to everyone's disbelief, a black homosexual man and a black heterosexual man can have a successful platonic relationship. It's a rarity with all the scares of black men being on the down low. I told Rod about my inclination toward men in our sophomore year in college. I was certain that he'd instantly oust me from our shared dorm room and dissolve our friendship. But Roderick lived by the ideology: "What one does in the bedroom is of little concern as long as he doesn't try to force his ways upon anyone else."

That was one of the things that I loved about Roderick. Even when I was in the wrong, as I was in this situation with Marcel, he'd never judge me. He'd remain open and neutral.

"So are you telling me that you aren't feeling Marcel any longer?"

I waited as our waitress placed our drinks on the table. Stirring my Long Island before taking a sip, I pondered Roderick's question. "Rod, I don't think that I allowed myself to fully give myself to him. It's like my adoration for him is on the superficial level. I don't want to get too deep and find myself being hurt."

"So every time you meet someone you're going to punish them for what he did to you? Sounds a little screwed up if you ask me."

I noticed how he always referenced Trevor as "he." "I'm not punishing anyone. I'm upfront with everyone in regards to being emotionally unavailable. If someone decides to ignore the warnings, or thinks that they can wear me down, it's totally on them. I only date adults, and as adults, they determine the paths that they want to venture down."

I watched Roderick take a large sip of his Madras cocktail. Something besides my love life was on his mind; I decided to press him. "So what's really on your mind tonight?"

"What are you talking about, Kent?" he casually asked.

"Come on; we've been homeboys for how long? I know when something is on your mind. So spill it!" I jokingly commanded.

Roderick took another sip from his drink and closed his eyes as he savored the chilled liquor sliding down his throat. When he opened them, I could see that his eyes were red as if he hadn't gotten any sleep or had been crying. Something was seriously wrong. Roderick was holding back the tears that were trying to push their way through his ducts. "I'm ending things with Elle."

"What! When? Why?" I rambled in disbelief.

"She burned me. I had a burning sensation exactly three days after we had sex, and I began leaking like a damn faucet. When I went to the doctor, I had to get the most painful shot in my ass with an antibiotic called Rocephin."

"How do you—"

"Come on, Kent! You and I both know that this wasn't lying dormant in her system for over three years. Plus, we've been tested on numerous occasions together. It's simple; she's whoring around behind my back."

I was astonished by Rod's admission. I had grown fond of Elle and had a great deal of respect for her. I couldn't believe that she would step out on him, but I couldn't stop from wondering how long he expected her to wait before he decided to actually follow through with their extremely delayed nuptials. Three years was a quite extensive time to be engaged and they'd dated prior to that for over a year. I honestly couldn't fault her.

"Rod, I'm going to be candid and put it out there." He nodded his head, prompting me to continue. "You never intended to wife Elle in the first place. If you did, you wouldn't be on the third year of your engagement."

Rod nodded his head in the affirmative.

"So why did you propose to her?" I inquired.

"Honestly, I did it out of guilt. I was experiencing remorse about forcing her to have that abortion, even when she was opposed to it. To this day, I don't think she's fully forgiven me."

"So now that it's out, what's your next move?"

"To move on. I'm not going to tell her what happened. I'm

sure she already knows, but this weekend, I'm going to pack my things when she's out of town and bounce. I'll stay in my cousin's old condo until I can locate a permanent place."

I remember how I used to always counsel my friends to not end a relationship due to one indiscretion, but after I fell head over heels with Trevor, I now realized that I had no idea of the magnitude of what my friends were experiencing. I didn't think it was possible to love someone as much as I loved him. I didn't know that I could feel so incomplete without him in my life. I now understood what was meant when someone said that another made them whole. I realized how much of myself I'd given up for the relationship. I'd learned since Trevor that another should never complete you, but they should complement you. They should only add to your state of happiness. More than likely, if they're given the power to complete you, when the relationship comes to an untimely demise, they'll also have the power to take away that state of euphoric bliss.

This reasoning was why I had kept Marcel at a distance. I enjoyed the time we shared with one another, but I wasn't going to allow anyone to open me up emotionally again. The next person who earned my heart would definitely be a dedicated one as my heart was barricaded behind an iron fortress.

I couldn't help but to notice the hurt embedded within Rod's eyes and the disappointment etched across his face. He was a bona-fide playboy before Elle and had traded in his player card for monogamy. From what he was now telling me, it was only a matter of time before he reverted back to his old ways. What better way to get over heartache than with uncommitted sex?

CHAPTER 15
Shawna

I was relieved when Anjel chose not to leave Temptationz. I was looking forward to spending time with Antoine. Since meeting, we'd spent countless hours on the phone, but due to his schedule, this was the first opportunity that the two of us could get up in person.

From the moment we entered the club, my eyes were constantly scanning the room for him. When I finally zoned in on him, I hastily excused myself from my girls so that I could be in his company. I didn't want to appear overly anxious, so as I strutted over to him, I made sure to take my time.

As I made my way from where my girls were seated, I could see that he was sizing me up from across the room; I was doing the same. His urbane demeanor intrigued me. Whenever we concluded our phone calls, I couldn't stop myself from pondering if he was as polished between the sheets as he was in person. I was getting the inkling that he was a sensitive, yet passionate lover. I couldn't recall the last time I'd had someone to actually make love to me. Lately, all I'd been doing was fucking; and a girl like me required more than manhandling. Most women would agree with me when I say that a man could light a woman's fire with a take charge-bad boy love style. But that was only in moderation. Sometimes we wanted to be kissed, held, caressed, and made love to. A man that only knew how to "beat-it-up" was a man, in my opinion, that needed to take a Lovemaking 101 class.

When I was within arm's reach of Antoine, he grabbed me and

embraced me in a firm hug. He kissed the nape of my neck and then whispered in my ear how good I was looking. I liked how he was staking his claim in front of everyone.

After Anjel assured the group that she was good, I had retreated back over to Antoine to get better acquainted with him. In some of our phone conversations, he always boasted about how good he was on the dance floor; I was going to test those skills tonight. As the deejay announced over the PA-system that he was going to take us back to the '90s and hit us with some jams from back in the day, I leaned over to ask Antoine if he was ready to demonstrate those skills he bragged about.

I was from Chi-town, but I was on point with my dance skills from all over. As the Quad City DJ's "C'mon N' Ride It (The Train)" erupted over the speakers, it seemed like the entire club got out of their seats to hit the dance floor. Grabbing me by the waist, Antoine led me to the center of the floor and we proceeded to get down. We were treated to Southern classics like 95-South's "Whoot, There It Is" and the 69 Boyz' "Tootsee Roll." The deejay strayed away from the Southern bass music and took us to the West Coast. Hitting us with Montell Jordan's "This is How We Do It," he brought us back to the East Coast with Salt-n-Pepa's "Shoop." Together Antoine and I worked the floor.

Impressive was an understatement for his skills. I could actually say that I had to work up a sweat to keep up with him. It was even harder trying to look cute in those damn pumps, not that I was trying to get low and scrub the ground. I was surprised that I was able to keep a smile on my face the entire time, even though my feet were killing me. But hell, if Beyoncé could work a stage for two hours without complaining, then I could endure the pain and put in a decent hour. I was ecstatic when the deejay played, "Tell Me" by Groove Theory. I was seven when the song came out, but I remember many days when my mother would croon along with Amel Larrieux. She played the song so much I had all the words memorized. Plus, the sultry groove gave me the opportunity to get closer to Antoine. I was grinding along to the beat, and he was grinding against my body from the back. I couldn't pretend not to notice his penis growing beneath his trousers as it pressed against my ass.

As Zhane's "Groove Thang" played, I grabbed Antoine by the hand and led him away from the floor. I was on the verge of sweating my hair out, not to mention that his body against mine was giving me flutters. Stepping away to refresh our drinks, I took the time out to check on my girls and to make sure they were all good. Earlier, I saw them out on the dance floor doing their thing. It was refreshing to see a smile on Anjel's face. It had been so damn long since she'd simply let loose. I was more astonished that she was able to keep a smile on her face with Mason in the same room hugged up with some tramp.

When I caught a glimpse of her out on the floor, it looked like she was causing the brother she was with to work up a sweat. I'd always known that she could do a little something, but tonight she was getting down. I admired how she could grind up on a brother, but still manage to look cute in the process. And brother was fine. She always managed to pull the prettiest of guys, regardless of their age. She made me sick—in a sisterly way.

"W'sup, ladies?" I panted out of breath.

"We should be asking you that. We noticed you trying to keep up with your boy," Alexandria teased.

"Right, I guess it's too soon to let him see you get low and drop it like it's hot," Noeshi chimed in.

"Whatever. It's easy for men. They don't have to try to dance while trying to balance themselves in a set of heels and remain cute at the same time. But maybe I need to take some lessons from Miss Anjel," I joked.

"Girl, please, you have me beat and then some."

"Uh-huh, I saw you working that brother. He was struggling to keep up with you. I had to do a double-take to make sure it was you."

"Shit, who are you telling? She was putting on a show for someone," Keri cajoled.

"Mmm, I wonder for whom?"

"Sounds like a bunch of haters," Anjel countered.

"Well, ladies, if it's okay, I'm going to head back over to my date now."

"We're good," they all managed to comment in unison.

When I got back to Antoine, he had a perplexed look across his face as he texted on his phone. Clearing my throat to grab his attention, he quickly looked up. "Hey, I was wondering where you headed off to."

"I went to check in with the girls. You should come and let me introduce you to them before the night is over."

"Sure, that isn't a problem, but I need to step outside to make a quick call. Is that okay?"

"No problem. I'll meet you back here in about ten minutes."

"Bet!"

Seeing that my girls had dispersed—some to the ladies room, some back on the dance floor, and some off on their own—I decided to head to the ladies room to freshen and touch-up my makeup.

Entering the bathroom, I could feel the tenseness in the room. A few of the ladies were looking my way and whispering to their girlfriends. When they saw me looking, they diverted their gaze. Standing in front of one of the mirrors, I started to get myself together. I was used to receiving shade from other females. It came with the territory of being on top of your game.

I pretended not to notice that one of the gossiping women had stepped up to my right. Continuing to reapply my lipstick, I could feel her gaze boring holes into the side of my head. When I finished, I turned around to address her. I was never one to back down from a fight. High-heels and a high-end dress weren't going to curb this tendency.

"Is there something that I can help you with?" I inquired with a hint of attitude.

"No, I only wanted to get a closer look at Antoine's latest bitch."

"Hold up! You don't fucking know me so there isn't any reason for you to disrespect me. If you have some type of beef with Antoine, then you need to take it up with him and not me."

"Honey, don't fucking tell me what I need to do. I'm standing in front of you so apparently, it's you that I have the problem with."

I couldn't have asked for better timing when Keri and Noeshi both came and stood next to me. I was certain they could sense that something was about to go down; I was already pulling my hair back in a ponytail.

"Is there a problem?" Keri questioned as she stepped to the unnamed woman.

"Am I talking to you?" she snapped back.

"No, but you're all up in my girl's face and we're rolling five deep so if you're looking to start a little trouble, we can certainly help you out with that."

"This bitch thinks that we're a little too bourgeois to snap a few heads back," Noeshi chimed in.

Taking the three of us in and noticing that her girls weren't coming to her rescue, the still unnamed sister spat out, "You tell your girl that she needs to close her fucking legs to married men.

She up in here grinding all up on my sister's husband and has no fucking shame in her game." With that being said, homegirl retreated but stopped to utter, "Who you think his ass ran outside to meet?"

I couldn't stifle my anger. I had been duped again. I realized that this shit was too good to be true. Taking a deep breath, my girls' attempts to calm me down were futile. Heading out of the bathroom, I headed to the club's exit. If Antoine was indeed outside meeting with his "wife," I was going to make sure that he'd regret publicly humiliating me.

CHAPTER 16
Anjel

I was relieved when the ladies left me to go on and do their own thing. They didn't know that running into Mason was no accident. I knew this was one of the places he frequented. There'd been plenty of nights where I had followed him to the club and watched him leave with some random girl. Plus, his assistant, Inola, had confirmed he'd be here. She had omitted the fact that he wouldn't be alone. I wasn't sure what was getting into him as of late. I could only assume that he was the latest one to discover that he was a sex addict. He was now following in the footsteps of Tiger Woods and Eric Benét.

I'd allowed him to have his fun long enough. The two of us weren't getting any younger and we had things to accomplish. I missed what we shared and what we were working to acquire as one of Orlando's power couples.

I ran my fingers through my hair. It was going to take a little time for me to get used to not having my free-flowing, shoulder-length tresses. I don't know what prompted most women to chop off their hair after a bad breakup. I wonder if Angela Bassett in *Waiting to Exhale* was the catalyst for this trend.

As I headed over to the bar in the VIP section to refresh my drink, I felt the eyes of many of the male patrons upon me. More than likely, they were watching my ass sashay from side-to-side. Even though I worked from home, I still took pride in my appearance. Prior to my break-up, I made an attempt to hit the gym at least three times a week. Approaching 30, everything on my body was still taut and smooth. Now ask me if it would remain this way after popping out a baby or two and the answer might be different.

As I waited for the bartender to finish with his current client, I felt a hand on the small of my back. I didn't need to look over my shoulder to know whose hand it was. I could recognize the invigorating smell of his cologne, Versace Man. There was something about the mixture of lemon, rosewood, and cedar leaves that always awakened my senses. I couldn't determine if his natural body scent complemented the cologne or if the cologne simply accentuated his scent.

I took a deep breath and told myself not to fall for his charisma. I don't know what it was about him that had me so enthralled. Every part of me was saying that I needed to walk away and leave him alone entirely, but I simply couldn't. It was unexplainable. I'd been in love before. I'd had my heart broken too many times to remember, and yet had managed to let go of those memories and the pain. So I couldn't understand why this time it was any different.

I turned slightly to my right and gazed into those chestnut eyes of his. His beaming smile made my heart flutter. It was like he understood what he did to me and, for this, I hated him. I hated him for not loving me. I hated him for not letting me go.

"It's nice to see you, Anjel," his tenor voice stated with authority.

At the sound of his voice, just like the cheesy cliché, I swear I felt lighthearted and weak in the knees. But I caught myself before I fell under his spell. I had to remember that those chestnut eyes were looking at some other woman, that his smile was no longer exclusive to me, and that his authoritative voice was whispering sweet nothings and making promises of forever to someone else.

"You as well, Mason. How have you been?" I inquired, turning my head back to the bar before he could answer.

"What can I get'cha?" the bartender asked, never breaking his stride.

"She'll have an Absolut Mixer," Mason interjected on my behalf, "and I'll have a Dakota."

It felt like old times, with him ordering my drink. I pulled myself from Memory Lane, remembering that this wasn't the time to abandon my plan. "Shouldn't you be getting back to your lady friend?"

"Is that where you want me to be?"

"Don't answer a question with a question. I don't do drama, and I don't need for you to be bringing any my way."

"Relax. We're cool. Regardless of how things ended, I still have love for you."

"Love? Is that what you call how you ended things? I'd hate to see what you'd have done if you hated me."

"Anjel, have you ever considered that it hurt me just as much to leave the way I did? We had problems. We needed time apart from one another."

"What are these problems that you are referring to? Our relationship wasn't plagued with yelling or fighting."

"You're right, but it was one that lacked truth. I loved you, Anjel, but I didn't love you the way that you wanted me to love you."

"And how was that, Mason?"

"You were ready to walk down the aisle, have kids, and buy accompanying graves. The whole thing was a little too much for me. Things were so much better before we got engaged."

We were interrupted momentarily as the bartender placed our drinks in front of us. "That'll be eighteen dollars!" he yelled out, already moving down to take the next order. I watched as Mason took out a twenty and placed it on the bar. I didn't want him buying me a drink, but if I even attempted to foot the bill, it'd complicate things between the two of us. Mason was such a man's man. He always had to be in control and the dominant one.

"So why did you do it?"

"What, propose to you?" he asked. His left eyebrow was slightly raised as if he was puzzled by the question.

"Yes. Why did you propose?"

"How could I not? You were good at leaving indirect and subtle hints. So, I guess you could say I did it because I felt like it was expected of me."

I tried to contain my anger. I didn't know how much of what he was saying was true or not. His eyes were telling a different story than what he was spitting in my face. The way we made love, not fucked, told a different story. That type of chemistry couldn't be fabricated. "Is that right, Mason?"

He broke our glance by taking a sip on his drink. "I like the new haircut."

"Thank you. Decided I needed a change. You know, switch it up a little."

"Well, it works," he commented. "It brings out your facial features more."

"Hey, baby, what's taking you so long?" his female companion interrupted. She made sure to let it be known that she was staking a claim on Mason by wrapping her arms around his waist.

"I'm sorry, Rhonda. I was talking to an old friend."

"It's Wanda," she annoyingly retorted.

Inside, I couldn't compress my laughter. Here she was giving up her pussy and he didn't even know her name. Sometimes broads left me baffled. I wish a man would try that mess with me; by the time the evening was over, he'd never forget my name or face.

"Uh, I'm sorry. I've had a little too much to drink," Mason retorted while mockingly slurring his words. "Anjel, it was nice seeing you again."

I watched as the two of them walked away with Mason's hand on the small of her back, and I wistfully remembered how he used to do that for me. Deciding that I was ready to leave, I began to seek out my girls.

CHAPTER 17
Kenton

I was still in a state in disbelief at my boy, Rod's, revelation about his fiancée. Even with their prolonged engagement, I truly hoped the two of them would go the long run. Meeting with him did nothing good for my current state of mind. All it did was affirm why I couldn't trust my heart with another. What was the point? It was sure to end with someone being left distraught and lovesick.

Relaxing on the sofa with my feet resting in Marcel's lap, I took a swig from my bottle of Heineken. Kai was lying on the floor right underneath me. She was pretty much exhausted. She had accompanied the two of us at Lake Eola Park. She was the center of attention, and she loved it. She ran around on her leash with her tongue out and her mouth fixed in a wide, clown grin. She always looked like she was laughing. When we brought her back home so that we could shower and head out, she immediately plopped herself on the hardwood floor of the dining room. She didn't even bother to trek upstairs and relax on her futon in her room. Some laughed at me because my dog had her own room and bed.

My eyes were stuck on the television. I was half paying attention to the show displaying on the fifty-two-inch LCD screen. Marcel loved watching the reality show *The Real Housewives of Atlanta* on the Bravo network. I told him before we left that I'd set the digital cable box to record it, but he'd insisted that we get back in time to watch it live. It was no big deal to me; I was more than happy to oblige. So after enjoying an early evening movie at Cinemark Festival Bay Theaters, we headed to Bombay Café on Doss Avenue, which specialized in Indian street cuisine. I loved cuisines from other cultures, and Indian ranked at the top along with Thai food in my book.

I ran my hand over Kai's gigantic head to stir her. She was snoring loudly as she normally did when she was fatigued. I looked over at Marcel who was completely engrossed in his television show and contemplated if I would be able to love him in the manner that he needed me to. I loved being in love. I even loved the concept of being in love, but I didn't love the hurt and pain that often accompanied it. I was reminded of a song that Gladys Knight recorded called "Love Hurts." At the time I could never relate to the lyrics, but now that I'd grown and experienced love, I understood what she meant.

Never in my wildest dreams would I have thought that something that was depicted to be so angelic and blissful could cause the type of heartache and pain that I'd endured in my short twenty-seven years. I wished someone would've given me the lowdown on this thing called love and told me how to protect myself. Unfortunately, like most, I had to learn the rules of love the hard way. But now that I had learned them, and felt its wrath, I was more determined to play the game of love on my own terms.

Looking at the clock, I knew that Marcel would want to retire for the night because he had work in the morning. That was one of the things that I loved about being my own boss. I worked whenever I wanted to work and didn't have to worry about a set schedule, although my hours could be a little unconventional depending on my clients' demands.

If anyone had asked me five years ago if I thought I'd be a CEO by the age of twenty-four, I'd have looked at them like they were stupid. But there I was, CEO of my own web and graphic design company. I had a staff of eight that worked remotely from their own homes, we catered to many small businesses, and were even targeting some of the Fortune 500 companies that were looking to cut their expenses by outsourcing.

Ideally, Marcel would be the type of guy I'd date, if I were looking to settle down. He was extremely smart. He had a master's degree in project management, had a broad scope on politics, current events, and economics, and he was a strong proponent of monogamy. Many nights, I asked myself, "Why can't you let go of the past and live for the future?"

It wasn't his fault that I'd been hurt before. It wasn't his fault that I'd been taken for granted, misused, or dealt an unfair hand in love. Even with this realization, I understood that I couldn't allow myself to fall in love again. In my heart, love no longer lived.

"Hey, babe," Marcel called, pulling me away from my thoughts. "I'm going to call it a night and head to my crib."

"You're not spending the night?" I asked, slightly surprised. Normally, I'd have to beg for some free time whenever he came over. So to hear him say that he wasn't spending the evening was a little out of character.

"Nah, not tonight. I didn't bring my clothes, and I need to go over some things in the morning before I go in. Remember, tomorrow I have to make a presentation in front of the board of directors and the investors."

"I don't envy your job in the least," I admitted. "Is your presentation ready?"

"Pretty much; I just hate speaking in front of people. It bothers me to have all those eyes staring at me, like they're trying to bore a hole into me. Not to mention, all the eyes of your peers hoping that you'll make a mistake so that they can step in and take your place. The corporate world is ugly."

"Especially in your field, but I'm sure you'll do fine." I removed my feet from his lap and stood up, stretching my arms over my head. Kai didn't even bother to get up. Normally, she'd be all over Marcel whenever she realized that he was about to leave.

I grabbed one of Marcel's hands and walked him to the door. Embracing him in a hug, I placed my hands on the side of his waist and he placed his around my neck; we exchanged a goodnight kiss. Feeling his body against mine caused my penis to stir. There was no denying that sex with him was off the chain. I could tell he could feel the bulging in my pants.

"Looks like someone doesn't want me to leave," he teased, squeezing my growing protrusion through my cotton lounge pants.

"Of course someone doesn't. Maybe you should give him a goodnight kiss before you go."

"Is that right?" he asked, placing his hand inside of my pants. We began kissing again as he fondled my semi-erect penis and tried to work it out of my pants.

When it was free, he broke our kiss, got down on his knees, and provided me with some of the best lip service that I'd ever experienced. The way he worked the muscles in his jaw, the way he twisted and twirled his tongue, made my head spin. I had to steady myself by leaning back against the wall. Fifteen minutes later, he rose up from his knees and headed into the half-bathroom to dispose of my seed.

That was one thing about him I was beginning to grow fond of. He was never too tired or too busy to make sure that I was satisfied sexually. When he returned from the bathroom, I gave him another firm hug and kiss on the neck before he departed for the evening.

Walking back into the living room, Kai hadn't been stirred. I bent down to wake her up so she'd follow me upstairs. As we made our way, I turned off the lights and turned on the alarm system. Tonight, I'd have no problem falling asleep, thanks to Marcel.

CHAPTER 18
Shawna

When I exited the club, I abruptly stopped to see where Antoine had run off to. I didn't need to look long; I could hear a female's voice yelling at the top of her lungs. I followed the voice to the side of the club, toward the adjacent parking lot, with my girls right behind me. When I was in full view of the angered female, I saw her pointing her finger in Antoine's face and shoving him.

I could see the tears in her eyes that she was desperately trying to hold back. She was asking Antoine for answers. She wanted to know why he was out at the club hugged up with someone else while she was stuck at home with their kids. She wanted to know why she was trying to build a future for them when all he wanted to do was to destroy everything with a quick nut.

I really pitied the woman. She was another victim of love, and she'd probably never fully recover from the damage it'd do to her heart. I'd come outside to rip Antoine a new one, but I could see there was no need to even do that. He was getting his at that very moment. Just as I turned my back to leave, I heard Antoine howl out in agony. Turning around, I saw Antoine on the ground and the woman hovering above him. She was pressing one of her stilletoed feet against his neck.

"We're done. I'm tired of having to keep tabs on you, having to chase after you, and putting up with all of your fucking indiscretions," she bellowed. Her voice was controlled and had an authoritative tone. She was a woman scorned one time too many.

For her sake, I really hoped that she was serious. There's simply too much danger involved in loving someone that doesn't practice monogamy. As I walked back to the club, Noeshi wrapped her arm around my shoulders to comfort me. They all realized how excited I had been to finally find someone that had me as besotted as Antoine had. Oh well, another one bites the dust, I concluded. I needed to get inside and find Anjel; I was so damn ready to bounce.

Just as the bouncer checked our club bracelets for reentry into the club, Anjel came barreling out with Alexandria closely in tow. She had a displeased look on her face. I didn't need to be a rocket scientist to know that her displeasure had something to do with Mason. No matter how hard she tried to front, she had a jones for him that simply wouldn't die.

"Ladies, you ready to fly this coop?" she asked.

"Yeah, let's get the hell out of here," I emotionlessly spat out.

We waited for the valet attendants to bring the cars around. Normally, we'd all leave and meet up at a twenty-four-hour diner, but tonight, we all wanted to call it a night. I wanted to get to my apartment and cry myself to sleep. I was by far no angel, but it seemed like the harder I tried at love, the more I failed. I didn't understand all the games that men chose to play, not to say that women didn't play them as well.

I remained silent as Anjel drove me to her place so I could pick up my car. We both had things on our mind that we didn't care to discuss. I glanced at the lit LCD of her satellite radio console. I forced back a tear as they played a song from back in the day. The late R&B singer Aaliyah's angelic soprano voice cooed through the speakers. I loved "The One I Gave My Heart To." Back in 2007, it was a song that had gotten me through my first breakup. Now here it was providing me the same comfort in my heart's distress.

"Are you okay?" Anjel asked, breaking the silence. She recognized when something was bothering me without me having to tell her.

"No, but I will be. How about you? Are you okay?"

"No. It still hurts, but I'm doing my best to move on. For some reason, my heart won't let me. I'm going damn crazy over a man that has made it plain and clear that he doesn't love me and never did. The sad thing about the situation is that when I looked into his eyes tonight, his mouth was saying that he didn't love me, but his eyes were saying differently. Or maybe I just convinced myself that they were."

"The eyes are windows to the soul. Isn't that what you and Kent are always telling me?"

"Yeah, you're right. That we do. So what happened to you tonight?"

"Some sister approached me in the bathroom, throwing me all kinds of shade. She got in my face, trying to start some shit. Long story short, she revealed that Antoine was married. When I went outside to confront him, his wife was out there ripping him a new asshole."

"Go figure. Men think that it's their job to sex as many women as possible. A ring, a vow of monogamy, and promises of forever don't mean shit to them. They utter these things like it's second nature, knowing that they have no intentions of keeping their word."

"Men are shit!"

"Mmm, are you thinking about switching teams?"

"As intriguing as my lesbian girls make it sound, I don't think I can turn away from a dick made of flesh to one made of rubber. Plus, I love how I feel when I'm grabbing a man's head and pushing his face deeper into my twat. So letting a woman eat the box isn't appealing to me at the moment. Not to say that I'd never experiment. Just not sure I want to call it quits on men right now."

"I feel ya, even if they aren't nothing but shit," Anjel commented.

"For someone with such an innocent name, you sure don't live up to it," I teased.

"You damn right about that. Let's just say I'm a fallen angel."

We made the rest of the drive in silence. We both needed to do some reflection and to map out what our next steps were going to be. I was tired of the life that I was leading with Kyler. Being available at his beck and call whenever he managed to ditch his fiancée was fatiguing. Plus, he could be the reason why I was having such shitty luck with men. I mean, why did I hold Antoine to different standards than I held Kyler to? They both were in committed relationships so it didn't make things any better. The difference between the two was that Kyler was upfront with his situation. Antoine went out of his way to deceive me and make a fool out of me.

In the end, if I couldn't respect and play by the rules of love, then how could I expect others to respect and play by them? Karma truly is a motherfucker! If I wanted to see a change in my love life, I'd need to reevaluate the way that I was going about trying to find love. I couldn't believe that I was once again in this fucked-up situation. I promised myself a long time ago that I wouldn't fall victim to love, and there I was again, helplessly on the hunt for the man of my dreams. A man that truly may not have even existed.

As we pulled up in front of Anjel's place, we gave each other a hug and then I climbed into my car. The latter part of the ride had helped me to make some major decisions. It was time to make some changes. I was going to have to give Kyler his dismissal papers first thing tomorrow. Sure, I was going to have to curb some of my expenses, but I had done a great job of putting some of what he'd given me to the side. I'd miss the monetary allowances he provided me, but I'd be graduating next semester so I'd soon be entering the workforce. I had enough to pay my rent, car note, credit card bills, and other necessities for the next year.

What could I say? My mama didn't raise me to be a fool!

CHAPTER 19
Anjel

As the morning sunlight seeped through my wooden faux blinds, I tried to convince myself to get out of the bed. I didn't have any pressing projects to do, and everything else could be postponed until later. Pulling the warmth of my comforter up to my shoulders, I blindly reached over to grab a pillow from the right side of the bed.

I was slightly startled when my hand connected with flesh instead of the softness of my feather stuffed pillow. Suddenly it all came back to me. Knowing that last night wasn't a dream, I slowly turned over in bed to see who was sleeping on the right side of the bed; on *his* side of the bed. I suppressed a smile as I looked down at the sleeping face of Mason. His breathing was light, and he seemed to be at peace in bed next to me.

As I watched him sleeping, a tear began to slip from my eye. As much as I tried to play the tough girl, there was no denying that, in actuality, I was nothing more than a vulnerable woman that had fallen helplessly in love with a man that didn't love her back. Reality set in. Last night was no different than the night we had shared three weeks ago. I was nothing more to him than a receptacle for him to deposit his seed. When he awoke, he'd get dressed and depart without an "I love you," a "see you later," or a simple "I enjoyed last night."

I couldn't understand why I continued to do this to myself time and time again. It was like I was a masochist addicted to being treated in this fashion. Time after time, I tried to give my all to him; and time after time, he eagerly took what I provided to leave me feeling depleted. I didn't know how to communicate how much I needed him. I didn't know what words to utter that would make him see the pain that the distance was bringing to me. I didn't know how to get it through his thick-ass head that the mere thought of him touching, kissing, or loving another woman frazzled me.

Turning away from Mason, I inched toward the edge of the bed. With my back turned to him, I slowly let the barricaded tears fall from my eyes. I wasn't sobbing uncontrollably with all the accompanying hysterics; I was quietly shedding a few tears at the realization that my heart was destined to remain in this tortured state. I never understood how the ones we chose to love were the ones who didn't choose to reciprocate and love us back.

I silently cried myself to sleep. When I awoke, I felt the warmth of Mason's body and his right arm wrapped around my waist pulling me closer into him. I lay there reminiscing about the past. Times like this motivated me to fight harder to recapture his heart at all costs.

I relaxed on the balcony of my bedroom sipping on a cup of specially blended Samurai Chai Maté tea from Teavana. Mason left around 10 a.m. that morning. The routine was exactly as I had predicted. I was becoming accustomed to it; the words that he'd utter; the awkwardness that would envelop the room; the look of regret that would be embedded within his eyes.

Pulling my silk robe closed, I blew lightly into the hot liquid before raising the mug to my mouth to take another sip. The spices, herbs, and citrus flavors blended together and teased my palate as the warm liquid slid down my throat. Looking at the sky, I could see the overcast that was beginning to set in and shield the earth below. The clouds protected the earth below from the sun's heat. Looking down, my eyes remained fixated on my rose bushes. Deep in thought, I concluded that something simply had to give.

Turning around, I headed back into the house to grab my BlackBerry. Using the trackball, I located Kenton's number. Once I found it, I opted to send him a text message in lieu of calling him. After completing the text asking him to clear his schedule this evening for dinner, I threw my phone onto the bed.

Kenton was a godsend. Not only did he handle the maintenance for my online blog, he also helped me with my website's layout and design. More importantly, he also was a good confidant. It was through him that I was introduced to his crazy-ass cousin, Shawna. I adored the both of them. So many times since my breakup, I'd leaned on them.

Flopping face first on my bed, I reflected on last night. I wasn't disillusioned like some women who thought that their pussy was strong enough to capture, or in my case, recapture, a man. Having sex with Mason wouldn't win him back. The sex had a purpose: to satisfy my physical needs and to simply see if the love was there. When Mason and I united, it wasn't like two strangers out to get theirs. The two of us made love. He was meticulous and passionate.

But I couldn't continue to do this—be the woman on the side. Seeing him every two to three weeks wasn't good enough for me. Having him next to me and inside me on a part-time basis wasn't satisfying. Knowing that someone else was occupying his bed was killing me.

The more days we spent apart, I became even more desperate to recapture our love lost. Nothing was coming out of me visiting the same places he frequented or from me staking out his place one or two nights a week. I didn't even know why I was doing this. It wasn't like I had taken the initiative to confront him. I hadn't gotten the courage to get out of the car and bang on his door until he let me in so that I could jump on whatever bitch he had with him. I hadn't even done any of the crazy things you see in the movies or hear about in the songs. Yet, all I continued to do was to torture myself.

I didn't know what else I could do to get him to turn his attention fully to me. When we were together it was like when we first began dating, nothing but smiles and passionate lovemaking. Throughout the years, Mason had learned not to make love *to* me but to make love *with* me. Making love to someone was nothing but taking the time out to please them physically. The other senses are often left neglected. Making love with someone entailed participation from both individuals in helping the other to get their zenith in all capacities—physically, emotionally, spiritually, and mentally.

I didn't quite know how long I'd be able to continue playing this game with Mason. Casual sex wasn't in my nature. Many times I thought about doing the unthinkable—something that I often criticized other women for doing. I was thinking about trapping him. It wasn't like we were using condoms when we made love. Placing my finger between my legs, I could still feel his seed within my walls. With our history we had evolved beyond using condoms. I used a vaginal ring so we didn't really run a risk of conceiving a child; but I must admit that bearing a child with Mason would easily fix our dilemma. Deep down, I knew that this was part of our separation.

When we first began dating, I made it known that I wasn't trying to have any children. It wasn't in my life's plan. Yet it wasn't something that I would totally rule out. I just didn't see them in my immediate future. I wanted to enjoy my time with my husband. I don't knock those who choose to have kids. It just wasn't for me. I wasn't the maternal type. Mason understood this and informed me that he felt the same way. But lately things had begun to change. Lately he'd been hinting around about how good it would be to start a family and how beautiful I'd look with child.

I brushed these comments off as if he were just going through a phase. I should've paid more attention to these side comments. Luckily, I wasn't the type of woman that would stoop that low to bring a child into this world with the sole purpose of capturing the attention of a man. Plus, there was no guaranteeing that once he got what he wanted, that he would stay. I refused to be anyone's life-long doormat.

I looked at my watch. I needed to soak in my garden tub for an hour or so before I met up with Kenton. Disrobing until I was fully nude, I sashayed to the bathroom to begin my stint of relaxation. Things had to change or I was going to totally lose it.

CHAPTER 20
Kenton

As I lay across the bed, I watched as a teary-eyed Marcel gathered the few belongings that he had left over at my place throughout our brief courtship. Things had been semi-good with us, but it was a constant battle for me to fully allow him into my world and into my heart. This was something that he constantly griped about. It was both vexing and draining. I tried to get him to understand that I wasn't ready to allow another individual the opportunity and power to put me in such a vulnerable and desolate state, but that wasn't why he was packing his things.

Things with the two of us had progressed, even with the many hiccups we'd encountered. Because of the amount of time the two of us spent with one another, I only thought it appropriate to give Marcel access to my place when I wasn't home. Most of our dates originated at my place and since he usually was home from work prior to me getting out of the gym, it was only practical that he wait inside the house for me. It was also great for my Boxer, Kai. Marcel loved to play with her and didn't mind stopping by to walk and spend time with her. I couldn't believe that he never took this as an opportunity to rummage through my things or invade my privacy. A few days back, I had set up one of those nanny cams to test him and he passed.

Last night happened to be a terrific evening, one filled with a romantic dinner and cuddling in front of the fifty-two-inch LCD with a bottle of Shiraz wine from McCrea Boushey. Together we retired to the bedroom. Ending the night with a very intense session of lovemaking, Marcel snuggly cuddled in my arms.

Waking up in the middle of the night, I couldn't manage to go back to sleep. After tossing and turning for over an hour, I decided to go into my makeshift office and surf the Internet. Growing bored of the gossip media blogs, I logged into my old account on Him4Now.com. It was a hookup site for gay and bisexual men. The message indicator notified me of new messages. I had a slew of them since I hadn't been on the site since Marcel and I had become somewhat of an unofficial item. There was no way I was going to be able to address the 198 messages sitting in my inbox. Hitting the "Select All" box at the top of the screen, a check box was placed next to each message. I then hit the "Delete Selected Message" icon. My inbox was now empty. With the message indicator no longer flashing, I proceeded to browse through the profiles of the members currently logged online.

Stopping on profiles of interest, I'd look at their collection of pictures and read what they had to say. I wasn't looking for anything in particular, and Marcel made sure that I was well satisfied in the sex department. After about ten minutes of browsing and laughing at the hilarity of some of the profiles, I saw my message indicator flashing again. I clicked on the icon and saw I had seven new messages.

I read through some of the notes, but was intrigued by the fifth one. The man in the picture was simply breathtaking and when I skimmed his profile, I was left astounded by the words, which had a poetic feel to them. I went back to his note and read what he had to say to me:

Good Evening, or should I say morning (lol). As I surfed the site looking at one profile after the next, I found myself infatuated with your picture and drawn to the simple, yet profound words on your profile. If the feeling is mutual, please shoot me a note.

Before I stopped myself, I was responding to the message. We continued with our exchange until he inquired if I had an instant messenger. Providing him with my username information, I signed onto my messenger account.

An hour into our cyber chat, I learned that his name was Demario, he was twenty-four years old, lived on the south side, and was originally from the Dominican Republic. We shared more personal information—if one another was single, our interests, both sexually and non-sexually, and what turned us on. Before bringing our chat to a close, we turned on our webcams. I asked him to show me what he looked like with no shirt. I was enthralled with his chiseled physique and without me asking, in one swoop, he removed his lounge pants. His body was flawless. He was smooth and hairless. When he turned around, I took notice of his muscular apple bottom. My dick instantly awoke.

When I relayed this to him, he asked to see it. I obliged and before I knew it, we were engaged in a cyber jack-off session. He leaned back in his chair, placed one of his legs up on the desk, and I watched as his balls slapped against his scrotum. Lowering my webcam, I positioned it so that he could see my engorged penis. We teased one another for about fifteen minutes before Demario's eyes rolled in the back of his head and his seed shot up onto his stomach and chest. Moments later, I joined him and my seed spit from my penis' tip and into the air. It splattered on my keyboard and my thighs.

Exchanging numbers, with promises to remain in touch, we both ended our session. I headed into the bathroom located in the hall to clean up and to get a washcloth to wipe up any incriminating evidence. I closed the website, clicked the "X" on my messenger window that recorded our virtual communication, turned off my monitor, and got back in bed with Marcel.

When I awoke the next morning, Marcel wasn't by my side.

Normally on weekends when he stayed over, he and Kai would retire to my office and he'd log on to my computer to catch up on his current events. I'd normally sleep in until mid-morning. Calling out to him, he didn't answer. Pulling myself out of the bed and slipping on a pair of gym shorts, I headed down the hall and into my office. When I opened the door, which was slightly ajar, I noticed Marcel seated at my computer but hunched over. Kai was lying down under the desk, her head resting on one of his feet. His shoulders were moving up and down and he was sobbing uncontrollably.

I entered the room thinking that he had learned something devastating about his family or a close friend. When I knelt down to wrap my arms around him, he jumped and pushed my hands away as if any touch from me would infect him with a deadly, incurable disease. I was dumbfounded. Marcel sprung from the chair and exited the room. I looked at the computer screen and a tight knot formed in my stomach.

Last night when I had closed down my messenger, I didn't sign out. I only hit the "X" in the upper corner of the window. This only minimized the messenger, placing it into my toolbar and keeping me logged in. I hadn't completely logged out. Apparently Demario had sent me a message this morning informing me that he'd enjoyed last night and that he hoped it didn't give me the impression that his interest was one grounded in carnal lust. Marcel had apparently seen the message and had gone through my message archive and read our entire conversation of the evening.

Even though he couldn't see the webcam session, he was able to read our comments back and forth and was able to fill in the blanks. Not only did Marcel read my conversation with Demario, he also read some prior conversations with other individuals. Some of these conversations with prior "pieces" resulted in booty calls, oral sessions, or jack-off sessions. In some of the conversations nothing sexual had occurred, but the dialogue wasn't necessarily respectful of someone that was kind of involved with someone.

I headed back into the room at a loss for words. I didn't know what I could say to Marcel to make him stay or to make him forgive me. As I watched him pack, I was slightly saddened. I didn't want to interfere with what he was doing. If the shoe were on the other foot, I'd be heading out the door. I watched Marcel bend down and give Kai a big hug and kiss on the top of her head. Without a word or a glance in my direction, he headed down the stairs and exited my abode. When I headed downstairs, I noticed my house key sitting on the breakfast bar. I had done to Marcel what Trevor had done to me. More than likely, Marcel would continue the cycle and do the same thing to his next lover.

CHAPTER 21
Shawna

As I trekked through the downtown alleys from my advisor's office, I came to terms with the fact that I was now a single and unattached woman. Not that I had previously been "attached" in the last few years. Growing up, I was always the girl that men would bend over backward for to be able to have me on their shoulder. Now that was all gone. I was the girl they simply wanted to bed.

My conversation with Kyler wasn't an easy one. He wasn't particularly pleased that our uncommitted rendezvous had run its course. He went into this long tirade about all the money he'd invested in me; I had to inform him that he chose to invest in me to keep me available at his beck and call. He negated to realize it was me that was forced to sleep alone, attend events for couples alone, and who had to deal with the title of being "the other woman." He'd lay down with me to only get up and go home to his fiancée.

Even though I was young, I deserved better than this. I deserved to be cherished and loved. I deserved to have a man to make love to me, spend the evening, and wake up next to me. I deserved to be with someone who could provide me with a future. Cutting through Pegasus Circle, I headed toward Gemini Boulevard where I had parked my car. I hated this damn walk across campus. Pulling out my iPod, I turned up my music and pretended not to notice the eyes of several passing men.

"One more semester," I muttered to myself, "and I'll be done." I'd have a degree in Business Marketing and a promised job with

Anjel and her online magazine. Right now, I did some freelance marketing work for her, but she guaranteed to put me on her payroll as soon as I earned my degree. Removing my headphones and climbing into my car, I took a deep breath before I made my way through the congested streets of Orlando. Merging onto I-4, I pressed down on my accelerator. I didn't have anywhere in particular to be, but I wanted to get the hell away from campus.

Deciding to get a few hours of study time in, I opted to do a study session at Starbucks across from my high-rise. I wasn't a coffee drinker so I always ordered the Chai Tea Latte with a dash of whipped cream and cinnamon. Anjel had introduced me to them. After getting my drink, I searched the room for a vacant table where I could get my study on.

Noticing that the majority of the tables were occupied with other patrons, I noticed that one gentleman sat alone reading a *Black Enterprise* magazine and sipping on his drink. It was refreshing to see a man of color reading something educational that didn't entail half-naked women, cars, and videogames. Debating on whether I should disturb the gentleman, I took him in from head-to-toe. He was dressed in business casual attire—an outfit that screamed out Banana Republic. He sported a shadow fade haircut, nicely trimmed facial hair, and nicely manicured fingernails. That was a pet peeve of mine. I couldn't stand a man that had fingernails that were bitten, dirty, or rough. This spoke volumes about their level of hygiene.

When a man stood before me naked, after taking in the obvious, I always took time out to explore his hands and feet. If a man couldn't take the time out to bend down to wash and lotion his feet, I couldn't guarantee that he'd take the time out to reach behind and wash his ass and balls. And an ashy man was definitely a turn-off. There were too many alternatives like lotions, shower gels, and oils to prevent chafed skin. It was an experience like no other having my man next to me in bed, spooning, and his soft feet intertwined with mine. It was an extra bonus if a man was secure enough with his sexuality to go get a manicure and pedicure along with me. But for those who couldn't get to that level of comfort, I didn't mind taking the time out to pamper my man and help him keep his hygiene up.

Taking the time out to check this stranger out, he glanced up from his magazine and a smile erupted across his face as he silently gestured with his hand for me to take the vacant seat. Relieved by his gesture, I made my way to the corner of the room to have a seat across from him. Pulling out the chair, I thanked him and he went back to reading his magazine. I noticed that he didn't have any jewelry on his fingers, but nowadays this meant nothing. Experience had taught me that he could have very well been married.

I tried to concentrate on writing my paper for my Marketing Research class. I stared blankly at my MacBook Pro, but I couldn't concentrate. The scent from his cologne permeated the air. It was so alluring, I couldn't help but wonder what it was. Clearing my throat, I shyly apologized for interrupting him and inquired about the scent.

This caused him to smile again before he answered. His teeth were beautiful. They didn't have the appearance that he'd had them bleached or had endured years of braces. They had this naturalness to them. They emphasized his dark chocolate complexion.

Taking a sniff from his shirt, he commented, "Givenchy Pi Neo. Does it not compliment me?"

"No, it definitely does. It is very masculine, yet has a softness that isn't overbearing."

"That's good to know. I'm not good at picking out colognes

and things of the nature. I guess I'm spoiled since my girlfriend always handled those things for me. Well, that is, until we decided to end things last year."

"I'm sorry to hear that. I know how that goes. Hopefully the two of you were able to remain friends."

"We're amicable. It wasn't a bad breakup, but we both realized that we're much happier not in a relationship with one another."

"Well, the good thing is you two are still amicable."

"That we are. I'm sorry but I didn't introduce myself. I'm Edrian, but only my mother calls me that. Everyone else calls me Dree."

"It's nice to meet you. I like Edrian. It's unique. I'm Shawna."

"Nice. Are you a writer?" he asked, gesturing toward my notebook.

He apparently fed into the stereotype that writers ran to Starbucks to churn out a bestseller. "I wish, but I don't have that creative bug. I'm working on a paper for class."

"What type of paper?"

"I'm working on a paper for my Marketing Research class. I attend Central University."

"That's a great business school. I got my MBA from there."

"Where did you do your undergrad?"

"I'm a Morehouse Man," he proudly boasted.

"My cousin went there as well. He's always talking about how great of a school it is. He wanted me to go to Spelman, and was quite disappointed when I didn't."

"Indeed he should've been. Spelman is a great school."

"I don't dispute that; it just wasn't right for me."

"Understandable. I hate to do this, Shawna, but I have to get back to the office for a business meeting. It'd definitely be nice if we could converse more."

"I'd like that."

"Here is my business card. It has my cell phone number and email address on it. Feel free to reach out to me when it's convenient to you. Maybe I can help you out with your paper."

I took his business card with a promise to utilize it within the next few days. As he backed away from the table and stood, I realized how tall he was. He had to be damn near 6'5". He was well over a foot taller than me. I watched him exit out of the coffeehouse. He surely filled up his dress slacks well. My thoughts became impure as I pondered what he'd look like in the nude.

Pulling myself away from those thoughts, I quickly pocketed his business card and delved into my paper. I made a mental note to have Edrian to look over it when I was done.

CHAPTER 22
Anjel

Pulling up to the valet parking attendant, I was late as usual. Kenton had already sent me a text message to let me know that he had arrived and was waiting inside. He had chosen to go to this new restaurant located in downtown Orlando that I had previously told him about. I raved to him about the create-your-own, American-inspired, stir-fry restaurant. I wasn't much of a cook, but there I got to put together different combinations that I could go home and try. Plus, their Martinis were to die for.

As I entered the restaurant, I scanned the waiting patrons for Kenton. Of course I should've known he'd be laying his charms on the host, and rightfully so. The host was truly a piece of eye candy. When he realized that I was watching, Kenton quickly exchanged contact information with the host and headed over in my direction. He looked like he was fresh out of the gym. His arms were swollen and his chest was poked out. Needless to say, he simply looked good!

As we embraced, I whispered in his ear, "It's such a shame you play on the other side."

Laughing at my comment, he squeezed me tighter. "All that matters is what side I'm on when I'm in the bed with you."

"Like hell it does," I gibed. "With a straight man, I only have to worry about these other classless tricks vying for my man's attention. With a bisexual man, I'd have to not only worry about them, but also men. I'd work myself to death trying to keep you to myself."

"Well, if the pussy is as good as you say it is, then I'd be hooked on it like an addict trying to score his next high."

"You're so damn crass."

"And you love it," he countered.

Our friendly banter was interrupted as the host showed us to our table. If I wasn't mistaken, he was throwing me some shade. I guess he thought Kenton and I were more than friends. It wasn't hard to not come to this conclusion based on the way we were interacting. Sliding into the booth, sitting across from one another, we held hands as we smiled in each other's faces. It seemed like forever since we'd last hung out. We had such a great professional relationship that entailed countless emails and phone calls, but we hadn't seen each other in the flesh in over a month.

We engaged in small talk as we waited for our drink orders to be taken. "How is that cousin of mine doing?"

"Just as bad as can be, but I think she had a revelation the other day."

"Really? What happened?"

I summarized the other night's events when Shawna had realized that her latest love interest was married and had been confronted in the bathroom by the wife's family and friends. I stopped long enough for the waitress to introduce herself and take our drink orders.

"Wow, drama seems to always follow that girl!" Kenton exclaimed.

Seeing a need to come to Shawna's defense, I informed him that this time she wasn't really the one to blame. She had no idea that the man was married and when she realized that he was, she had backed away with the quickness.

"Yeah, but did she tell you about what happened late last month?"

"No. What happened?"

Kenton told me about the night he was awakened in the middle of the night to rescue a stranded Shawna. He told me about the events that transpired leading up to her having to be rescued at such an ungodly time of the morning.

When Kenton finished, I realized that I had been so consumed with my own troubles with Mason that I'd really been neglecting my friendship with Shawna. We'd always had a sisterly type of relationship, but lately all that I could think about was Mason. That had to be hard on my friends and associates. Every conversation resulted in wasted energy regarding him and how I couldn't simply let him go. But I was truly coming to the realization that I had to let him go. I had to allow him the opportunity to miss me and to chase after me.

Without a doubt, we still shared love for each other; especially the passionate sex that we'd shared last night until the wee hours of this morning. I didn't want to divulge to Kenton that I had tripped up again and fallen into bed with Mason; he would've been disappointed.

I wasn't too surprised when he informed me of his latest breakup with his latest sexual conquest, Marcel. Sometimes I had to detach my own personal situation whenever I listened to Kenton. He was behaving similarly to Mason and it was behavior that was hard for me to condone. Hurting another to spare your own heart from getting hurt wasn't right.

After catching up, we both headed to the stir-fry station to concoct our evening's cuisine. I successfully put together a meal that consisted of flat noodles, assorted chopped vegetables, a scrambled egg, shrimp and tilapia, dry red pepper, and a light teriyaki sauce. I was pretty pleased with myself. I made a mental note of everything that I had chosen to be stir-fried by the cooks so that I could attempt to replicate it at home.

When we finished eating, we both reclined back in the booth; our stomachs were full, and we sipped on our second round of drinks. "So…" Kenton asked.

"What's up?"

"As much as we enjoy one another's company, I'm certain there was a reason behind this meeting."

"Not really. I needed something that would get my mind off of Mason. He's been flooding my thoughts."

"When was the last time you two…"

"That I thought of him?" I interjected, playing stupid. I realized that he wanted to know when was the last time we had sex.

Kenton raised his eyebrow and the look in his eye silently read: "Bitch, you know what the fuck I mean."

Without him having to verbally ask me, I divulged the truth. "It was last night. He popped up unexpectedly, as usual, after the club."

I could see the scowl forming across his face. Then his face softened. "Part of me wants to rip you a new one, but another part of me remembers what it is like to be in love and how hard it is to let go of someone who isn't any good for you. No matter what anyone does or says, the choice to walk away must come from within."

"I came to the terms today that I must, in fact, walk away from him. It's like when we are making love, things are back the way they used to be. But the next morning, it's like we're two strangers waking up from a drunken stupor, realizing the stupid mistake we made the night before.

"This morning when he left, he was so unemotional and detached. I could see the look of sorrow in his eyes. I can't even explain how his look and demeanor made me feel."

"Did you mention it to him?"

"No. I didn't want to cause an argument or make him feel even more uncomfortable. But Kenton, I'm exhausted. I'm so tired of chasing him. I'm tired of trying to make him see what he's been missing. I'm tired of not being able to live my life, and skulking around in the dark chasing after him."

"What do you mean 'skulking around in the dark'? What have you been doing?"

Now I was slightly embarrassed; I meant to omit that part. I never told Kenton about visiting Mason's place and sitting outside in the middle of the night, about slashing his tires, or about my other shenanigans. Now that I had opened this chapter, I decided that it was finally time to bring Kenton fully up-to-date.

When I was finished, he looked at me in bewilderment. My actions were so unlike myself, and more importantly, I was risking my livelihood and reputation. But, at the time, I was convinced that these things would help heal my tattered heart. I hated the look in Kenton's eyes. It made me feel dirty.

"Have you been seeing that counselor I recommended?"

"I've seen him a couple of times. It seems like a waste of time and energy. Frankly, I do the same thing with him that we just did. Except with him, there's a lack of friendship, great food, and of course, alcohol."

"Do me a favor and give him a chance. You're looking for a quick fix and you forget that you didn't fall in love overnight, so you will not fall out of it overnight."

Everything that Kenton was saying was true, but I wasn't completely comfortable divulging such intimate and personal details with a complete stranger. Yet, on the other hand, that could possibly be what I needed—someone who was neutral and could offer suggestions and advise me in an impartial manner.

Finishing our drinks and paying our tab, we embraced one another in a loving hug. Promising to text the other when we made it home, we exited the restaurant and headed in our own directions.

CHAPTER 23
Kenton

It's funny how people turn to the things that they know aren't good for them. I lay on the right side of my bed, my penis now limp between my legs. I was partially propped up, my right hand providing support for my head. The glare of the moonlight lit the room and I watched as Demario slept beside me with his bare back facing me. His breathing was steady and deep. Sporadically he would let out a light snore. I had been watching him sleep for the past forty-five minutes, wondering what he was dreaming about. His soft lips formed a small smile. As I watched him sleep, he appeared to be at peace with everything.

I'm not certain what had made me allow him to spend the night. Marcel had reminded me of how good it felt to have someone to hold at night. It could have also been a vain attempt to replace the emptiness that I was feeling now that Marcel and I were no longer dealing with one another.

I was a little apprehensive about allowing him to come to my house. I was still feeling a little guilty and panged about the demise of my courtship with Marcel. He was truly such a wonderful guy, and although it wasn't my intention, I had hurt him. After me, he'd be just as jaded as I was—afraid to love and afraid to fully trust another with his heart regardless of how true their intentions might be. But wasn't this what love was about? Is it really love if it doesn't hurt? Sometimes we have to go through a shit-load of hurt before we come out victorious with the love of our life lying next to us. I'd never known anyone to say that they'd gone through the rigors of love and come out completely unscathed.

That was the misconception that many people failed to realize. Love isn't always going to make you smile. It isn't always going to be joyous. There'll be times when infidelity comes into play, maybe a little jealousy, and certainly times when what we think is the truth becomes nothing but lies. Sometimes we'll find ourselves crying more than smiling; but when it all comes down to it, we know that we can't live without the one who is causing all of our heart's distress.

As I became engrossed with my thoughts on love, I didn't notice that Demario had awakened. I felt him pushing his backside against me. Slowly he began rotating his hips in a slow motion until he felt my penis growing to a full erection. Feeling my manhood against his ass caused him to let out an audible moan as he pushed his head back against my chest, his back slightly arching. I couldn't believe that he was still horny after our session earlier, which resulted in me ejaculating twice. It appeared that Demario was what I dubbed a marathon ejaculator. It took him forever to reach his moment of climax. Shit, sexing him was putting a hurting on my back. I wasn't sure if I'd be able to keep up and match his relentless stamina.

When I failed to embrace him, Demario reached back and between my legs to slowly massage my penis. When he felt the pre-cum emerging from its tip, he moved his hand up to my head and pulled me closer until my face was in the crook of his neck. My lips connected with his neck and his body shivered. He began gyrating faster and leaning back, and then he whispered seductively, "Can I have some more?"

Never one to disappoint, I rolled over and reached into the nightstand for some lube and a condom. I never went in without a raincoat. It "felt better" without one, and there was nothing like erupting and filling your lover with your seed, but there was too much going on to be doing that with just anyone. Hell, even with your lover, you had to be careful. I was terrified to go to my doctor and reveal that I had a discharge or that I needed a shot of penicillin in the ass because I had been careless. There wasn't anything that I loved more than my own life—excluding Kai, family, and God.

As I ripped the magnum wrapper open with my teeth, I quickly rolled it on my penis and then applied my favorite lubricant, ID Slide. Now that I was safely protected, I began sucking on Demario's neck harder as he allowed his hips to guide me inside him. His walls were still open from our session earlier so I didn't have to work as hard to enter him. I usually didn't like to have sex without getting a little head and a little foreplay, but I'd need all my energy in order to get Demario to his climax. When we were totally united, I began moving in and out of him slowly. He matched me thrust for thrust while clenching the bed sheets.

He moved onto his stomach without missing a beat and I moved atop, still remaining inside of him. Aggressively pulling him toward me, he raised his lower half into the air until he was on all fours. This was my favorite position. Not wanting to ruin the moment by ejaculating too soon, I began to slow my pace.

Gyrating my hips in circular motions, Demario stammered, "Damn, baby, you hitting my spot." He uttered some things in his native Spanish language. Most of it I didn't understand. Arching his back even more, he let out a loud moan that was intermixed with pain and euphoria. In less than twenty minutes he had managed to cum. I stopped my gyrating as his body convulsed in the aftermath. When his body had subsided, I began to pull out.

He reached back to stop me. "You have to cum, too," he managed to utter, trying to catch his breath.

Exiting Demario, I turned him over. I grabbed him by the ankles and pulled him toward the edge of the bed. Pushing his legs up in the air and placing them on my shoulders, I grabbed his hips, and lifting his lower half off of the bed, I reentered him in one swift movement. He sucked in the air as I pushed my entire girth inside of him. Now that he had gotten his, I was going after mine. With a force of a sledgehammer, I began beating the brakes off of him. He cooed about how good I felt and urged me to fill him up. Stroking my ego in every sense, I finally let out a loud moan as I erupted for the third time. Exhausted, I collapsed onto Demario. We both were winded from our session.

We struggled to catch our breath; my dick was nearly limp and had fallen out of Demario. Removing the condom, I picked him up and carried him to the bathroom. Running the water in the shower, we both got in and took turns bathing each other. When we were done, we again took turns drying one another off before heading into the guest room. I was too tired to change the sheets. Our late-night romp had ruined them, leaving them wet with perspiration and his ejaculation. As we climbed into the bed, we were joined by Kai who took her place at the foot of the bed. Together we all relaxed. Demario stroked my neck with his hands, but stopped abruptly. Bolting upright he looked down at Kai and then back at me. In unison, we both broke out in laughter as Kai loudly snored. She sounded like a grown-ass man that was exhausted from a long day of work.

"She'll quiet down in a few," I informed him. "Just be lucky she's not in her pooting mood." I laughed.

Resting back in my arms, Demario eventually fell back asleep. I couldn't refrain from thinking that the other night it was Marcel who was lying beside me. As fatigue consumed me, eventually, I also fell asleep.

CHAPTER 24
Shawna

It took me two days to finish my paper, and deciding to get out of the house, I grabbed my car keys and jumped in my car. I didn't want to be left alone at home with my thoughts. I was still upset about Antoine. I was on a search to find true love. I'm talking about the type of love that Deborah Cox sang about in "Definition of Love."

As I wandered about the streets, I found myself in the vicinity of Kenton's home. I hadn't had the opportunity to stop by and talk to him about what had gone down with him and Marcel. Although I never met Marcel, from what Kenton told me, he seemed to be a genuine guy. He would've been the perfect guy for my cousin pre-Trevor. Trevor had definitely done a number on Kenton, and the hopeless romantic that I once knew had died along with that failed relationship. That was quite unfortunate for Marcel.

Kenton was now in the game to win it. He didn't care how many hearts he broke in his quest to not be made a fool again. He wanted to love on his own terms, something that he had adopted from me. I wish he'd take notice and see that trying to control love was futile.

Pulling into the driveway of my cousin's home, I noticed that the porch light wasn't on. He must've still been out running the streets. Hopefully he was remaining out of trouble and not breaking any more hearts. Entering through the front door, I immediately disarmed the alarm system. The chirping from the system must've wakened Kai. She stood at the top of the stairs; doe-eyed, she stared down at me. Her threatening statuesque stance let any intruder know that she was prepared to defend her home.

When I called to her, the recognition of my voice caused her little stub of a tail to vigorously wag back and forth. When she got downstairs, she sniffed at my feet before jumping on me to greet me. I rubbed her enormous head and her folded ears relaxed back as she grinned in appreciation.

"Hey, girl. Where's your daddy?" I asked her in a mock baby voice as if I were speaking to a toddler. "Come on. Let's go potty."

Rushing toward the back door, she waited until I opened it so that she could go out and relieve herself. As she did her business, I pulled out my cell phone to text my cousin to let him know that I was here. The last thing I needed was to disrupt his flow if he decided to come home with some random guy. Lately, Kenton put shame to the character Ricky, from the Logo channel's gay-themed television show *Noah's Arc*. Kenton loved that show and was devastated when it was cancelled after two seasons. Needless to say, he had both seasons on DVD as well as the 2008 movie.

When Kai was finished doing her thing, she came back into the house. Running up to her room, she was no doubt looking for one of her toys so we could play tug-of-war. Running back down the stairs, she had a plastic squeaky ball in her mouth. Heading back outside, I tossed the ball back and forth for her to catch. Kai loved playing fetch, but she hadn't learned that when she brought the ball back she was expected to let go of it. In her world, bringing it back meant for the tosser to pry it from her mouth. Even with her being just shy of a year, this proved to be a feat. Her teeth were massive, and her strength was overwhelming.

I attempted to get the ball from Kai's clenched teeth as she pulled back from me and friendly growled. I decided to give up.

This always angered her into dropping the ball so that it could be tossed again. As I tossed the ball for the fourth time, Kai chased after it, picked it up, and ran around the yard in circles. Feeling my phone pulsating twice against my hip, I pulled it out to read the text message. It was Kenton asking me to walk and feed Kai as he was running late. He promised to be home within the hour so we could catch up.

I played outside with Kai for another twenty minutes before tiring myself out. With reluctance, she came back inside the house. Going into the garage, I pulled out her bowl and her food. She got half a can of wet can food and a half-cup of dry food. Kenton had drilled this into me so many times that now it was embedded within my memory.

As Kai ate, I kicked off my sandals and started upstairs to relax in the loft-like den. Making my way upstairs, I was impressed by my cousin's decorating skills. The downstairs had a very eclectic feel to it. Most of the colors consisted of browns, dark reds, and clay-like oranges. In the lower half of the house, the living room and dining room were connected, and each had an accent wall in the color of light brown. It was a little darker than the skin of a baking potato.

His furniture consisted of an oval glass dining room table with a mahogany-brown wooden base. The chairs that surrounded the table were some type of dark orange. Because of the colors and design, it was evident that the set had probably come from Rooms to Go. The table was set as if he was expecting a dinner party. On the accent wall was an abstract painting that tied every color in the two rooms together.

The living room consisted of an LCD television mounted on the wall and a brown leather sofa and loveseat; both had brown cushions and multi-colored brown pillows. Both were placed at the edge of a throw rug that consisted of all of the rooms' various colors. In the middle of the sofa and loveseat was a brown, oversized leather ottoman, which Kai had claimed as her own. Above the fireplace's mantle, a large mirror with a dark brown trim was centered.

Before heading into the upstairs den, I went to the guest bathroom for a washcloth. Kai would be making her way up to me with food plastered all around her mouth. Plopping down on the den's worn microfiber cloth sofa, I flipped through the channels as I waited for Kai to come and keep me company. If it was not for Kenton's disdain for entertaining downstairs, I would've been sprawled out on the sofa, which was extremely more comfortable than the worn-out thing I was currently on.

"It's a damn shame," I muttered. With hundreds of channels, nothing seemed to interest me. I tossed the remote into the reclining chair at the same time Kai wobbled upstairs with a full stomach, and as expected, a dirty face. I took the washcloth and wiped the remnants of her dinner from her face. After tossing the washcloth in the dirty clothes hamper, I plopped back onto the sofa to take a nap while I waited for Kenton.

As I slept, Kai had apparently gotten lonely and had plopped her big ass on the sofa to cuddle with me. When she rested her head on the small of my back, I was startled awake. Looking at the clock, I noticed that a few hours had passed and Kenton still hadn't come home.

Remembering Edrian, the guy from Starbucks, I wondered if he was available to meet up tonight. Digging into my purse, I pulled out the card that had his number on it. Dialing the cell phone number, I waited as his phone's ringing came through my receiver. After the fifth ring, I prepared to leave a message when suddenly a male voice bellowed into the receiver, "Hello."

CHAPTER 25
Anjel

My late lunch with Kenton had opened my eyes. I truly had to do some soul-searching. I needed to decide what I was going to do about Mason. I didn't know whether to leave or to stay. I was certain that, in time, he'd come around and things would be back to the way they used to be. But did I really want them to be the same?

Did I want him to have the same privileges that he once possessed? This time apart was hell for me, so now I was uncertain if I wanted to give him the opportunity to run his shenanigans on me again. What if he decided after a few months, or even years, that he once again needed space? At the club, he said that he had only proposed to appease me. So what if taking him back was another attempt of him trying to pacify me?

He was tired of us haphazardly running into one another. And he definitely wasn't a fool. I'm almost certain that he speculated that it was me that was wreaking havoc with my mischievous acts. Then again, maybe he didn't know it was me. He went through women like most people go through a roll of tissue.

Pulling into the RaceTrac gas station to fill up my tank, my eyes made contact with a familiar face. Smiling, I waved at him as he waved back. As the pump authorized my card, I unscrewed the cap to my gas tank. When I was about to remove the 93 Premium gas handle, I was startled as the familiar face informed me that he'd take care of it for me. Who said that chivalry was dead?

"Are you filling up?"

"Yes, I am, Bryce. I appreciate your kindness." I batted my eyes and flashed my signature smile.

"It's my pleasure. So how have you been, Anjel?"

"I've had better days, but complaining won't do any good."

"I feel you on that."

While pumping my gas, he seemed to be nervous and avoided making eye contact with me. "Is everything okay, Bryce?"

"Yes, I'm fine. So did you and Mason wind up working things out?"

"Unfortunately, we did not," I revealed with a frown.

"I'm sorry to hear that…I hope I'm not stepping out of line, but would you consider going to dinner with me Friday evening? Not on a date, but to catch up?" he nervously stammered.

I hesitated before I responded. Bryce was a former coworker of Mason's and although the two weren't the best of friends, they had hung out a few times. When I questioned why they had stopped, Mason informed me that he thought that Bryce had a thing for me. As put together as Mason was, he could get extremely jealous. I didn't think anything further of it, and didn't question what had made him come to that conclusion. Now, I realized that Mason's assumptions were valid.

"Sure. I'd love to," I answered. What better way to fuck with Mason than to date an old acquaintance of his? I'd make sure that we'd wind up "accidentally" running into Mason. What Mason didn't know was that his personal assistant, Inola, fed me his schedule on a weekly basis.

Inola was a widow, and had taken quite a liking to me. She was devastated when I informed her that Mason and I had broken up. She was even more distraught when I revealed the details of how he had decided to end things with me. She vowed to help me in any way that she could to win Mason back. In fact, it was Inola who had suggested the drive-bys and accidental run-ins to remain a constant in his life. She revealed that she'd also had to resort to these tactics to win back the affection of her husband, and after she did, they were happily married until he died in a car accident.

When my tank was filled, Bryce and I exchanged contact information. I promised to give him a call tomorrow to finalize things. With a smile, he opened my door and waited until I pulled away. Bryce was a very nice guy. He was extremely handsome if you were into the stereotypical light-skinned guy with the green eyes type. I could tell from the fitted shirt he was wearing that he either worked out, or was heavily into sports.

But going beyond the physical, Bryce was a little too…weak for my tastes. He was the type that needed to be told what to do and did it without fighting back. He was more of the passive type of guy and I needed one with a take-charge attitude. Mason was somewhat like this when I met him, but I saw his potential and had taken the time and put in the effort to mold him into the man he was today. Presently, I didn't really have the time to train another man to only have him to leave me for another woman.

The thought of this angered me as I thought about all the bitches that were reaping the benefits of my hard work and sacrifices. I needed a drink. I zipped through the traffic to get to the nearest package store so that I could replenish my dwindling home supply of alcohol.

Using my car's built-in phone Bluetooth system, I called Alexandria. "Hey, girl, what are you up to?"

"What do you think? I'm studying as usual."

"I'm not going to waste my breath on trying to convince you to get your head out of the books and to get out and have some fun."

"Good; I don't need to hear it. I took your advice and decided to get my ass back out in the game. That's why I'm trying to get my studying in now so that I will be free for this weekend."

"And what's happening this weekend?"

"Well, I didn't want to say anything until I knew what the deal was, but I met this guy that goes to my gym. We've been talking for a few weeks and have been out on a few dates."

"You've been holding back," I chided.

"Not intentionally. I didn't want to jinx things."

"You still haven't told me what's going down this weekend."

"Oh, my bad. I'm going on a romantic weekend getaway to Amelia Island."

"Romantic? Does that mean that you're going to give him some?"

"Hell yeah! I'm going to give him some. I wanted to give him some the first time we went out. I have a weakness for a sexy, chocolate brother with a toned body, but the major selling point is that he's into women with curves."

"Now that's what I'm talking about. I was waiting for you to stop trying to compete with these anorexic wannabe Hollywood broads running around here."

"It's kind of hard not to when that seems to be all that most men want."

"Apparently not all men. You've found the exception."

"We shall see. But what's going on with you? Did Mason do something?"

That was a shame. My life had been so consumed with Mason that whenever I called one of my people, they automatically assumed that I was calling them to whine about him. "No, I didn't call you about Mason." The phone went silent. "Hello…hello…hello," I repeated into the receiver.

"I'm sorry. I'm here. I'm in shock," Alexandria teased.

"Whatever. You can go to hell. I'm trying to get your advice," I told her. For the next five minutes, I gave her the rundown on what had happened at the gas station and also about Mason and Bryce's history. "So, what do you think?"

"To be honest, I don't see a problem. Mason and him aren't friends anymore, and when Mason decided that he was ready to move on, he lost all claims to you. I couldn't care less about his feelings, and you shouldn't even give a fuck about what he'd think if he found out that you were going out with one of his old hang-out buddies."

"You don't think that it is...I don't know...lowdown?"

"Why would I? Anjel, you need to do you and stop worrying about how he's going to react. Hell, I hope he hits the roof when he does find out. Maybe this will be what it takes for him to get his act together."

"I hear you." Alexandria was right. I was going to go ahead with my date with Bryce and was going to go forward with making sure that Mason knew it. A by-chance encounter would more than likely require at least another two or three dates; I was certain that I could manage to put up with Bryce for that long.

Disconnecting with Alexandria, I turned up my radio and pressed down on the accelerator of my sports coupe. I was feeling like a rock had been lifted off of my shoulders and like I could finally breathe again.

CHAPTER 26
Kenton

I was headed to Lucent, a club located in the southern outskirts of the city. I had never heard of it, but when Demario suggested that I meet him at the club, I obliged. I was always down for experiencing something new.

Immediately when I pulled up to the club, I could tell that it was nothing more than a hole in a wall. It was situated in the back of a rundown and abandoned strip mall. There wasn't any valet parking. It proved to be quite frustrating trying to find a place to park in the pothole-filled lot. I was going to have to take my truck in for service to fix my alignment that weekend.

Managing to park, I headed toward the club's entrance, performed the routine search procedures at the door, and then paid the ten-dollar admittance fee. As soon as I rounded the corner where the dance floor and bar were situated, the dank smell of marijuana and sweat hit my nose. The weed brought about wistful memories of my college days back in Atlanta when I had attended Morehouse. I don't know how I would've made it through my four years without the help of weed to get me through the stressful periods.

I glanced around the club; house music blared from the speakers, causing the walls to vibrate from the heavy bass. I watched as the mixture of Black and Latino bodies gyrated to the music. The sweat was dripping off of their bodies and rolling down many of their shirtless chests. The glow of multi-colored glow sticks lit up the floor. The expressionless dancers were in a trance as they let loose and got lost in the music.

"See something you like?" Demario asked. His accent was thicker than usual. It could've been due to the liquor or maybe it was because he was in an environment filled with other Latinos.

"I was looking for you?"

"Mmm, last time I looked in the mirror I didn't look anything like that guy." He pointed at the guy behind me.

He was referring to the guy on the dance floor who had briefly caught my attention. Even as Demario spoke to me, the guy continued to stare at me. I wished that Demario would've picked another time to find me. The guy on the dance floor was truly something to marvel at. He had to be at least 6'7", sported a low, faded haircut, and was slimly built. I loved a tall, slim guy; especially if he had a nice ass. I couldn't tell if he did or did not; he was wearing baggy jeans that sagged around his lower extremity. From the appearance of it, he didn't have any underwear on and I could get the full frontal view of his upper torso all the way down to the "V" that formed between his lower abs and groin.

"You're right. You look better than him."

"Nice save," Demario voiced with a hint of sarcasm in his tone.

"Hey, you're the one who invited me here. Don't get mad if I look at some of the eye candy."

"That's fine as long as you make sure that's all that you do."

What was it with the guys that I was meeting lately? It seemed like they wanted to put immediate claims on you just because they gave you a little ass. What happened to the days of dating and getting to know someone for compatibility before trying to engage in a full-blown relationship?

"What are you drinking?" I asked, pointing at the blue concoction in his cup.

"A Blue Motherfucka. Ever had one?"

"What's in it?"

"I'm not sure. All I know is that it's strong as hell and after I'm done with it, I'm sure to be fucked up."

"How many drinks have you had?"

"I'm on my second. I had some Hennessy and Coke earlier."

Either he was an experienced drinker, or truly a novice. Mixing drinks was never a good thing, and mixing white and brown liquor was asking for a hangover in the morning. Feeling the need to loosen up some, I decided to get a drink. "I'll be right back. I need to go get a drink. You need a refresher?"

"Maybe later. I need to go and take a piss," he slurred.

As he stumbled away, I made my way to the bar. I hope he didn't get too drunk. If he did, I could count out having sex. I couldn't stand drunken sex. It was always sloppy and rushed.

Standing at the bar, I waited for the bartender to take my order. I wanted to know what exactly was in a "Blue Motherfucka."

"Is that you?" I heard a voice to my right ask.

Turning in the direction of the voice, it was the guy on the dance floor. He had been bold enough to approach me, even though he had seen Demario indirectly make claim on me. "What do you mean?"

"Is that you…the guy? Are you two together?"

"In a way. Nothing serious." He must've been raised in the States because his voice had no trace of an accent. This was a major disappointment. A Latin accent would've propelled his level of sexiness. Without it, he was just another attractive guy in a club filled with other attractive guys.

"So if it isn't anything serious, then he won't mind me giving you my number, right? Maybe you can ditch him sometime tonight and we can hook up at your place."

With that, he handed me a napkin that had his name and number scribbled on it. I looked at the paper; his name was Tomás. I stuffed the napkin into my back pocket as Tomás went back to the dance floor to join his friends.

"What can I get you?" the burly and unattractive bartender barked.

"What's in a Blue Motherfucka?"

"Gin, rum, tequila, vodka, 7-Up, sour mix, and Blue Curacao," he quickly rambled, "Is that what you want?"

"Yeah, let me have two."

The bartender quickly turned away to mix the drinks as Demario approached me. "That damn line was long as hell."

"You didn't piss in your pants, did you?" I teasingly asked.

"Funny. You get your drink?"

"He's fixing it now. I got you another one."

"Are you trying to get me drunk so you can take advantage of me?"

"Why do I need to get you drunk to do that? I can get what I want without the alcohol."

"Cocky, aren't we?"

"*No, señor. Yo soy confianza.*" No sir. I am confident.

"Oh, so I was wrong? I didn't mean to mistake cockiness for confidence. I didn't know you could speak Spanish."

"*Yo hablo espanol un poco.*" I speak Spanish a little.

"*Muy bien. ¿Quieres bailar conmigo*? Very good. Do you want to dance with me?

"*¿Què?*" What?

"I asked if you wanted to dance with me."

"Sure, let me get the drinks and I'll meet you out there." I slapped the bartender twenty dollars and followed in the direction that Demario had headed.

With a drink in our hands, we grinded on the dance floor as the deejay played a hip-hop song by Miami-based Latin rapper

Pitbull. I was a little disappointed with Demario's rhythm, or lack of rhythm. I struggled to help him find the rhythm with the song. He definitely didn't have the "Latin flare" that many Latinos bragged about. Maybe it was the alcohol that had him a little tipsy.

Five songs later, I had grown tired of trying to help him to find his rhythm. I excused myself to the balcony to get some air. Making my way through the sweaty bodies, I endured many pats on the ass, and guys accidentally bumping into me. When I got outside, the air was muggy and laden with smoke. I found a bench in the corner where I could relax and unwind with my drink. I liked to people watch; especially when I was in the company of so many sexy men.

Pulling out a Black & Mild wine-flavored, wood-tipped cigar, I asked the guy sitting across from me for a light. I wasn't really a smoker, but in a setting like this, I did enjoy a strong drink and a cheap man's cigar. When I looked up, I caught a glimpse of Demario watching me from the door of the club. I guessed that he was trying to make sure that I wasn't trying to get my flirt on. I pulled out my cell phone and sent him a text message assuring him that I was good and he could relax and have fun with his friends.

He texted me a smiley face and disappeared back into the club. I could still feel his eyes watching me. I reclined back on the bench and enjoyed the effects of the alcohol running through my system.

I didn't want to stay out too late. Shawna was at my place, and I had texted her almost four hours ago telling her that I'd be home shortly.

CHAPTER 27
Shawna

I was in my car, headed toward Universal Studios City Walk where I was supposed to meet Edrian. I had sent Kenton a text that I'd have to catch up with him later. After fifteen minutes on the phone, Edrian had convinced me to come out and meet him for a drink. So kissing Kai on the head, I grabbed my keys, armed the home alarm system, and jumped in my car.

Parking my car in the garage, I trekked in the direction of Bob Marley: A Tribute to Freedom. Once I entered, I could see Edrian seated at the bar checking his watch. I'm sure he was a little nervous that I was going to stand him up. Creeping up behind him, I bent down and seductively whispered into his ear, "Waiting on someone?"

His face lit up when his eyes focused on me. When I looked into his eyes, as cheesy as it sounds, I felt butterflies. It was a feeling that I wasn't really familiar with. I sat down on the stool next to him. I was very apprehensive, and deciding not to waste any of my valuable time, I became very direct with him.

As the house band took a break, I took the initiative to get some questions out of the way before the music drowned us out. "So before we waste one another's time, let's go ahead and get this out of the way. Are you married, do you have a fiancée or a girlfriend? Are you bisexual or do you engage in any gay-for-pay activities?"

With a laugh, Edrian placed a hand onto my thigh. "I take it you've had some bad experiences with guys in the past?"

"That's an understatement. I don't know what I'll do if I run into another man that has a wife, girlfriend, fiancée, or boyfriend."

"Well, you can put down your guard. My answer is no to all of your questions, but I must admit that I have no idea what 'gay-for-pay' means."

"Gay-for-pay is when a straight man will perform certain sexual activities with another man for money. Basically, he's being paid to be gay but sees himself as being completely straight," I taught Edrian.

I was relieved he had answered "no" to my questions and I took a deep breath to calm my nerves. I knew not to get my hopes up when it came to men. Love and men only equated to pain. I so desperately wanted it to change for me, but I had stopped believing in fairy tales a long time ago. There was no knight-in-shining-armor. I doubted that I'd ever live the American dream that I desperately wanted.

"So, Shawna, why don't you tell me something about you; whatever it is that you want to tell me."

"I've got something better," I countered. "How about we take the time to learn the things about the other that we want to know. I mean, I'm so tired of having to go through the routine interview questions. Seriously, I don't think I can endure the same old 'where are you from,' 'what's your favorite movie,' or any of the other typical questions that one asks on a first date.

"I'd love to meet a guy that takes the initiative to learn that whenever we go out to eat, I always inquire if the food has onions. I'd like for a guy to take the time to notice what color the majority of my shirts are, the types of music I shop for, and what ticks me off."

"Okay. I understand where you're coming from. So instead of me asking you what your favorite food is, you want me to actually take some time out and learn that."

"There will be things that I'll have to tell you. I can't expect you to read my mind."

"So with your request, are you willing to reciprocate and to do the same?" he questioned.

"I don't ask for what I can't give so, yes, I'm willing to get to know you. Who knows? Romance might not be in the cards for you and me, but we could end up being great friends."

"I second that. So, Shawna, what prompted you to try this new style of dating with me?"

I wasn't sure if I was ready to divulge the truth about what had made me reconsider how I now chose to date, but if we were going to get to know one another, I didn't want to start things off by lying. I opted for the truth with some omissions.

"Well, let's just say that I'm growing tired of men asking how to please me or what will make me achieve an orgasm. I'm tired of dating men that can't comprehend that the simple act of sending me flowers for no reason will make me smile. I'm tired of dating men that don't understand that they don't have to open their wallets to try and buy my affection with extravagant gifts. I like nice and expensive gifts, but they don't leave lasting impressions on me. It is the simple things that count. Something like a man trying to cook dinner for me on my birthday, or remembering the first day we met even if he has to program it into his BlackBerry or put it into his email calendar. For me, it's simply about putting forth the effort." I left out any details centering on Kyler, my male sponsor, and Ryan, my heartbreak.

"Okay. I'm game for trying things your way."

For the rest of the evening, we shared our past relationship experiences and what we expected to find the next time we decided to fall in love again. I shared with him what had happened between Antoine and me, and how I was supposed to be taking some time out for myself.

"So, if you're supposed to be taking this time out for yourself, why are you here with me?"

"Let's just say that it was something in your approach that took me off-guard."

"But it was you who approached me at Starbucks. I was simply sitting down reading my magazine on my lunch break."

"Touché, you're right. Well, maybe it was the way you responded. With other guys, before they left the coffee shop, they'd have spent the majority of the time talking to my chest and the remainder trying to figure out how to get me back to their place and into their bed. With you, you seemed capable of repressing the hormones. But time will tell if this is merely a mask that you're wearing or if it truly is you."

"I can see getting to know you will be like walking on water—impossible. I'm willing to put in the effort in getting to know you as long as you don't make me pay for every man that you've previously dated and their mistakes."

"I'm not making any promises, but I can try."

For the rest of the night, we sipped on drinks and enjoyed the live music before Edrian and I strolled through City Walk. After two hours, he walked me back to my car. I promised to call him when I made it home safely. As I headed to my lonely apartment, I smiled to myself for not totally giving up on love. I was looking forward to seeing where it'd take me this time. I'd be damned if it left me heartbroken and jilted again.

CHAPTER 28
Anjel

I debated on fixing a light cocktail to calm my jumping nerves. I don't know why I had consented to Bryce's invitation for dinner. I also didn't understand why Alexandria hadn't talked me out of it. She had even called in reinforcements later that evening; all my girls had conferenced in on the call and had made me commit to not pull out. I tried to explain to them that I didn't think that I was ready to get back out in the dating game when my heart still remained with Mason. But as Bryce put it, this wasn't a date.

I called him that morning to touch bases and to inform him what time I would be available. Throughout our brief conversation, we broke the ice with some small talk. In the past, the two of us had never really shared much conversation. Our dealings were simple pleasantries as he stopped by to hang out with Mason. From our current phone conversation, I could see that he and I had a lot of similarities.

When he inquired about my likes, I divulged that I had a new interest in wine tastings. This prompted him to suggest that we ditch our dinner plans to attend a wine pairing at The Grape at International Plaza in Tampa. He levied that this would give us the opportunity to get comfortable with one another during the hour-long drive. This would also mean that we would be going to a mutual place. Despite what he had said, I surmised that this was shaping up to be a date.

I hoped that I wasn't leading Bryce on. I didn't want him to think that anything serious could actually come of this other than friendship. I didn't feel comfortable dating someone that used to be an acquaintance of the man that I still loved, and more than likely would always love. My grandmother always told me that you only get one shot at true love and when you find that love, you will do anything and everything to keep it. My antics lately had illustrated this. I was fighting the temptation to kick them up a notch.

There is no doubt in my mind, or in my heart, that my "true love" was Mason. I wished that my grandma hadn't passed away. I had some questions about her views on true love. I mean, what were you supposed to do if you found your true love and that true love didn't share the same feelings? I wondered how she'd explain this. How could you love someone unconditionally that wasn't willing to love you back in the same fashion? Hell, in my case, it was simply getting him to love me *period*.

I glanced at my watch. I expected Bryce to be knocking on my door any minute. I got up and headed to my half-bathroom. I bent over the antique-style sink to glance into the mounted mirror. My makeup was spot on. My hair was fashionably styled.

As each day passed, I grew fonder of my new haircut. Next time I'd try some auburn highlights to bring out my complexion and the color of my eyes. Smoothing out my straight-legged jeans and my maroon, cotton turtleneck sweater, I felt my phone vibrating on my hip. Taking the phone from its leather encasement, I saw that it was only Inola, Mason's assistant. I didn't want to be bothered with her at the moment so I let her call roll to the voicemail. Just as I placed the phone back inside the holster, my doorbell sounded.

I wondered if Bryce would be as apprehensive tonight as he had been at the gas station. I headed to the door. "Just a minute!"

I called out. I needed to put on my heeled boots, which I had left at the door so that I wouldn't scuff my hardwood floors.

Quickly stepping into them, I opened the door to see Bryce trying his best to look calm. "Sorry for the wait. I would invite you in, but we have quite a ride ahead of us."

"It's no problem. Shall we?" he asked, signaling toward his Range Rover.

"We shall, but I hope you don't mind if I drive. You were kind enough to drive all the way here. It's the least I can do."

"It wasn't a problem, and I don't mind."

"But I do. I'm not the selfish type." I noticed that he was a little taken aback by my aggressiveness. So, to ease the tension, I threw in, "Plus, it'd give you some time to relax and to get rid of that anxiety."

"You noticed, huh?"

"I did. It was out of character for you. From our brief run-ins, I'm used to this boisterous guy. At the gas station, I thought we were back in high school."

"That bad?" He blushed.

"Yes, it was that bad." He laughed at my comment and seemed to shake off some of his apprehension. "See, you're lightening up some."

I quickly turned on the house alarm and locked the front door. Bryce extended his hand to assist me in walking down the porch stairs. His chivalry wasn't going unnoticed.

Standing side by side, even with the three-inch heels of my ankle boots, I still hadn't managed to match his height. As I led the way to the driveway, I could feel his eyes watching me. For added effect, I put a little extra bounce in my step. I had to admit, it was nice having someone of the opposite sex to show me some real interest.

Usually at this time of the year, Orlando was pretty warm in the early part of March, but a cold front had caused temperatures to drop into the low-fifties. This was way too cold for me to let the top down on my convertible. So to make this road trip, I decided to use my Jeep Liberty. I loved my mini-SUV. Although it was a jeep, it drove like a car.

Climbing into the driver's seat, I waited for Bryce to get into the passenger side and to adjust the seat for his height. As I backed out of the driveway, I teased, "The next time you stare at my ass like that, I'm going to have to charge you."

"Do you take VISA?"

"Now see, I was going to be crass, but I don't want you thinking that I'm being un-ladylike."

"Don't put on a front for me. Be comfortable and speak your mind."

I briefly diverted my attention from the road and looked at him. His green eyes met mine, and his picture-perfect smile greeted me. To make matters worse, he had dimples. I had never noticed them before; possibly because I had never paid him any real attention in the past.

This "not a date" thing was starting off on a good note. I wondered what he'd say or do to cause it to end sourly. He was a man, so it was inevitable that would happen.

In my head, I made a bet to myself that he wouldn't get through two hours before I suddenly had to pull the "I have cramps" line.

CHAPTER 29
Kenton

I was pulling away from Demario's apartment. He was totally inebriated and I thought that it was best for him to sleep it off at home. If there was one thing that I hated, it was a sloppy drunk. My father was a drunk, and when he drank, he would become aggressive. So aggressive that he would hit on my mother in his drunken state.

I remembered a time when I was no more than four years old and he and my mom had gotten into a heated argument. My mother shouted for me to go to my room, but my father instructed me to stay. He demanded that I remain seated. He told me that I needed to learn how to "keep my woman in check." I'm not sure what kind of checking he was referring to; by the time the fight was over, my mother had done a number on him.

That day was imprinted into my memories. I had forgotten plenty of other things but I remembered things like that. I remembered another fight when I was a little older, and again my parents were going at it full throttle. My father was always the instigator. My mother screamed for me to call the police, but I was scared of my father so when he told me to sit my ass down, as usual, I did.

My father had ripped the downstairs phone from the wall jack; as my mother scrambled around upstairs for an operable phone, my father took it upon himself to scramble my siblings and me into his beat-up, brown 1989 Isuzu Piazza Nero. He knew this would devastate my mother more than any type of beating. As we drove away from the brownstone, I remembered the song that was playing on the radio. The song and its lyrics would forever be embedded in my mind. It was "Hey Little Walter" by the R&B trio Tony! Toni! Tone!

As we reached the main street leading to the highway, the chorus began playing. I would never forget those lyrics. Even today, I cringe every time I hear the song.

At the very moment the hook ended, my father's hatchback was surrounded by four Chicago police cruisers. They forced my father out of the car and handcuffed him in front of my two brothers and me.

I remembered an officer returning us home to my badly beaten mother, who was waiting with open arms and tears falling from her face. Before entering the house, I looked back over my shoulder at my father sitting in the back of one of the police cruisers. It was an image that no little boy should have to witness.

From that moment, I swore to never drink to the extent where I wasn't coherent. To this day, I'd only broken that vow once. Seeing Demario in his current state brought back those memories. In the car, as I drove him home, he became very belligerent and accusatory. He thought that I went out on the patio to flirt with other guys. I didn't add fuel to the fire by telling him that even if I had chosen to do that, I was within my rights. He and I weren't an item.

I couldn't believe that I had chosen Demario over Marcel. He was genuinely a nice person, but he still needed to do some living and some growing. His bouts of jealousy and tantrums were a huge turnoff and deterred anyone from wanting to love him beyond the physical. I never said that he was ever going to be more than a piece of ass, but he was in the running for a temporary replacement for Marcel.

I opened the sunroof to allow the cool evening chill to seep into the cabin of the SUV. Tonight it was a full moon. It sat so high in the sky amongst a plethora of stars, yet it appeared to be alone. I couldn't help wondering when I'd be able to let down my guard and to stop imitating the moon and become like the stars surrounding it. When was I going to trust in love again and find my star?

The irony about my situation is how I was advising Anjel the other day to get over Mason and to move on. Regardless of how much I wanted and how much I prayed, I couldn't get Trevor off of my mind or out of my heart. He had hurt me deeply. I thought I knew what pain was before him, but the day I walked in on him getting fucked by someone else, he had literally torn my heart in two.

It was unsettling when I thought back to the man that I had become, all in an attempt to prove my love to him. I couldn't shake the way that I felt when I gave my body to others so vicariously, thinking that this would make him love me more. I needed to let it go…to let him go, but I didn't want to risk feeling such pain ever again.

Tonight was a night I didn't want to be alone. I didn't want to feel the way that I was feeling. So like an alcoholic turns to the bottle for a means to escape, I turned to the body of another. When I approached a stop sign, I reached back into my back pocket to retrieve the number Tomás had given me.

I was going to take him up on his offer. There was nothing like some carefree, no-strings sex to get your mind off of an old romance. With one hand on the steering wheel, I used my free hand to dial Tomás' number. After a few rings, he answered.

"Hello."

"What's going on? Is this Tomás?"

"Yep, and this is…?"

"The dude from the club that you gave your number to at the bar?" There was a brief pause from him. "That many guys, huh?" I asked. I wasn't probably far off in my insinuation.

"Funny. I was actually trying to remember if you had given me your name."

"Nah, I didn't. Is it really needed? You didn't seem too interested in getting to know me for dating."

"True; I don't date dudes. Fuck with them, yeah. So, what's on your mind?"

"Tryna take you up on your offer. Feel me?"

"Nah, I'm not feeling you…yet. So, what time you talking, playboy?"

"What you got going on now?"

"Shit, not much. My girl's still out with her peoples. So if you down with scooping a brother up, we can make this shit happen."

"No doubt. Where do you live?"

I listened as he gave me directions to his place. He was all the way on the other side of town. It'd take me a half-hour to get to him, bring him back to my place, and take him back home at a decent hour so he wouldn't get the third-degree from his girl. I relayed this to him, suggesting that we possibly make it another night.

"Hell no! I want that dick tonight. Shit, why do you need to take me back to your crib? We can handle this anywhere. By the time you get here, I'll be showered and this ass will be tight. We can let things play out and whatever happens happen."

I was down with his thinking. I wasn't sure what he had in mind, but it seemed like he was a pro at getting his nut on the low. I wasn't a fan of bisexual men, but hey, we weren't meeting to date. We were meeting to fuck. We didn't need to exchange names or numbers. The responsibility I had in regard to him was making sure that I wrapped it up.

Him cheating on his girl, or boy, had nothing to do with me. I was nothing more than a stranger passing in the night. I wouldn't be surprised if his girl didn't already know what the deal was with him. But then again, if she was a sistah, she was probably mesmerized by his light complexion, nice hair, and his physique. You'd be surprised at how many Southern sisters were more concerned about having a light-skinned baby with good hair than they were in making sure that the man they laid down with at night was, in fact, solely into women. Or it could simply be that he had a big dick and knew how to use it—this seemed to always get any woman's attention.

It was wrong for me to stereotype, but behind every stereotype is some truth. This was all the reason why I kept my ideologies to myself. As I made my way to Tomás' crib, I got a text from Shawna notifying me that she was bouncing and that we would have to catch up later. I couldn't wait to hear whom she was running off to meet. This made things even better because now I could definitely bring Tomás back to my place.

The night was getting better by the minute!

CHAPTER 30
Shawna

Tossing and turning in my king-sized canopy bed, I buried my head under the covers. I don't know what was going on with me tonight. I glanced at the alarm clock and noted that it was only 3 a.m. I didn't really have anything to do tomorrow, but if I didn't get some rest, I'd be dragging through the entire day.

Turning onto my back, in the darkness, I stared up at the ceiling. I could see the light fixture due to the ray of moonlight, which penetrated my bedroom from a break in the curtains. I had so much on my mind, it kept me perplexed and left me troubled.

I was still feeling the aftermaths of Antoine. I thought for the first time that I could truly begin to let go of my past and to venture down a path of happiness. I don't understand why he felt the need to deceive me. Expecting him to be upfront and tell me what the deal was upfront was ludicrous.

I wish men would realize that their actions caused many women to be jaded. Because of Antoine, I was now wondering what Edrian's intentions were. He seemed like a decent guy, and I'd be a straight-up fool to say that I wasn't attracted to him. After our date this evening, I was certain that it was possible for us to complement one another romantically.

Look at me. Here I go again. I don't know why I always seemed to run when I should be walking. It was like a never-ending story. I swore that my love life was on repeat. I would meet a guy that caught my eye based on the physical, we'd talk and vibe some, and I'd realize that we had some things in common. From there it all went downhill. I'd find myself catching feelings for someone that I truly hadn't taken the time out to learn.

It was a mistake that I often made. It was a mistake that I needed to correct, and hopefully by doing so, I'd break this ongoing cycle. Was I really wrong? Isn't it innate for people to want to be loved and to feel loved? As much as I put on a show pretending to be the bad girl, when it came down to it, that is exactly what it was—a show.

I needed to love and to be loved. I needed consistency and repetition. I wanted to wake up in the mornings and know who was going to be on the other side. I wanted to experience the ups and downs that came with being in love—morning kisses with the morning breath, frivolous arguments that ended with make-up sex, and using the restroom when the other was in the shower.

Ultimately, I wanted a ring on my finger and the lifetime commitment that came with it. There was no uncertainty in my mind that I would be able to remain monogamous—even though I had become a love'em and leave'em type of woman over the years. This was merely done to protect my heart from having to succumb to any further unwarranted emotional distress.

I knew firsthand about the dangers that came with love. I'd had my bouts with them, witnessed Kenton fall victim to its alluring spell, and I was seeing firsthand, my girl Anjel, battle with the laws of love. After awhile, the heart becomes numb to the pain and remains hardened. I wasn't quite there yet. I still had some feelings, but the feelings were slowly dissipating.

The questions that left me perplexed tonight centered on Edrian. He was such a gentleman, but you could tell that if pushed too much, he could get straight-up hood with the best of them. The whole night I couldn't break our eye contact. His eyes told a story.

It was a story that I was anxious to find out. When he placed his hand on the small of my back, I could feel his confidence as he guided me. We walked though City Walk hand-in-hand like we were two lovers on a late-night stroll.

Closing my eyes, I eventually drifted back to sleep only to be awakened again. This time it wasn't my anxiety that had awoken me; it was my upstairs neighbor. I glanced at the clock. It was 4:47 a.m. and here she was getting her rocks off. If I was promiscuous, she was a bona-fide slut.

"Yes...Don't stop...Beat this pussy up..." she sang to her lover of the night.

"You have to be fucking kidding me!" I screamed to the ceiling. My protests were falling on deaf ears. This heifer was very animated and vocal when she was getting hers.

"You want this dick? Tell me you want this dick!" her male companion's voice boomed through the ceiling.

"Yes, I want it. Give it to me. Fuck me, boy! Fuck...me...good!"

This was going to last for at least another twenty minutes before they took a break and, like always, she'd be back to screaming again within the hour. Listening to the two of them get it in was beginning to turn me on.

Normally her sexual encounters wouldn't have bothered me because I'd be getting my freak on, or would've just finished getting mine on, so I'd be too exhausted to care about what she was doing. It was a shame at how much I paid to live in what was described as a luxury high-rise by the sales agent, and the walls were paper-thin. I'm sure if I'd farted, all my neighbors would've heard it as if they were in the room with me.

I listened to my neighbor cry out in pleasure as she and her lover fucked. My room was filled with the sounds of their call-and-answers. Fully awake, my thoughts began to reminisce about my night with Edrian and they weren't as pure as they were earlier in the evening. I remembered how he made me quiver when he placed his hand on the small of my back last night. I wanted to know what his touch would do to other parts of my body.

I brought my left hand up to my right breast and slowly circled my nipple. Imagining my fingers were his, I softly pinched my nipple. Bringing a finger to my mouth, I sucked on the tip of my finger before moving my hand back down to my breast and softly squeezing my nipple again. I let out a barely audible moan. I wondered if his hands would have this same effect on my nipples.

Intensifying things, I squeezed my nipple harder and now my moans were louder. I rotated back and forth, kneading my breasts and playing with my nipples until both nipples were hard as rocks. Slowly taking the tip of my finger, I traced it around my upper torso down to my belly button and across to each of my oblique muscles. I squirmed from my own tantalizing touches. I wondered if his touch would have this same effect.

Escalating things further, I moved my hand down to my neatly trimmed bush. I felt the moistness between my legs. I wondered if his touch would make me wet. I rubbed two fingers up-and-down the lips of my pussy. Arching my back, I moved one of my fingers inside. I then inserted another finger, and while my left hand played between my legs, my right hand toyed with my nipples. Masturbation was never first on my list, but in hard times, you had to do whatever it took.

Physically I was the one bringing about this euphoric feeling, but in my mind it was Edrian that was making me feel like I hadn't felt in years. It was him that was making me warm and wet. It was him that was teasing and pinching my nipples in an effort to make me cum.

Stopping for a quick moment, I rolled over to the other side of the bed, and pulled out my vibrator and a small bottle of K-Y

Jelly from under the pillow. Lathering the makeshift penis and turning it on, I replaced my fingers with it. I felt the battery-induced vibrations pulsating throughout my body. Starting between my legs, it simultaneously reverberated downward to my toes and upward to my head.

I was growing lightheaded as I moved the vibrator in and out of my walls. My heart rate was racing and my breathing quickened. My toes were curling. My right hand was squeezing my right nipple, the more sensitive of the two. I tried to slow down, but it was too late. The electric vibrations were sending me over the edge as I reached my climax.

I lay in my bed, my body still convulsing from the aftershocks of my orgasm. I tossed the vibrator covered with my juices to the floor. After my heart rate slowed and I caught my breath, I would make my way to the bathroom to clean up. Apparently that hadn't happened when the sound of my television awoke me. I ended up drifting off to sleep. My television was set to automatically turn on at 6 a.m. so that I could listen to the news while trying to fully wake up. Sometimes this was a depressing way to start the morning off. It seemed like all there was to report about were killings, the skyrocketing unemployment rates, and the increasing number of people losing their homes to foreclosure. As depressing as this might have been, I still needed to be aware of what was happening around me and within the community.

In national news, the male anchorman reported on the latest ruling by the Georgia Board of Regents in regard to illegal immigrants being allowed to attend state universities in Georgia. Hearing the message indicator of my phone, I picked it up. It was Edrian sending me a text message wishing me a good morning and informing me that I was heavily on his mind.

"Now this is how you start a morning!" I screamed to the four walls.

CHAPTER 31
Anjel

I was startled and awakened by a hand grabbing me from behind. It took a minute, but slowly I was able to remember what had gone down last night. As he slept, his arm was protectively wrapped around me. His breathing was light. When I was certain that he was back in a deep sleep, I slowly and quietly escaped his comforting hold.

Turning around to make sure that he was still asleep, I took in his boyish features. He was even more handsome than I had given him credit for, and his body was simply delectable. After we had spent hours at The Grape, there was no way that either of us would be able to make the drive back to Orlando. To not risk getting a DUI or one of us falling asleep behind the wheel, I suggested that we simply get a hotel room to retire.

We managed to drive a half-mile from The Grape to the hotel. There was a major citywide convention going on, and the hotel ironically had one room with a king-sized bed. Entering the room, I don't know if the alcohol had an effect on me, but the two of us began joking around. Joking around led to us wrestling. The wrestling led to our clothes coming off. I couldn't resist him once his shirt had come off, revealing a chiseled and solid chest. His hardened nipples pointed out from his massive pecs. They were erect as they set atop of his well-defined chest.

I wasn't sure who had seduced whom, but somehow Bryce and I had ended up naked and horizontal. When he first disrobed, I had to take a step back. Brother was nothing like Mason. Bryce was definitely a well-endowed brother. He gave a new definition to the term "third leg." Normally, an uncut penis would have turned me off, but something about Bryce drew me near. It wasn't the physical that had me interested. It was the way he smiled when he looked at me. The way his eyes lit up when he caught my gaze.

I hadn't felt…so attractive in years. In a relationship, things that you do when you are in the dating stages slowly fade out as the days, the weeks, the months, and years pass by. It is as if you take your partner for granted and don't realize that you need to tell them that they look beautiful or handsome, tell them how much you love them, and tell them what it is about them that brings about happiness.

Tiptoeing, I slowly crept into the hotel room's bathroom. Quietly closing the door, I turned the sink's faucet on so that the trickling water would drown out the sound of me peeing. Sitting on the toilet, I waited until I heard my urine break the sitting water. I glanced around the cramped bathroom. It was a wonder how they managed to fit a sink, toilet, and bathtub inside.

As I relieved myself, I thought about Bryce. What exactly was I doing? He was a genuine person, and it was obvious from our conversation last night that he was interested in more than a random roll in the hay. He revealed to me last night what I had already known to be true; that he'd been attracted to me for years. He even told me that he realized that I was still in love with Mason, but that didn't matter to him. He was determined that if I gave him a chance, my love for Mason would dispel with time.

He seemed convinced of this, but I didn't have the heart to tell him that last night was what it was—a one-night stand. My heart was with Mason and no matter what I did, or how hard I tried, there was nothing that was going to change that. I'd been in love several times, and there was nothing that could surmount the intensity and adoration that I held for Mason. He was my one true love.

After I finished wiping between my legs and washing my hands, I headed out of the bathroom. There was that light in his eyes and that smile again. This was going to be harder than I thought it was going to be. I wasn't in the business of breaking hearts, but I would need to nip this in the bud soon before I was guilty of leading him on.

"If you aren't in a rush to get back to Orlando, I'd love to go to breakfast. There's this little eatery that I love; it's known for their pancakes, homemade grits, and chicken sausage," Bryce suggested.

He was beaming and I didn't want to ruin the moment; especially when we had to make the ride back to Orlando. There was nothing like being trapped in a car with tension in the air. "I'm game," I replied, "but what are you going to do about fresh clothes and freshening up?"

"Me? What about you? I'm sure you want to be so-fresh and so-clean yourself."

"Now what woman do you know that doesn't have a travel bag in her car? You never know what kind of accidents you're going to have or when Mother Nature will play an evil trick and come early."

"I got'cha. So you're covered. I'll have to go down to the hotel gift shop and see what they have."

"Tell you what, you go take a shower and call up for some toiletries and I'll handle the rest."

"Wow, already dressing me?" he teased.

I playfully threw a pillow at him. He wasn't the lame person that Mason had described him as, or whom I had him pegged to be.

As he headed to the bathroom, I took notice of his well-developed assets. I loved a man with a firm ass. If he opted to, he could actually do some modeling.

"Why do I feel your eyes checking me out?" he asked over his shoulder.

He had caught me in the act. "Oh, like you weren't checking me out when I went to the bathroom?"

"I was asleep."

"Yeah, pretend sleep. Funny how you were conscious enough to come over to my side of the bed and wrap your arm around me."

"Prove it," he shot over his shoulder as he entered the bathroom to shower.

I heard the shower start, and I quickly threw my clothes on. Grabbing my purse and car keys, I left the room, taking the room key with me. I remembered when we had arrived last night, we had passed a Target two blocks from the hotel. Unfortunately, at 8 a.m., no major department stores were open so he'd have to deal with an improvised outfit from Target.

Finding my car in the parking lot adjacent to the boutique hotel, I headed to Target. Once there, I quickly found some khaki pants, an off-brand polo shirt, and some boxer briefs. I didn't think to inquire about his size. But I considered myself an experienced shopper so I didn't think I'd have a problem picking something out for him.

After choosing an outfit, some socks, and some boxer briefs for Bryce, I made my way back to the hotel. I was having an epiphany and had come to the conclusion that I didn't want to use Bryce in my scheme to evoke jealousy with Mason. Pulling up to the valet attendant, I handed him my keys as I pulled the Target shopping bag from the passenger's seat, rounded the rear of my Jeep and got my spare bag of clothes. It had been so long since I'd worn them, I hoped they still fit.

When I entered the room, I could smell the fresh-scented smell of the hotel soap. Bryce was lying across the bed with a white hotel towel wrapped around his waist. I had to admit he was truly a sight to see; it didn't hurt that the sex had been better than I expected. I had an underlying feeling that there was more to Bryce than the eyes could see. I was certain that he had more than a little freak hidden within.

As I closed the door, he turned his attention away from CNN and toward me. A smile exploded across his face. Something deep within me stirred. I remembered how Mason would smile at me whenever he caught sight of me. Why didn't men realize that it was these small things that got inside of a woman's head? Shit like this would make a woman fall in love. Unfortunately for Bryce, the only love that remained in my heart was for a man who wanted to go on a sexual exploration with every skank in the state of Florida.

"There you are. While you were gone, your phone has been ringing off the hook."

"I'll check it later; I was hoping that I could get you to wash my back," I seductively informed him, beckoning him to follow me into the bathroom.

Taking my invitation, Bryce stood up, let the towel that was wrapped around his waist fall to the floor, and followed me to the bathroom. Climbing into the cramped shower, we immersed ourselves in the tepid water.

Grabbing the hotel's liquid body wash, he poured the sudsy liquid over me. Moving his hands in circular motions, he covered my body with the soap. Taking a washcloth, he cleaned every inch of me. When he was done washing my feet, he remained on one bended knee and raised my right leg and placed my toes inside his mouth. I leaned back against the shower wall to keep my balance. His tongue danced across my toes.

Moving his tongue from my foot up to my calves, then up my thighs, he stopped when he reached the lips of my vagina. Using his tongue to tease me, he suddenly plunged his tongue inside. He lapped at my clitoris like a deep-sea diver looking for fish. I grabbed his head as I rode the waves of ecstasy. With his tongue deep inside me, his hands toying with my nipples, I gripped the shower curtain and the shower walls as I bucked against his face.

As the water pelted down on me, I couldn't control it any longer. I climaxed—hard. Bryce continued to French kiss me between the legs as my body violently convulsed. When my convulsions subsided he stood up and we kissed. I tasted my juices on his tongue. I was spent from the climax and I didn't have the energy to return the favor and pleasure him back. He sensed my weakness and smiled at me to let me know that it was okay.

"You did a good job last night taking care of me," he whispered in my ear. "There's no way I could bust again until I had a little time to recoup."

Together we finished showering and took turns applying moisturizer to one another's body. When we were done, I wrapped myself in a robe, grabbed my phone, and headed to the balcony. I didn't know who'd be calling me with a sense of urgency on a Saturday morning. I hoped everything was okay with my family and friends.

"Excuse me, Bryce; I need to make a personal phone call." I drew back the curtains to the sliding glass window and stepped out on the room's balcony.

When I unlocked my phone, I noticed the missed calls indicator notified me that I had five missed calls. Checking the log, I was surprised they were all from Mason. His timing was perfect. Hitting the TALK button, it automatically called the last number that had called my phone.

After two rings, Mason answered.

"Where the fuck are you?" he snarled into the receiver.

"Excuse me? Good morning to you, too."

"I'm done playing these damn games with you, Anjel. This time you've gone too far. It has been long enough. Don't you think it's time that you move on?"

"Where is all of this coming from? What do you mean by 'move on'? You're the one that shows up at my place unannounced in the middle of the night. And what do you mean, 'gone too far'?"

"Look, I know what you've been up to. You're responsible for the water in my gas tank, the slashed tires, and the broken house and car windows. I didn't press charges because I realized that you were venting and that our breakup had hurt you. But I can't take this drama anymore. I called the police."

"For what? You fuck any and everything that has a pussy. That shit could've been done by any of your tricks," I spat back into the phone.

I turned to make sure that Bryce wasn't eavesdropping on my conversation. He was fully dressed and his attention was back on the television.

"Anjel, this has got to come to a stop. Directing your anger toward me is one thing, but now you're lashing out at my fiancée. That's unacceptable."

I used the rail of the balcony to steady myself. I had to be hearing things incorrectly. I thought he had said "fiancée." My ears had to have been deceiving me.

"Fiancée? What the hell are you talking about?" I kept my voice level. I didn't want him to know that his statement had rattled my nerves.

"I was going to tell you when the time was right, but I rekindled things with an old girlfriend. She was before you. She was the main reason that I decided to end things with you. We've been communicating back and forth for almost a year via Facebook."

"So you were emotionally involved with her while we were together?" My head was swimming. I could feel my legs turning into rubber, but I maintained my balance.

"It is what it is. Let's not dwell in the past. If you pay for the damages, I won't tell the police that it was you."

"I have no idea what damages you're talking about, you sonofabitch. And what past don't you want to dwell in? How am I the past when less than a week ago you were waking up next to me? I'm the past but you were fucking me in the middle of the night. I was the one you were depositing your nut inside."

"One of many that I've done that to," he crassly retorted. "Janine hadn't officially relocated here and I needed to get that out of my system."

"So, I was just a mere fuck? Fuck you, Mason! If you burned me again, you will regret it. This, I promise you.

"As for calling the police, do whatever the hell you need to. The next time you decide to contact me, it better be through my lawyer. And take this for what it's worth, but you better make sure your bitch knows who I am. I can't believe the two of you were cheating together while we were together. If she sees me out and about, she better get the hell out of my way," I snapped into the phone before terminating the conversation.

The tears were welling in my eyes, but for the time being, I needed to put on a show. I didn't need for Bryce to see me in such a vulnerable state.

CHAPTER 32
Kenton

As soon as Tomás entered my bedroom, he wasted no time undressing. When he was in the nude, I reclined back on the bed, still fully dressed, as I took him in from head to toe. He had a moderate amount of hair on his chest, lower legs, and arms. He had taken great care in trimming his pelvic area and his ass appeared to be as smooth as a baby's bottom. That was a major plus for me. I couldn't stand a man with a hairy ass. It seemed to be unhygienic.

I was always left wondering how they were able to keep the area clean after defecating. Just the thought of seeing broken tissues or remnants of their bowel movement between their legs brought a frown to my face.

"Something wrong, papi?" Tomás questioned after obviously observing the look on my face.

"It's all good on this end. You've got a sexy body," I told him as I stood up and went to him. He grabbed the bottom of my shirt and lifted it over my head. He ran one of his hands down my chest and stopped when he got to my belly button.

My body was naturally smooth, except in certain areas. One of the few areas that had a little hair was right under my belly button. It was a small trail that led down to my penis. Bending down, Tomás brought his lips to mine and we kissed. It was a little sloppy at first, but when I placed my hands around his waist, we found our groove. We savored one another. His breath was laced with a peppermint Altoid. Mine still had the taste of alcohol on it.

With our lips connected, Tomás' hands moved down to my belt buckle. Clumsily, he unbuckled the belt, and then attempted to unfasten my jeans. Sensing his trouble, I assisted him with loosening my jeans and pulling the zipper down.

My jeans fell down to my feet, and my penis protruded against the fabric of my boxer briefs. Tomás' hand caressed the head of my penis as his tongue playfully darted in and out of my mouth. With my tongue, I licked at his lips and softly placed kisses on the tip of his nose and on the bottom of his chin.

As we kissed, his penis protruded, poking me in my abs. I moved one of my hands away from his waist and reached around. I ran a finger up and down between his buttocks. A moan escaped from Tomás' throat and I could feel his body relaxing. Pulling away from me, he looked me in the eyes. At that moment, I could see the pain that was embedded within them. He was a man living a double life and was uncertain of where the future would take him.

At the moment he was in bed with me, but in a few hours he'd be back home, lying next to his girl. I could tell that from the look in his eyes that home wasn't where he wanted to be. He was merely going through the motions that so many men went through. He didn't want to face the ridicule and persecution from society so he played by society's rules. He had chosen to live a life that his heart wasn't into.

Breaking our eye contact, I pulled away from Tomás. Bending down, I unlaced my shoes and kicked them off. Pulling my boxer briefs down, I removed them along with my jeans and socks. Now I was also completely nude.

"Can we keep the lights on?" Tomás requested.

That was an unusual request, but if that was what he was into, then I was game. Seeing that his request puzzled me, Tomás interjected, "I love to see your skin on mine. It's like we're a

Reese's Peanut Butter Cup," he observed. He smiled up at me.

He was actually correct. My skin tone was the perfect shade of chocolate and his was the same as peanut butter. Moving over to the bed, I aggressively pushed him onto the mattress. He was on his back; his feet were slightly hanging over the side.

"Hold on," I instructed as I went to the other side of the room. I could feel his eyes watching me as I walked away. I wasn't a gym rat, but I did what I could, including the routine body maintenance. I did 500 sit-ups a day, 250 pushups, and ran two miles every other day. When Kai was a little older, she'd join me on these runs. Presently, she'd tire out close to a mile into the run.

I turned on the mounted stereo and Alicia Keys' voice softly erupted from the speakers that were strategically placed around the room. With the lights on, I couldn't really set the mood, but I'd do what I could. I wanted to make sure that I gave Tomás a night that he wouldn't be able to forget before I sent him home to live his double life.

As I headed back to Tomás, I stopped at the nightstand adjacent to my bed to pull some body oil from the bottom drawer. Placing a small amount in my hands, I rubbed my hands together. Climbing onto the bed, I instructed Tomás to turn over onto his stomach. With his face buried in the pillows, I mounted him. As I sat atop of his buttocks, I softly rubbed the lavender-scented massage oil over his neck, shoulders, and back. Then I gently, but firmly, began to massage his upper body until the oil was completely rubbed into his skin. As I massaged his neck, I leaned forward, allowing my hard-on to press against the top of his ass.

Each time I did this, I could feel Tomás squirm under me. His body language was letting me know that he was ready to get down to business, but I was going to take my time. I operated on my own terms and not on anyone else's. When I was done with his upper body, I turned around and repeated the same actions to his lower extremities, starting with the balls of his feet.

Nothing turned me on more than a man that took the time out to take care of his feet. It took a few seconds in the shower for a person to rub a pumice stone across the soles of their feet to smooth out the calluses and to get rid of the dry skin. It took even less time to apply some oil or moisturizer to keep them soft and unchafed. A few minutes more were needed to keep the toenails clean and trimmed.

Tomás' body seemed to fully relax as I rotated from foot to foot. From time to time, when I added a little additional pressure, he'd let out a soft, appreciative moan. When I was finished massaging his feet, I moved up to his calves, his hamstrings, and finally to his buttocks. When I was done, I instructed him to turn over.

As I reached for the massage oil on the nightstand, he grabbed my arm and pulled me to him. Engaging me in a full-blown kiss, his hands explored my body. I could sense his level of excitement from the way he kissed me. He kissed me hard, our tongues no longer slow-dancing but now doing an oral grind in one another's mouths.

Taking control, Tomás roughly pushed me down on my back. Hovering over me, he eyed me from head to dick to toe. Liking what was pointing right up at him, he bent down to show it love. Welcoming me inside his mouth, I could feel the warmth of his breath before I felt the wetness of his tongue. After he engorged my penis in his mouth, something happened. Not even after a minute of Tomás giving me fellatio, my dick began to go limp.

I couldn't believe it. I was about to have some uncommitted no-strings sex and I couldn't maintain an erection. My limp penis fell out of Tomás' mouth. He continued to softly flick his tongue at the head, hoping that my erection would return.

"Is something wrong?"

"I...I...don't know," I stammered. It was an understatement to say that I was embarrassed.

"Okay, let me try something else."

For the next twenty minutes, Tomás tried several different sexual acrobatics to help me get an erection. With me on my back, he straddled me and tried grinding. Even though our pelvic rhythms were in sync, I still couldn't get aroused. He tried licking on my scrotum, sucking on my areolas, talking dirty to me, and he even tried seductively dancing along to the soft music. No matter what he tried, nothing would make my dick rise.

Defeated, he reluctantly gave up. In silence, we both put back on our clothes. He must've sensed my embarrassment because he hugged me at the door and whispered in my ear. "It's okay. You might have a lot on your mind. Maybe you're feeling guilty that you're hurting your boyfriend from the club."

"Yeah, that's it," I lied.

My emotions had been numbed for so many years, that there was no way that any type of guilt about cheating on Demario was the cause of my lack of an erection. I knew one thing for certain and that was I needed to get to the root of my problem.

With no more exchange of words, the two of us climbed into my truck and I made the trek back to his home to drop him off. I truly did give him a night he wouldn't forget.

CHAPTER 33
Shawna

"So what does this mean?" Keri asked me.

I didn't exactly know how to answer her question. I didn't know what this newfound interest in dating really meant. I had promised myself to just play the game and not get too heavily involved with anyone. But my actions lately were speaking differently.

"Keri, I'm not really sure. I'm trying to remain detached, but it's obvious that my heart is telling me differently. Think about it; first there was Antoine and now it's Edrian."

"I knew you weren't going to be able to keep that fence up for long. I told you too many times that you're a lover and not some loose playgirl. Now, go ahead and tell me that I'm right."

"Part of me hopes you are right and another part hopes that you are completely wrong. Falling in love is the easy part, trying to remain in love is the hard part, and falling out of love and trusting again seems to be impossible," I revealed.

"Aren't you the optimistic one?" Keri joked.

"I'm not trying to be a pessimist or an optimist. What I am trying to be is a realist. Love hurts in so many ways; and I'm the first to admit that I'm damaged."

"Now, Shawna, you know that you aren't damaged."

"Girl, when you look at me, you're seeing the damages of love gone wrong. I've given and given in every relationship, but it seems that all I get back in return is a shattered heart. So please understand my reluctance in giving my heart to another."

"Shawna, you keep trying to govern love and you're going to

end up enduring more hurt than you ever have before. You can't control love, and your experiences over the last year should've taught you this. You entertain attached men and have sex vicariously. This isn't the Shawna that I know. I'm hoping…no, I'm praying, that Edrian is the one that will bring back the Shawna that I used to know."

"I hear you, Keri. I'm simply going to go with the flow. I'm going to casually date him, but I'm not going to commit to anything until after three months. In these first three months, he'll be free to date and sex whomever he wants, and I'll be free to do the same. I refuse to rush into a monogamous relationship again."

"And what is the purpose of 'casually dating'?" Keri asked.

"Well, when we get to the point of commitment, if we get to that point, then we'll both know that we've tested and played the fields, but ultimately, we'll both understand that we've chosen one another."

"Interesting," Keri retorted. "I'm curious to see how that will fly with Edrian. I don't know any man that is going to be okay with his girl getting dicked down by another man."

"Unfortunately, that's something that I'm unwavering about."

"See, there you go, trying to dictate love again. If he isn't okay with your proposition, then you compromise and work with him until you two can agree on something that will work for the both of you."

That was one thing that I loved about having older friends. They always knew when to draw me back whenever I wanted to go about things in my bullheaded manner. Keri was absolutely right. I couldn't set rules for someone and demand that they play by them without getting their input. I wouldn't want anyone to do that to me, so I definitely didn't want to do that to anyone else.

"Why the silence?"

"I'm thinking about what you said. For once, I can truthfully say that you gave me some advice that I'm going to actually follow," I teased.

"I'll believe it when I see it. You're one helluva stubborn girl."

"That I am. But why are we talking like this? I haven't even had an invitation for a second date."

"There you go again, rushing things. Give the man the opportunity to make a move."

"He's moving too slow for my liking."

"You two only got together last night. Damn, if he asked you out first thing this morning, you'd be thinking he was thirsty. Don't forget, you're no longer dealing with the little boys; you're now dealing with a grown-ass man."

"We'll see how grown he is. Well, Ms. Keri, I'm here at the gym. I need to get to my cycle class so I can keep this body in shape."

"I don't know how you can do all that working out. My men love a little jiggle, and my jiggle is in all the right places."

"Hold on…I think I just threw up in my mouth thinking about your jiggle," I joked.

"Fuck you. Take your skinny ass in the gym and lose the little curves that you have. I'll talk to you later."

I ended my phone call with Keri and headed inside the gym. After checking in at the front desk, I headed back to the ladies locker room. I couldn't help but to notice the eyes of some of the men who were checking me out as I walked through the gym. There was nothing sexier than a sweaty man with muscles pouring out of his wife beater. Not to mention a tight ass sitting up high in a pair of knee-length gym shorts.

I flashed a smile at the few that could possibly be worth my time and continued to the back of the gym to the locker rooms to change. Before I could make it there, I felt a hand gently grabbing my arm.

"So you don't have any love for me?" Quincy, the head personal trainer, asked.

"Quincy, the last time I checked, you had several pieces here at the gym. The last thing I need is for one of your chickens to start acting all ghetto and chasing me around the gym with a dumbbell trying to bash my face in."

"See, you talking to the wrong people. I'm not going to lie; I've dated some women here, but I'm not currently involved with any of them."

I started to reveal to Quincy that I knew that he dated more than *some women* in the gym. One day while I was visiting my cousin Kenton, he was showing me this online social chat site for gay men. He wanted to show me this "fine brother" that he'd been chatting with. When he pulled up the profile and clicked on the private picture, I almost fell to his home's office floor when Quincy's face was staring at me from the LCD monitor.

There simply was no way in hell that I was going to get involved with a man that played on both sides of the field; especially when that man didn't respect the woman enough to lay the truth out in the beginning. To me, Quincy, like so many other men who played on both sides of the field, was nothing more than a coward.

"Quincy, I know more about you than you think I do. We would never work out."

"Damn, you threw me to the curb without even giving me a chance. Shit, since I can't be the gentleman and get a date, then maybe we can be friends with benefits."

I laughed louder than I should have. "Quincy, like I said before, we would never work out. I don't seem to have the right equipment," I informed him, grabbing my crotch like I was in a Michael Jackson video.

With that being said, Quincy stopped in his tracks and I again made my way to the locker rooms. My class started in five minutes; if I didn't hurry up, there'd be no more cycles left.

CHAPTER 34
Anjel

Engaged? Was he fucking kidding me? Just last week he was telling me how I was pressuring him to do something that he wasn't ready to do. Now he drops this shit on me while accusing me of doing something that I hadn't done.

If he thought my antics before were annoying, he hadn't seen anything yet. He had pushed me over the edge and I wasn't going to allow him the satisfaction of treating me like garbage. All in all, I was glad I didn't allow his phone call to interrupt my remaining time with Bryce.

I successfully feigned my way through breakfast and convinced him to drive us back to Orlando while I pretended to sleep. I didn't want him to see me rattled. He seemed like a nice guy and the last thing I wanted to do was to introduce my drama to him. Who knew, maybe I'd grace him with another date. We had an uncanny good time.

When we arrived at my place, I gave him a peck on the cheek and a hug, promising to give him a call later that evening. It was something I might actually do. He seemed a little taken aback by my coldness, but I'd worry about reassuring him later. Right now, I needed to calm my nerves.

Soaking in my bathtub, I tried my best to allow the Epsom salt to soothe my muscles. The shades were pulled down and my scented jasmine candles cast a dim light on the walls. The only thing to make this afternoon a perfect one would be a glass of white wine, but I had made a promise to myself earlier in the week to not drink any alcohol until after 5 p.m. I was doing my best to cut back on my drinking. I had even promised Shawna that I'd rejoin her at the gym on the weekends.

Placing a damp washcloth over my eyes, I rested my head, which had a towel wrapping my hair, against the tiled wall. I slipped lower into the water until it covered the top of my breasts. I allowed one knee to dangle over the side of the garden tub.

In the background, I had the sensuous voice of Robin Thicke playing from my Bose speakers. If I were ever to jump on the other side of the color line, that man would have to have a voice like Robin's. It also didn't hurt that he wasn't bad-looking. I did my best to sing along as he crooned about his woman "shaking it for daddy."

Before I could get to the end of the song, I heard the doorbell ringing. Scrambling out of the tub, I grabbed my terrycloth robe and slippers. Heading downstairs, I peeped through the curtains to see who was knocking on my door unexpectedly. Taking a deep breath, I opened the door. Preparing myself, I readied for the drama that was about to ensue.

"Good afternoon, officers. What can I do for you?"

"Afternoon. Are you Ms. Anjel Russell?" the thicker of the two asked. I nodded my head up and down. "We need to talk to you about an incident that happened last evening or sometime early this morning."

"Does this have to do Mason Wright?"

"Yes, ma'am, it does," the other officer, a slim Asian man, confirmed.

"Can you do me a favor and call Mr. Wright over while I go back inside and put on some clothes. I was in the middle of a bath."

"Well, ma'am, you're welcome to go back inside and put some clothes on, but we don't need to involve Mr. Wright at the moment."

"Don't worry about it. Give me a minute." I slammed the door and headed upstairs. Grabbing my cell phone, I called Mason.

"What now?" he yelled into the receiver.

"You have the muthafucking police at my door. You need to bring your black ass over here, now! I want to hear from your goddamn mouth in person what you're accusing me of."

"You're not saying a thing. I'll be there in less than ten minutes."

I headed back downstairs, and opened the door for the officers, who were still on my front porch. "Officers, I'm sorry for storming off and slamming the door," I calmly stated. "I needed to make a phone call."

I motioned for the both of them to come inside. Leading them to the living room, I asked them to have a seat while I headed back upstairs to change my clothes. Ten minutes later, I descended the stairs wearing a spaghetti-strapped shirt, some loose-fitting jeans, and my hair was now under a headwrap.

"Gentlemen, can I offer you a drink? I have bottled water." When both declined, I excused myself to go get a glass of Chardonnay.

As soon as I took a seat on the sofa across from the officers, there was a knock on the front door. Excusing myself once again, I went to open it. I didn't even need to inquire about who it was because I recognized Mason's knock.

Slinging the door open, the smugness on my face was instantly removed as my eyes set sight on his "fiancée." How dare he bring her to my home? Without uttering an invite to either of them, I turned away, leaving the door open.

When everyone was situated in my living room, I inquired why they were here interrupting my day. "Let's not beat around the bush; why in the hell are you all here in my space?"

"You know damn well why we're here." Mason rose up from his chair and pointed his finger in my direction.

"If I knew why you all were here, I wouldn't be asking," I retorted, my annoyance lacing my response. "Can we stop beating around the bush so I can continue with my day?"

"Well, Ms. Russell, we've received a complaint from Mr. Wright alleging that you have been harassing, stalking, and vandalizing his property."

"And when did I allegedly do all of these things?" I feigned, knowing pretty well that I was guilty of all his accusations excluding the last occurrence.

"Well, ma'am, the latest complaint occurred either late last night or earlier this morning. Mr. Wright reported that some obscenities were written on his home and some derogatory remarks written on his fiancée's car while they were asleep, but Mr. Wright is stating that this has been an ongoing ordeal."

"If this has been an ongoing ordeal, then why doesn't he get an order of protection against me? Oh wait, if he did that, then he couldn't come over to my place for a late-night booty call after the club like he's been doing since we've broken up."

Looking at his fiancée, I chimed in, "Yes, honey, we've been intimate, with the last occurrence being less than a week ago."

Mason looked like he was about to shit his pants and the phony-ass smile that his fiancée had been wearing this whole time now had become a frown. "Look, officers, I don't know what happened last night at Mr. Wright's residence, but I can tell you that I was not involved. I wasn't even in the city."

"Is there anyone that can attest to that?" the thicker officer inquired.

"Yes, there is. I wasn't alone, I was on a date, but if I can, I'd prefer not to involve him."

"Without anyone to corroborate your story, then it really has no validity," the Asian officer now piped in.

"What do you mean? Can't you do like they do on television and track my cell phone signal and see what towers it hit?"

"That would take time and money; it'd simply be easier to produce the gentleman you were with. Do you have any receipts?" the Asian officer continued.

Damn, Bryce had been ever so much the gentleman and had picked up the tab at the winery and the hotel room. I had paid for his clothes at Target with cash, and didn't know what I had done with the receipt. I was never one to retain things like that, which always got me in trouble; like now.

Sighing loudly, I got up from where I was seated and headed upstairs to grab my cell phone. Dialing Bryce's number, I apologized for inconveniencing him, but asked if he could stop by briefly within the next few minutes. I was grateful when he had obliged.

Going back downstairs, I informed them that he was on his way. Leaving them once again, I went into the kitchen. I needed something stronger than the glass of wine I had been sipping on. After pulling a tumbler from out of the cabinet, I went to my refrigerator to get some crushed ice. Filling the glass halfway with ice, I covered the ice with the Absolut Vodka that I kept in the cabinet next to the refrigerator. Normally, I'd add some cranberry juice or some orange juice, but at the moment, I wasn't in the mood for anything sweet.

Taking a seat on one of the barstools that was situated in front of the island counter in the middle of the kitchen, I sipped on my drink. I needed to formulate a plan on how I was going to justify all of the things I had done.

It was going to be hard explaining why I had pried open his gas tank and filled it with three gallons of water, why I had broken into his house and wrote "Fuck You Asshole" on all of his mirrors in red lipstick, why I'd keyed his car, why I'd use a steak knife to puncture tiny holes in his tires so that when he got on the road they'd deflate leaving him stranded, and why I had been lurking around his house at all times of the night. Lucky for me, Mason never used alarm systems. I'd be surprised if he even had one installed. When we lived together, he claimed that it was simply a waste of money because it always took the police close to an hour to arrive whenever it sounded.

My nerves were jumping. I came to the conclusion that I wouldn't admit to anything until it was presented to me with proof. Finishing my drink, I placed it in the sink at the same time the doorbell rang.

I walked through the living room toward the front door. My strides were filled with a newfound confidence. I was slightly elated that I was about to be exonerated from the accusations that I had participated in whatever had gone down at Mason's place. It was just like I figured; he'd pissed off enough women with his games and now he was feeling the wrath of their vengeance.

Opening the door, I gave Bryce a hug and thanked him for coming on such short notice. I could see the concern etched across his face. He probably could sense something was wrong with the police cruiser parked outside and with me sporadically requesting that he come over.

I reassured him that everything was okay, and led him inside. Mason's face almost dropped to the floor when he recognized who I had been out with.

"Officers, this is who I was with all the way from yesterday afternoon until this morning; that's why it's impossible for me to have done the things that I'm accused of doing."

"Hello, everyone," Bryce interjected. "Nice to see you again, Mason. I hope all is well." His demeanor was secure. I'm sure it had something to do with Mason's presence.

Mason didn't respond but angrily glared at Bryce. For the next fifteen minutes, the officers grilled Bryce about our whereabouts over the last twenty-four hours. Bryce even presented them with his credit card receipt from the wine shop and used my laptop to log into his bank account to show the charge on his debit card for the hotel room and breakfast.

Becoming annoyed with the officers' invasive questioning, Bryce crudely responded, "Look, I don't know why we're even going through this. There's no way that Anjel did anything last night or this morning. She was with me until eleven o'clock this morning. If you need anything else, then call the hotel and request to check their cameras. I'm sure you'll see both of us checking in and out."

With that being said, both officers thanked us and headed out. Mason and his fiancée followed. Before leaving, Mason grabbed me by the arm and pulled me to the side. "This isn't over!" He was seething at the thought of me lying up with another man; especially one that was once an associate of his.

CHAPTER 39
Kenton

"Kenton, I can tell you what happened," Roderick informed me.

I knew he'd have his own take on what went down with me two nights ago. It was one of the most embarrassing moments that I've ever endured within the bedroom. It was even more embarrassing than my first time having sex, which only lasted about fifteen minutes. No one ever prepared a guy for the overwhelming excitement that would push him over the edge sooner than later.

"I'm listening?"

"Well, you've been at this love'em and leave'em thing for a while now, but the problem is, that this isn't really who you are. You're a romantic and no matter how hard you try to elude this with random booty calls, you won't. Back in the day, the old Kenton would never have entertained messing with a bisexual guy."

"What can I say? Things change and so do people. Why should I be excluded from evolving?"

"No one's saying that you can't evolve, but why does your evolution have to be a deviation from who you truly are? Usually, when something evolves, it's for the better."

"Or it evolves to adapt to its surroundings," I threw in.

"Yeah, I guess you're right, smartass. But let me ask you this, how many times have you thought about calling Marcel?"

"It's been less than two weeks since we broke up, but I want to call him at least three or four times a day."

"So, why don't you?"

"He deserves someone better. He doesn't need someone that's

only concerned with trying to love on their own terms. Plus, I haven't told you why we really broke up."

"What did you do?"

I spent the next ten minutes telling my homeboy why Marcel had broken up with me. I filled him in about Demario and finished up where we had started our conversation—with Tomás. I could tell that he wanted to curse me out for my reckless behavior, but he remained silent until I finished.

"So, it wasn't Marcel you were cheating on with Tomás; you were cheating on this Demario fella, who you cheated on Marcel with?"

"Yeah, I guess that pretty much sums everything up."

"Kenton, are you telling me that you aren't seeing a pattern?"

Sadly, now that Rod had mentioned it, I was. I was spiraling out of control and I needed to find a way to get back on track. I wanted to be in love again, but my heart was lethargic. I didn't want to go through the rigors of dating a person, finding out their interests, their likes and dislikes, and in the end, having things not work out and having to repeat the cycle over and over again with someone else.

Let's not mention the disagreements, the sacrifices, the pain, and the heartache that accompanied love. But, what I was doing wasn't getting any better. Look at what it had gotten me? More sexual encounters than I could count, a list of nameless faces, and the guilt of inflicting the same hurt that I'd had to endure onto another.

I glanced at Rod, who was seated on my loveseat. He had one of his legs propped up on the leather ottoman that was in the center of the sofa and loveseat. The LCD television was on mute and the cocoa-flavored candle in the window sill scented the room. We both sat in silence, reflecting on what we were going through internally.

"So, how are you dealing with the breakup with Elle?"

"I'm good," he quickly stated.

"Come on, dude; you can keep it real with me. How are you *really* dealing with the breakup?"

Clearing his throat, he looked as if he wasn't sure that he wanted to tell me. "I miss her, Kent. I'm not used to putting myself out there emotionally. I did that for her, and in the end, it wasn't even worth it."

"Rod, every relationship is going to have its ups and downs. The decision is yours to make if you can work through them and work past them."

"Come on; are you telling me that you would've worked things through with Trevor?"

"No, I wouldn't have worked things out with Trevor. My relationship with him and the one you shared with Elle are on two different levels. In my relationship, if you can call it a relationship, things were one-sided. I was the only one that was emotionally and mentally invested in it. What you share with Elle is on another level. You two have history. At one point, you two were completely invested in the relationship and in one another. She messed up; now you have to decide if her error is something that can be worked through, or if you really want to end things."

"I'm hearing you, man, but I'm not sure I can trust her again. Every time she tells me that she's out with her girls, or she's going to the store, I'll be thinking she's going to hook up with some random guy."

"I never suggested that you jump back in like nothing happened. I'm saying that you two owe it to one another to sit down and decide if the relationship is still salvageable. If it is, then take things slowly. Try dating again, don't rush to move in with one another, and take your time to rebuild the trust."

"You mean start over from the beginning and negate all the

history and memorable moments that we've built over the years? Seems like it could be a waste, if the trust never comes."

"No, I didn't say to forget everything that made you two fall in love in the first place. I'm saying to use the same formula to help you fall back in love with one another. Tell me, do you think Elle's indiscretion had something to do with the prolonged engagement and you not wanting to commit to a date?

"Maybe she felt that she was wasting her time because you weren't ever going to actually marry her. It's been a minute since you've popped the question. When were you actually going to finalize things?"

Rod sat in silence. What I said had hit home. He had never once considered that Elle's infidelity could've had something to do with him stringing her along. A woman was only going to wait so long before she realized that her man was complacent with the current status of the relationship, and he would continue to make empty promises in an attempt to appease her. Elle's stepping out was a wakeup call for Rod. He now realized that if he wanted to keep Elle in his life, he'd need to step it up and actually take things to the next level.

True, Elle should've told him what was on her mind or in her heart before seeking comfort from someone else. Her actions now only complicated things. If Roderick had a problem with commitment before, now he was even more reluctant about giving himself to another completely. But no matter how long it took, things would work out between the two of them. They had too much love for one another to simply give up.

"So now, back to you? What are you going to do about your problem?"

"I don't know. I don't think it's something medically wrong so going to a doctor won't help. Plus, it was only one time. You got any suggestions?"

"Yeah, I do; slow the fuck down! Take the time and learn these dudes. Don't allow your first date to be in the bedroom. Marcel sounds like he was a good dude. Forget that you two met in an unconventional way; the fact is that it was beginning to turn into something real. And the more real it became and the closer it began to resemble a relationship, the more you did any and everything to cause things to come to an end.

"Have you really considered making that call? Maybe apologize and do the same things that you suggested I do with Elle?"

Now, it was my turn to be silent. I never knew that my feelings toward Marcel were so obvious. I really did miss him and I hated the way that things had ended between the two of us. Kai broke my thoughts of self-reflection as she came bumbling down the stairs.

"Well, Rod, I've got to get my ass in the shower and hit the road. I'm finally going to catch up with my lil' cuz, Shawna. She met some dude, and she's been ghost for a minute."

"There isn't anything lil' about your cousin besides her height. If she wasn't your cousin…let's just say, I'd be back in player mode."

"Yo, leave my cuz alone. I'd hate to have to beat that ass," I jokingly warned.

"Shit, I'm not worried about you. I'm worried about Shawna's feisty ass."

We gibed with one another for a few more minutes before I escorted Roderick to the door. Headed back upstairs, with Kai closely in tow, I walked into my master bathroom to prepare for a night of family fun.

CHAPTER 36
Shawna

"What's going on? I swear you've been ghost," Kenton heckled me.

"It's not even like that, cuz. I've been a little preoccupied with school."

"*And*...?"

My cousin knew me better than anyone else. He knew when my time was being spent on someone of the opposite sex. "And by Edrian," I gushed.

Kenton took a seat in the booth across from me. He was dressed very stylishly. I didn't know how to categorize his sense of fashion. I wanted to say it was metrosexual, but it was more masculine than the average metrosexual type of garb. One thing I loved about my cousin was that he could never be placed in a box. It seemed that as soon as you had him figured out, he'd switch things up.

He and I were closer than most brothers and sisters. Although we were four years apart in age, we practically were glued at the hip while growing up. Our family was huge. We had plenty of cousins, but the two of us seemed to mesh. I always wanted to hang out with him and go wherever he went. My mother couldn't stand that I was such a tomboy. Growing up, Kenton wasn't into dating men. He was such a charmer, and almost all of my girlfriends had the biggest crush on him. He was one of the most popular guys in the neighborhood.

I was distraught when he left for college. Every chance I got, I would fly down from Chicago to visit him down in Atlanta. And on major holidays, he knew that he had no choice but to come back home. When he finished college and told me he was moving to Orlando, I immediately began looking for colleges in the vicinity. I was an only child, and he was the closest relative that I had to a big brother. He was there to teach me about boys, teach me how to spot when a guy was spitting game my way, and whenever I needed to get into a guy's face, he was there to handle that for me. Kenton was no pushover.

Contrary to what most people believed, not all gay men were flamboyant like the men you saw depicted on television. Through Kenton, I'd learned that there are different types of gay men. In the beginning, I was astounded by some of his friends. Most of them were the antithesis of what I was taught gay men were. I thought that Kenton was a rare kind, but I quickly learned that he was just one of many. Some of the guys he hung out with, you wouldn't be able to tell that they were gay unless they verbally told you that they were into the same sex.

"So, who is Edrian and why am I just now hearing about him?"

After we placed our drink orders with the waiter, I took the next few minutes bringing him up to speed on how I had met Edrian. I revealed to him that the night I flaked out on him, it was to meet Edrian. That was our official first date.

"So how is the sex?"

"We haven't had sex," I admitted.

Kenton almost slid out of the booth. "How many times have you two been out?"

It wasn't like me to not take a test drive in the beginning, but the chemistry that I was getting from Edrian was causing me to rethink the way that I did things. I realized that there was nothing wrong with waiting before jumping in the bed. Until the time came, I was satisfied for the moment using my vibrator.

"We've officially been out one time. But we talk on the phone several times a day. I can tell there's an interest on his end."

"Now don't get caught up in one of these whirlwind romances," my cuz cautioned.

"I'm not. The last thing I want to do is to put myself out there again and end up hurt and wondering what I didn't do right and what I could've done differently."

"You're preaching to the choir," he sounded. "Remember, I've had my share of letdowns. It definitely is a road I'm not trying to travel down again."

"So, what's going on with you? I never got the opportunity to talk to you about Marcel. What did *you* do?"

"Why do you think I did something wrong? Maybe the two of us mutually decided that it wasn't working."

"Kenton, I know you better than that; if it was someone else, I could believe what you just suggested."

As we sipped on our drinks, Kenton brought me up to speed on what had occurred between him and Marcel. I learned about Demario, who had caused the friction between the two. Then he surprised me with his "incident" with club piece, Tomás, the other night. I couldn't stifle my laughter when he told me that he couldn't keep it up. I laughed so hard, tears began to fall from my eyes. Never in my wildest dreams would I have imagined that of all men, Kenton would be admitting to having a problem like this.

"It's not that funny," Kenton interjected. I could tell by his tone that he was serious.

"I'm sorry. I can't believe that you fucked around so much that you broke the damn thing," I continued to tease. "But all jokes aside, Kenton, do you think that it's more of a psychological thing?"

"That's what Roderick was saying. He thinks it has something to do with my breakup with Marcel."

"Well, does it?"

Kenton sat across from me in silence. I had never seen the look that was within his eyes. He had slipped into a trance and there was a glistening in his pupils. I could tell that in their short courtship, Marcel had really gotten to him.

"Kent, you should call him."

"I don't know. I wouldn't even know where to start."

This was weird. I was used to Kenton giving me relationship advice and now here the tables were turned. "How about an apology to start things off," I suggested.

"I don't think that's going to do it."

"I didn't say that it was. I said as a start. He'd be stupid to accept you back into his life with open arms like nothing happened. To be honest, if I were him, I'd make your ass work for my forgiveness.

"I haven't said anything in the past, but you've really been an asshole lately. Trevor did a number on you and you've been making every guy pay for it. Don't get me wrong; I'm not all that innocent myself. My problem is that I sex them and leave them. You, on the other hand, sex them and if there's no chemistry, then you leave them. If you think there's a potential for additional fun, you string them along and then when you sense there are feelings involved on their end, you bail out."

"Isn't this some bullshit? I'm being given love advice by you. When did the tables turn? I guess now you're going to suggest that I start dating guys without having sex in the beginning."

"Now, I wouldn't go that far. I'm going to be honest and say that I myself probably won't make it past the third date. I don't see anything wrong with being intimate within the first few dates. So many people try to pretend that sex doesn't hold a big bearing on a relationship, but we all know that they're only shitting themselves. Sex is just as important as the emotional and mental."

"I'm not sure that I'm liking this newer and more mature side of you," Kenton ribbed. "I like things the way they used to be."

"Hey, what can I say? Things change and so do people. So are we going to order something to eat or what?"

"I'm not really feeling the menu."

"Let's get the hell out of here then."

Kenton requested the check and, after paying the tab, we headed out for a night on the town. It was like the old days before all the heartbreaks. I cherished nights like this.

"Hey?"

"W'sup, Baby Girl?"

"Let's not go this long without hanging out again, okay?" I requested. As adults our lives could get pretty hectic, but I didn't want them to become so busy that our relationship boiled down to random text messages, voicemails, and an occasional dinner.

"Okay. I forgot how much I enjoy being around you," he in return admitted.

I climbed into the passenger seat of Kent's SUV. When we were done with our evening, he'd drop me off to pick up my car. I reclined back in the seat as Kenton zoomed onto the interstate. No doubt we were headed to our old stomping grounds off of International Drive.

CHAPTER 37
Anjel

It had been nearly a week since I revealed to Mason that I had been out on a date with Bryce. I had successfully been dodging phone calls from him and Bryce ever since. Bryce was interested in getting together again and, of course, Mason wanted to do nothing more than to sabotage any chance of me moving on.

At the moment, I didn't want to be bothered with either of them. Bryce was a decent guy, and the sex was better than I actually thought it would be. Hell, it was actually some of the best mind-blowing sex that I'd had in a long time. But I wasn't ready or prepared to jump back into the dating game on a full-time basis.

To keep my mind off of things, I had thrown myself into my work with a vengeance. There was so much that I had put off and I needed to get back on the ball. That was one of the things about being your own boss and managing a company virtually—sometimes the discipline seemed to be lax. I was fortunate for my assistant, who worked out of Birmingham, Alabama.

He was truly a godsend. If it weren't for him being such a perfectionist and a diligent worker, I would've been in some major trouble. The best thing about our relationship was that we rarely communicated via phone. We were both tech junkies and utilized the Internet to the fullest. Most of our conversations were done via text messages, emails, and instant messenger.

Just as I had hit the SEND button on my latest email to him, my doorbell rang. With my house shoes slapping against my hardwood floors, I left my home office to see who was at my door. Peering through the peephole, I braced myself; my peacefulness was about to come to an abrupt end.

As I opened the door, I was instantly pushed aside as Inola invited herself into my home. Inola was Mason's personal assistant and closest confidante. He didn't make a move without her knowing of his whereabouts. She was the one that was feeding me information on how to win him over. I had been checking in with her daily, but since my date with Bryce, I had been ignoring her as well.

There was something about her that perturbed me. I didn't trust her. She came off as an innocent Native American Indian, but her name fit her perfectly. Mason once told me that her name meant "Black Fox" in Cherokee. Just like a fox, I was learning that she was just as sneaky and conniving.

"So, you don't answer your damn phone anymore," she barked.

"Inola, I've been preoccupied and the last thing I needed was to be concerned with Mason."

"I take it you heard that sonofabitch is engaged to some tramp from the past? I told you to step it up, and now look what happened. Now, things are going to be a lot more complicated."

"Why would they be more complicated? Unless I'm mistaken, it's a done deal. She has the ring."

"That conniving whore trapped him. She got knocked up. He was devastated when he found out. The last thing he wanted was to have children with her. Their chemistry is awful. Just imagine an earthquake and hurricane hitting at the same time."

"Inola, how do you know so much about his fiancée?"

Inola looked at me like I was the stupidest person on earth. I had forgotten how long she had been Mason's assistant. It was long before me.

"Sometimes I swear you aren't the sharpest knife in the drawer. You'd think you were a dumb blonde."

I had to remind myself that I had to mind my elders. If it weren't for my upbringing, Inola would've been all kinds of bitches and hoes. Here she was showing up at my home uninvited and disrespecting me.

"Inola, to what do I owe this unexpected *and* obtrusive personal visit?"

"I came by to see what the game plan is. When I learned that trick was back in the picture, I had to take things into my own hands."

"So you were the reason behind me being accused of the vandalism at his place last week?"

"I plead the fifth; next time, answer your damn phone. I tried to give you a heads-up, but from what Mason tells me, you didn't need one. Word is you were out on a date with Bryce."

"Why does Mason tell you all of my damn business?"

"Darling, there isn't anything that I don't know when it comes to the people in Mason's life. So again, what's the plan? I hope that Bryce isn't going to be a major distraction."

"No, Bryce is a nice guy, but I'm not looking to get involved with anyone else at the moment. And to answer your question, there is no plan. It's evident that Mason has made his decision. She gets the ring and she gets his baby."

"Do you really think she's pregnant? She's a sneaky one. If I know her, she probably got knocked up by a nobody and now needs for someone to play daddy to the little bastard."

"To be frank, I couldn't care less. I'm tired of playing this game, I'm tired of the ups and downs, and riding the emotional roller coaster over and over."

I never thought I'd hear myself utter those words, but I had. I was really tired of being Mason's safety net. When he needed someone to hold at night, when he simply wanted familiarity within the bedroom, or when he just wanted companionship, he always ran to me. Like an idiot, I had allowed him to do it. I was no different than a store with a revolving door. He'd come in, do his business, and leave.

Over the last few months, I had allowed things to go too far. I had consumed my life with Mason. I had lost total control of my life and had lost myself in all of the scheming. I was better than this. I deserved better than this. As much as I wanted love, there was no way that I was going to continue to throw myself at a man that had potentially knocked up some other woman.

"So, you're saying that you've been wasting my damn time. You came to me for my help. Now that we're reaching the finish line, you want to pull out. I'll be damned if you think that this is the end of this!"

"Inola, let it go. Mason already knows that I was the one responsible for the other things. If I hadn't been on that date with Bryce, I could be facing potential jail time. This is getting way too deep. We need to take a break from things and see how things play out between Mason and whatever her name is."

"Like hell I will. Like hell you will. We're going to finish this!"

Inola marched out of my house, slamming my door behind her. I don't know what business it was of hers whether or not Mason and I were together or not. I hoped that this would be the last time that I had to deal with her demented ass. I needed to make another appointment with Dr. Lynn. I must not have been totally lucid to have allowed her to talk me into her shenanigans.

I locked my front door, and once again my house shoes began slapping against my hardwood floors as I headed back to my office. I was at peace with my revelation. I was ecstatic that it had taken Mason committing to someone else in order to get me to move on.

The only thing I needed was to mend my broken heart. As I reached the top of the stairs, I wiped away the tears that were beginning to fall from my eyes. I couldn't believe that she'd be the one to give him his first child. Even though I wasn't ready for kids, I didn't want someone else giving birth to his. How could he do this to me? To us?

CHAPTER 38
Kenton

I was awakened by someone pounding on my front door and ringing my doorbell repeatedly. My head was spinning from my late night out with Shawna. It had been a minute since we went club-hopping. We bounced from straight to gay clubs—in no particular order. I don't think I've been sleep more than a few hours.

Pulling myself out from the bed, I stumbled downstairs. Kai was already at the front door barking at whomever was on the other side. Before opening the door, I snatched the yellow Post-It note from the door.

"Just a minute," I managed to mumble while massaging my temples. "Stop ringing my damn doorbell!"

I was still in a daze due to my lack of sleep. My body wasn't fully awake and my movements were sluggish. Reading the note, I saw that Shawna had gotten a ride to go pick up her car from the restaurant.

Peeking through the sheer curtain, I saw Demario was at the door. Commanding Kai to go upstairs, I opened the door.

"What's wrong with your ass?" I yelled.

"How you going to fucking do me like that?" he shouted at me. His Dominican accent was thick. If he weren't yelling at me, I'd have thought it to be sexy.

The beaming sun caused me to squint. "Bring your ass inside and stop acting so ghetto."

Walking away from the door, I left it open, signaling to Demario that he was to follow me inside. Taking the hint, I plopped down on the sofa. Drawing my left foot under my right hamstring, I reclined back against the cushion of the couch. Kai had come back downstairs and had made herself comfortable next to me. She rested her big head on my lap.

Patting Kai on her head, I turned my attention to Demario. I could tell that he'd been crying and the new black shiner that accented his left eye caught my interest. "What happened to your eye?" I questioned with concern.

"Don't change the fucking subject. You dropped me off the other night to go fuck with that trash from the club? I saw you two talking at the bar when I went to the bathroom, but I didn't think you'd let him talk you into fucking his HIV-infested ass."

"I didn't fuck him," I admitted. I wasn't lying. I really hadn't fucked him. I wasn't concerned about him having HIV; I always used condoms. It would've been nice if he had revealed that detail to me. Then again, Demario could've been lying. Screaming that someone was HIV positive was usually the first thing that a gay guy called out when he wanted to bring harm to another's reputation. They'd tell people that someone had the "package" in an attempt to deter others from messing with him.

"You're a fucking liar. He was all up in the mall boasting about how the two of you had linked up. He could even describe your crib and your dick."

"I didn't say we didn't meet up or that we didn't fool around. I said that the two of us didn't fuck, and I'm not lying about that," I annoyingly retorted. "So, you decided to fight him; I see how you ended up with a black eye." I was growing tired of this conversation.

"Yeah, I got the black eye, but I'm not the one who had to go to the hospital to get stitched up."

"Demario, why are you here? We mess around, but we aren't together in a monogamous relationship. We're both free to talk to whomever we please."

"So, it's like that? You got what you wanted and now you're done with me?"

"Come on; what did you honestly expect? When we met, I was with someone. He and I broke up because of you. Remember?"

"So, it was my fault that your ass was on the chat site when your dude was laying up in the bed. It's my fault that his ass left you? You must've not cared too much for him…how long did it take for you to invite me into your bed?"

He was right. Everything he was saying couldn't be disputed. Hearing him say how much of an ass I was hit straight home. I needed to end this cycle. I needed to heed Shawna's advice. If I was going to play, I needed to play and leave. Don't invite them to stay over and don't lead them to believe that it was more than it actually was. If I had only known what I was getting into from the beginning, my invite would've never extended beyond that night.

I blamed this all on Marcel. He had reminded me what it was like to hold someone at night, to wrap my legs around them, our feet touching under the sheets, to wake up to them the next morning. He had reminded me of what it was like to have companionship. That was something that I truly missed. I tried to use Demario to fill the void that Marcel had left.

"Demario, I'm sorry about your eye and I'm sorry if I led you to believe that we were more than what we actually were. I think it's best if we call it quits now."

I watched as Demario, who was still standing, glared down at me. I could see the tears sweltering in his eyes. He was still young and he'd bounce back. To be honest, he needed this experience in heartache to make him a better and more experienced lover.

Without another word, Demario walked out of my residence. Once again, I was the one inflicting the same hurt and pain that so many in the past had inflicted upon me. The damage caused by love would continue and the cycle of pain would continue. I wasn't part of the solution, but I was part of the problem. So many times I had the opportunity to break the cycle of pain and hurt and, like all the times before, I never did.

I had the chance to stop so many hearts from enduring the trauma that mine had to undergo and, yet, I hadn't risen to the occasion. Instead, I dastardly took the easy way out. I could have been a man and come out and told these men that I was damaged goods. I could have told them what to expect from falling in love with me or what catching feelings would entail. But, I didn't. The sad part about the ordeal was that I would probably do the same thing to the next unsuspecting heart.

Locking my front door, I turned to head upstairs. I was stopped when I heard a large crash coming from outside. It sounded like glass was breaking. I rushed back to my front door and outside. As I stood in my driveway barefoot, I saw Demario standing at the bottom of my driveway. He had thrown a brick from my landscaping through the windshield of my truck. I could've killed Shawna for not parking my ride in the garage. I was so tired last night that all I wanted to do was to climb into my bed.

Before I could stop myself, with Kai at my heels, I ran to the bottom of the driveway and had backhanded Demario.

"What the fuck is wrong with you?" I yelled at him. The force of my blow had knocked him to the ground.

As I continued to yell at him, Shawna pulled up in her car. Just as I lifted my foot to kick Demario in his face, Shawna tackled me, knocking me to the cemented driveway. The moment I hit the ground, I realized what I had done. I had used physical violence to defend something material. This wasn't like me and I couldn't believe I had stooped down to this level.

"Little boy, go home!" Shawna yelled at Demario. "Kai, let him go. Go inside now."

I hadn't noticed that Kai was holding onto Demario's pants leg. I had never heard her growl so menacingly before. She must've sensed my anger. Any other time, I would've been proud of her, but this time, I was in the wrong.

"Kai, let him go," I sternly commanded.

Sensing the tone of my voice, she did as she was told.

"Demario, go home!"

Scrambling to his feet, Demario spat the blood from his mouth and ran to the car that was waiting for him across the street. Following his lead, I also pulled myself up from the driveway and retreated into my house. I hoped that none of my neighbors had called the authorities. I did live in a nice neighborhood. In fact, I was one of three black residents in the subdivision.

Going back into my house, I fought back the tears that were welling in my eyes. I was from a family of domestic abuse, and had promised myself that it would never be a trait that I'd adopt from my father. This morning, I had failed. Today, I had become my father and it overwhelmed me.

Shawna held me as I cried my heart out behind closed doors. Once again, Kai, sensing my distress, laid her head in my lap and whined. She didn't know what was wrong, but she realized that something was hurting me.

"Kenton, it's okay. Let it go." Shawna tried her best to console me.

"Come on, repeat after me: Our Father who art in heaven, hallowed be Thy name.

"Thy kingdom come. Thy will be done, on earth as it is in heaven. Give us this day, our daily bread, and forgive us our trespasses, as we forgive those who trespass against us, and lead us not into temptation, but deliver us from evil…"

I repeated after Shawna. We were saying the "Lord's Prayer." A prayer that our deceased grandmother had made us memorize by the age of three. As kids, we had to call her every night and recite it to her before we went to bed.

CHAPTER 39
Shawna

Two days had passed since I was pulling my cousin Kenton off of, who I later found out, was Demario. I had never seen him so upset over something as trivial as a busted car windshield. I finally convinced him to make an appointment and talk to his licensed therapist, Dr. Lynn, because he appeared to be losing his cool.

I'm sure that his inability to perform last week had something to do with it, as well as his pent-up feelings for Marcel. I hoped that his therapist could talk him into simply picking up the phone and giving Marcel a call. It would be beneficial for Kenton to properly disclose his true feelings; if nothing else, to tell Marcel how he truly felt.

I was sitting in my living room, propped up so that I didn't wrinkle my outfit. I wasn't dressed in anything fancy. I merely was sporting a pair of jeans and a form-fitting cotton shirt. Topping off my outfit were some sandals to show off my freshly done pedicure.

I was waiting for Edrian to come by, for what was to be our second date. I expected him at my front door by eight o'clock and looking at my cell phone for the current time, I saw that it was only seven-fifteen. I had been extremely anxious and had jumped the gun. I didn't want to take a risk of him arriving early and me not being ready.

So now there I was, impatiently waiting. My right leg bounced up and down and my nerves rattled me. I don't know why I was so nervous. It's not like it was the first time that we'd been out. I was curious to know if he truly was the knight-in-shining-armor that would rescue me from this life of solitude.

Looking around my apartment, it was the opposite of what most people would think a college student's apartment would look like. I had some of the latest technology, and my sofa, although a hand-me-down from Kenton, was still stylish and expensive-looking.

Inside my closet were hangers draped with designer dresses, blouses, and pants. Not to mention, the lavish shoes that were spilling out from the closet. One pair of shoes could pay someone's rent.

Kyler had done a good job of keeping me fashionable. I wasn't extremely keen on the type of shoes I wore, but he had a shoe fetish and wanted me in a different pair whenever we hooked up. He especially loved when I wore a pair of stilettos when we were having sex. Being the pleaser that I was, I always obliged to most of his requests.

I was down when he asked if he could bust in my mouth. I told him that as long as he didn't expect me to swallow, then we were cool. I was even game when he asked if we could get it in on my balcony, which overlooked the pool. Of course we had to wait until it was dark. I didn't need the police knocking on my door. The only time that I had to use the "no" word was when he wanted to go beyond our normal freakiness and delve into new territory.

I should've drawn the line when he requested that I entertain his curiosity for shower play. Naïve in that area, I obliged, thinking that it was nothing more than lovemaking in the shower. What I didn't know was that his request to engage in wet showers was actually a request for me to participate in golden showers.

I clearly remember being on my knees giving him head as the water poured down on me. He had already shot his load and wanted me to continue sucking on the head until his penis was entirely limp. The shower water had turned cold because we had been in there so long. Holding me by the top of my head, he instructed me to close my eyes and to lean my head back. Following his instructions, I did so.

Seconds later, I felt something warm hitting me in the face. Opening my eyes, I realized that he was pissing on me. Scrambling around in the shower, I got to my feet. In my struggles, I had caused him to lose his balance and ended up pushing him outside of the shower. He was tangled in the shower curtain and I was gagging. Tears were flowing from my eyes as I got under the head of the shower to cleanse myself.

Even after all those months, it still pissed me off—no pun intended. I didn't see how he would think that it was okay to piss in my face. There was nothing more degrading in my eyes that a man could do to a woman. It was like he was a dog marking his territory. It took him a month of phone calls, flowers, and lavish gifts to get me to speak to him again. I never forgave him for disrespecting me in such a way. A lot of people are into things like that, but excreting your wastes on another person, especially on me, caused my stomach to turn.

Heading into my kitchen, which resembled the galley of a ship because it lacked any shape and was narrow, I opened the refrigerator to grab a bottle of water. The moment I closed it, my cell phone began ringing.

Dashing into the living room to get it, I wanted to answer it before it rolled to my voicemail. "Hello!" I yelled into the receiver louder than I meant to.

"What's going on, Baby Girl?"

I could sense that Edrian was smiling on his end of the phone. "I'm good; so how close are you?"

"I'm about twenty minutes away, but I have a request, if you don't mind."

"I'm listening," I reluctantly responded.

"It's raining like crazy out here; do you mind if we have what I call a 'cheap date'? You know, watch a movie, order some take-out, and sip on some wine? I realize that it's quite early to be doing that, but if you look out the window, you'd see that it's barely visible outside."

"I didn't even know it was raining. I was so preoccupied," I told him, looking out of my window. It was exactly like he said. I could barely see the pine tree that was no more than ten feet away from my apartment. The lightning flash caused me to jump back from the window.

"I don't mind us doing a 'cheap date.' The last thing I need is to get out in all that rain after spending all day in the salon. Are you going to be okay driving my way?"

"I'm good. I'm going well below the speed limit and I've driven in much worse. Plus, I'd drive through a tornado to get the chance to spend some time with you."

I laughed out loud. He was being extra corny now. It was good to see him let down his guard a little and allow me to experience another side of him. "Well, don't let me distract you. Did your GPS system pull up my address?"

"That it did. Hey, before you go, I have one more request."

"Aren't we full of those this evening?" I joked.

"This is simple. Can you dress down for me?"

"What do you mean?"

"I want to see you not all dressed up, looking all fancy. I want to see you like I would see you if we were dating for three months and you were lounging around the house."

This was an unusual request; I was always on top of my game

when I was with my man. I usually would wake before him and make myself presentable and even my loungewear was fancier than what most women would wear.

"I'll see what I can do."

Hanging up my phone, I went into my closet to find something that was considered typical loungewear. Not finding anything, I went to my dresser. Opening the bottom drawer, I managed to find an old pair of baggy Florida State sweatpants that my ex had left over. I hadn't built up the strength to throw them away after all that time.

I used to hate when he would wear them. There wasn't anything bad about them. It wasn't like they were tattered or full of holes. Whenever he put them on, it meant that he wasn't going to do anything but sit his ass in front of the television and watch sports all day.

Undressing down to my underwear, I slipped into the sweatpants. They were so baggy that they slid down my waist and rested at the top of my ass. Pulling the drawstring as tight as I could, I managed to situate them onto my hips. More rummaging through my drawers produced an old and worn T-shirt.

Satisfied with my last-minute wardrobe change, I headed into the bathroom to wash off the little bit of makeup I had applied earlier and to wrap my hair with a headwrap. There'd be other opportunities to look cute for him. Plus, I took this as a sign that Edrian was more into a down-to-earth and laid-back type of woman.

Going into my living room, I was not as meticulous as I was before about wrinkling my clothes. Plopping down on my sofa, I hit the power button on the television's remote and waited for Edrian to arrive.

CHAPTER 40
Anjel

"Anjel, I'm glad that you finally decided to meet with me. I didn't mean for you to find out about Janine like that."

"Like what? Oh, you mean when you blurted it over the phone while accusing me of harassing the two of you, or did you mean when you brought her to my home uninvited last week?"

"Look, I didn't ask to meet with you to argue. It seems like that's all we ever do. What happened to us remaining friends like we both promised when we called it quits?"

"I love the way that you say 'we called it quits' whenever you talk about us ending things. If we had ended things mutually, do you think I'd allow you to use me sexually whenever you saw fit? Do you think that I'd allow you into my bed knowing that you had done the very thing that you accused me of pressuring you to do with someone else?"

"Anjel, she's pregnant…"

"So I've heard. Tell me, was she pregnant the last time we fucked?"

The tears flowed freely from my eyes. I wasn't ashamed that I was letting him see me in such a vulnerable state. The months of separation, being used, and having my feelings toyed with were all getting the best of me. All the time I'd been keeping things pinned inside, and now I was letting it all out and didn't care who witnessed my emotional meltdown.

Mason rose from where he was seated to come and comfort me.

"Don't you fucking touch me!" I hysterically screamed at him, pushing him away from me. The mere thought of his touch caused my body to shiver. His touch no longer warmed my body and sent electricity through me. Now, his touch was cold, and I felt chills when his skin touched mine.

"If I had forgotten before, you just reminded me why we didn't work out," he muttered, turning away from me.

"What did you say?" The tears in my eyes had momentarily stopped. My anger was escalating.

"Don't worry about it. I see that trying to talk to you was a big mistake."

Mason turned away from me and bent down to grab his car keys from the coffee table. When he turned back in my direction, my open hand met his face.

"Are you out of your goddamned mind?" I yelled at him. "How the hell did you expect me to react, knowing that you've been sleeping with me realizing how I felt about you, and all the time you had proposed to someone else and gotten her knocked up? Getting married was the so-called primary reason for our breakup, according to you."

Mason looked at me. For the first time since we'd broken up, I could see the hurt within his eyes. I could see the wetness in them. Sitting back down, he brought his hands to his face and rubbed his eyes. His body slumped into the cushion of the sofa.

"Anjel, I had to propose to her. I got drunk one night when she was in town and we had sex. We had unprotected sex and she ended up pregnant. I tried to convince her to get an abortion and she refused. I asked that she put the baby up for adoption so that the child would have a loving home and two loving parents that would adore it; again, she refused.

"She told me that she was keeping the child and even went a step further to tell my parents. You know how religious my family is. My mother was devastated and made me promise to 'make an honest woman out of Janine' to save the family from disgrace. So to appease my family and Janine, I relented and proposed to her. Now for the next eighteen years, I'll be trapped inside a marriage where there is no love."

Silence entered the room. I sat on the opposite end of the sofa. I was turned so our eyes met. No words were exchanged as we sat, looking at one another. I didn't really know what to say, or how to comfort him. Mason was the only child, and his parents had gone through great extremes to conceive him. After several years of fertility treatments, his mother was finally able to carry a child to full-term. Ever since learning about his mother's difficulty to conceive, Mason had made it his mission to do whatever he needed to do to make his parents happy.

With such a religious family, they wouldn't recognize a child that wasn't a product of marriage. To stay within his parents' good graces, Mason had to marry Janine so that his unborn child would be welcomed and acknowledged by his family. The last thing that Mason would ever do was bring shame to his family.

"I can only imagine how you feel, Anjel. I didn't intentionally play with your feelings. We broke up because I needed some time to play the field and to test the waters. I always came back to you because there was no doubt in my heart that it would be you that I'd spend my life with. When it was all said and done, you would've been the one to bear my first child.

"I was selfish. I don't need anyone to tell me that. I wanted to be single and free to mingle, but I also wanted to hold onto you as well. I didn't plan for this to happen and now that it has, I don't know what I can do. Every night that she's with me, I realize more and more how much I love you.

"I pray to God every night that I will love this child, even though

I hate his mother. As cruel as it sounds, in the beginning, I wished that she'd miscarry. What kind of man am I? What kind of man wishes for the mother of his child to miscarry or, better yet, to die during childbirth?"

I didn't know what to tell Mason at this point. His problems could have simply been avoided if he had manned up and stopped trying to pacify his parents. Looking at the defeated man sitting across from me, I realized that I had dodged a bullet. No matter how many children we had, no matter how much we loved one another, no matter how hard I tried, I would've always come second to the wishes and desires of his family.

"Mason, I don't know what to say to you. Your unhappiness can simply be avoided if you stood up for yourself and stopped putting your family first. I wish you and Janine the best and that you'll find some way to be happy."

Mason rose to his feet, and I stood up as well. I walked him to my front door and before he exited my home, and hopefully my life forever, we embraced. Our hug lasted longer than it should have. Lowering his face to my ear, Mason whispered. "I'll always love you, Anjel."

If we were in a movie, now would've been the time that Whitney's rendition of "I Will Always Love You" would have begun playing in the background. But we weren't in a movie and this wasn't a fictionalized story. This was reality, and sadly our time had run its course.

I watched as Mason climbed into his car. The feeling was bittersweet, but it was something that needed to be done.

Closing the door, I went into my dining room to get my cell phone. Locating the number I needed, I hit the TALK button. The phone rang three times before I heard Bryce utter a "hello."

CHAPTER 41
Kenton

I sat at the bar nursing my drink as the soloist crooned out Chrisette Michele's "Blame It on Me." Accompanied by the lounge's house band, she wasn't doing such a bad job. Looking around the lounge, I caught a bout of nostalgia. The atmosphere reminded me of the Apache Café in Atlanta. I used to love amateur night when local musicians would take to the stage and perform their original songs, or their rendition of a well-known song.

I don't know why I was here. It'd been over a year since I'd visited the lounge. Although the music was nice and the drinks were strong, the small lounge would often become too cramped. By midnight, it'd take a person almost a half-hour to get from the bar to the bathroom. Dancing was almost impossible, but still, you had those who attempted to shake their asses in the restricted space.

"How have you been, Kenton?" a familiar voice asked from behind.

"I'm aiight," I shot back. I didn't even look over my shoulder to see who it was that was giving me the salutation. I didn't want to be bothered and wanted to spend the next hour or so enjoying my drink and the music.

"So, it's like that?" the individual continued.

Taking a sip of my rum and Coke, I turned around and started coughing excessively as the liquid entered the wrong pipe. Standing before me was a face from the past. It was a face that had brought and had continued to cause me extreme pain.

"You okay? I'm sure you missed me, but I didn't think seeing me would cause you to get all choked up," he teased.

All the things that I had practiced that I would say when I saw him again fled from my thoughts. I was speechless and could only stare at him. He flashed his signature smile that used to make me stutter. Looking at him, something looked different. He looked like he had aged horribly.

"Tre…Trev…Trevor? What are you doing here?" I managed to stutter. I needed to pull it together.

"I'm in town and I've been cramped up in my hotel all week. The concierge told me about this place and I thought I'd check it out. I didn't know that I'd run into an old face."

"Well, it's nice to see that you're doing okay," I managed to lie. I could not give a fuck about how he'd been doing. Seeing him standing before me with his faded looks sort of brought me some sadistic satisfaction.

"So, are you going to invite me to have a seat?"

"It's a free world. The seat is empty so if you want to have a seat, then it's your decision."

"I see you're still salty. You'd be so much happier if you let go of the past and focused on the future. Shit happened. We didn't make it. Let's just say that me leaving the way I did was me doing *you* a favor," he reasoned.

"How do you figure?"

For the next ten minutes, Trevor revealed to me how he had began engaging in "party and play"—also known as PNP when having sex. PNP was a sexual experience that used chemicals to enhance the overall experience. Most often the choice of drug was crystal. He revealed how he started with crystal and then would also occasionally snort a line of cocaine. He was doing all of this while the two of us were together. This was why he couldn't maintain his erection with me. He had become dependent on the drugs to stimulate him and without them, he couldn't perform. He knew that I wouldn't be into a PNP session, so that's why he'd suggested the threesomes. While I wasn't looking, he'd pop an ecstasy pill to stimulate himself.

"That still doesn't explain why I walked into my house to find you getting fucked by that guy in my bathroom shower."

Taking a swig of his drink, he cleared his throat. I guess he thought I was going to let that go without an explanation. But I needed closure so that I could completely move on.

"Let's just say that things had really gotten bad. I had gotten some cocaine on credit and had fallen behind. I couldn't ask you for the money. So in exchange for an extension, I had to let dude fuck me in the ass."

"I always thought you'd kill a guy if he ever tried to fuck you," I joked.

"No, I'd been fucked before. It was when I was in my first relationship. We both took turns doing one another. But I've never been one to enjoy getting fucked in the ass. I only did it with him because I loved him. Believe me when I say that I've never had a dick that big in my ass. I felt like he was going to split me in two.

"Much love to the kats that don't have a problem taking them Mandingo dicks up in them, but I don't want to take a fart and risk taking a shit because my ass is so worn and loose."

I was expected to be upset, but I had to admit that Trevor's conversation was enlightening. For so long I had been holding such animosity and anger toward him for the way he left, and now I realized that my anger was what was preventing me from moving forward and finding true love.

"So, do you still PNP?"

"Hell to the no! I don't touch any type of narcotics. I almost lost my life and hit rock bottom because of that shit. Now that I've been given another chance, I'm not going to do anything to mess it up."

"So, where are you living now?"

"My job has me on assignment in Charlotte, North Carolina. My contract ends in three months and there's talk about me being assigned to Jacksonville, Florida."

As a male group took to the stage to perform an old Dru Hill cut, "In My Bed," we both sat at the bar in silence. We continued sipping on our drinks as the group put their own stamp on the classic jam from the '90s.

"Kenton, I really am sorry about the things I put you through and the pain that I might have caused you. I really hope that you're able to put it behind you and find someone to make you happy."

"I appreciate you saying that. I'm still single, but I'm at a point now where I can do like you said and let go of the past."

"Why are you single?"

"Because I wouldn't allow myself to fall for anyone like I fell for you. I remained detached in my encounters and wouldn't permit my heart to feel anything for another. I'm man enough to admit that you really put me through some shit. The sad thing is that I did the same thing to so many others. I had several opportunities to break the cycle of pain, but I chose to continue it. Now those hurt individuals will only treat someone else the way that I treated them."

"Wow, it's a never-ending cycle. Well, I hope that after tonight, you'll be able to stop your participation in that cycle of hurt."

"It's funny. I've spent countless hours rehearsing an entire spiel on what I'd say whenever I ran into you, but now I see that all those hours of being upset and angry were a waste of my time. I'm glad that we ran into each other and had the opportunity to clear the air."

"Same here. But what would make this night even more perfect is if we went back to my hotel room, for old time's sake. I'd even give up some ass for you."

I looked at Trevor. Looking into the eyes of the broken and damaged man staring back at me caused no feelings to arise. Pulling from our past, nothing made me want to bed him. I didn't even have the heart or energy to go back to his hotel room and fuck'em and leave'em. I still felt like he owed me some ass, but I was more content with the closure that he'd given me.

"How about we end things on a good note," I countered. "It was really nice seeing you and I'm glad that you've been able to get yourself back on track. Let's leave the past where it belongs. The last thing I want is for us to sleep together and when I don't call you, you'll be the one continuing the cycle."

"I agree about the past. But if we go into it knowing that there'll be no next-day phone calls, emails, or text messages, then there will be no ill-feelings or cycle to continue. Plus, I don't think my wife would like you falling in love with me again."

"Your *wife*?"

"Yes, I'm married and she knows about my past. I'm all about full disclosure and she knows that I occasionally mess with men. We have an open relationship. She sometimes likes messing around with women as well."

"That is really some agreement."

"Well, it's what I call 'new love.' Today, with so many couples not making it and the divorce rates at an all-time high, we've tried to reinvent dating and courting so that we're together and exploring our sexual inhibitions."

"I'm really happy that you've found real love. I wish the both of you continued success and happiness."

"Thanks. It really means a lot."

Standing up from the bar, I left a twenty on the bar top, gave Trevor some dap, and headed toward the exit.

"Hey Kent?"

Turning around, I saw that Trevor was following close behind me, trying to catch up with me.

"W'sup?"

"I need to ask you one last thing."

"Go 'head."

"Will you forgive me?"

CHAPTER 42
Shawna

Oh my God! What the fuck was that? I lay in bed asking myself. The highlight of the show was, in actuality, the letdown. How could a man so fine and with the right-sized tool not be able to complete the job?

When Edrian arrived, I was ecstatic. I had obliged to his request and dressed down. When I opened the door, he also was casual and not overly dressed. In his hand, he had a bottle of wine and a white rose. The gesture was hackneyed but still sweet.

It's nice when a man puts forth some type of effort. The night was off to a smooth start. We spent the majority of the evening getting to know one another. I learned that he was part owner of a company that managed a chain of local gyms. When he was in college, he had married his high school sweetheart and the two of them had a beautiful daughter. Things didn't last, and two years after tying the knot, the two found themselves at each other's throats. After divorcing, the two of them managed to remain the very best of friends. She had remarried, which probably made things a lot easier for him when it came to dealing with her.

We traded stories from our childhood and early dating years. The Cabernet wine was helping us both become more comfortable with one another. The television was on, playing some movie that we had ordered from On Demand, but neither of us was watching it.

I was relieved when he got up the nerve to move closer to me. Sitting on separate ends of the sofa was a little too adolescent for me. I had done everything to show him that I was open to him making a move, but up until that point, he had ignored my hints. I didn't know what else I could do or say to cause things to progress. I laughed at his jokes, placed my hand on his leg, batted my eyes, stuck out my chest whenever I spoke, and did a handful of other so-called tricks; they all went over his head.

Sitting less than a few inches from me, the level of intimacy increased. Reaching for the wine bottle to refresh my drink, he realized that we had drained the bottle. I excused myself to go into the kitchen to get a bottle of sparkling Moscato wine from the refrigerator. Being the gentleman that he was, he took the corkscrew and bottle from me and opened the bottle of wine.

Taking a sip, the bubbles from the wine tickled the back of my throat. I smiled as I watched him swishing the wine back and forth in his mouth. Noticing me watching him, he put down his glass and leaned forward. Our lips connected and our tongues interlocked. I could still taste the sweetness of the lingering alcohol on his tongue. I sucked on his tongue as he wrapped his arms around me and rested them around my waist. With a little pressure, he pulled me closer to him.

The man could kiss. His initial kiss was sweet, soft, and gentle. As I kissed him back, it was as if I had excited him. His kisses—still meticulous, were now more passionate and intense. I moved my hand to the crook of his neck and used the other to place my glass of wine on the floor. Now with my free hand, I gently coaxed him closer to me. Before I knew it, we were both reclined back on the sofa, kissing and groping one another through our clothes.

It was all too sweet and romantic. I felt like I was back in high school, making out with my boyfriend after school before my parents got home. As Edrian grinded on me, I could feel his manhood fighting against the cloth of his jeans. Running my hand down his chest and then below his waist, I gently squeezed his dick. A small groan of appreciation escaped from his throat.

Breaking our kiss, he uttered, "Keep that up and it's going to want to come out and play."

"Is that right?" I coyly asked, slipping from beneath him.

Standing to my feet, I pulled him up and led him to my bedroom. Falling backward on the bed, I propped myself up on my elbows and seductively looked at him. He was truly a male Adonis if there was even such a thing.

"Hold on," he instructed, running back to the living room. He returned with the bottle of Moscato and placed it on the nightstand.

"Take off your shirt," I commanded.

"Bossy, I see. That's kind of hot," he threw back, pulling his shirt over his head.

I sat up and ran my fingers across the width of his chest. His nipples were hard. I toyed with the little patch of chest hair that rested between his pecs before trailing my fingers down his abs. His stomach wasn't solid as a rock, but there was still some definition. This turned me on. It was nice to see that he was into fitness in moderation, but wasn't an obsessive gym rat. From my own experiences, I knew that most gym rats had too much of an "all about me attitude."

Tracing my finger around his belly button, I moved down to the waist of his jeans.

"So what about these? Looks like something wants to be freed," I taunted, pinching his restrained dick.

"Nope, those are staying on until you match me," he countered.

"Are you asking me to take off my shirt?" I smiled up at him.

Our eyes met and he bent down to kiss me. As our lips reconnected, his hands pulled my shirt over my head. Continuing to kiss me, he moved his lips from my mouth and then to my neck. As his tongue flickered across the nape of my neck, I squirmed. That was a very erogenous zone for me. Sensing this, he used one of his hands to wrap around my back and to hold me in place.

"Ohhh, Edrian," I cooed.

Edrian moved from my neck down to my breasts. I still had my bra on, but that didn't stop him from brushing his tongue across the little flesh that was exposed. I leaned back, and my upper body became concave as I pushed my chest forward and my back arched inwardly.

I placed a hand on his hand, letting him know that he was welcome to explore the entirety of my body. Luckily I was wearing a bra with a front clasp. There was nothing like a man with clumsy fingers trying to unhook a woman's bra from the back to kill the mood.

Successfully freeing my breasts, he pulled the straps from my shoulders. Removing my bra, my breasts were his for the taking; without any prodding, he used his hand to bring my left breast to his awaiting mouth. As he serviced my left nipple, he massaged the right breast with his other hand. He switched and repeated the same actions. His tongue and hand switched. He moved his tongue in circular motions and used it to dart at my nipples like he was a cobra sensing its prey. Applying some pressure, he sent electric chills down my spine.

My hand still on his head, I pushed him down to my torso. Taking the hint, he traced his tongue down to my belly button. Deviating, he moved to the sides of my oblique muscles. When his tongue lapped at the bottom of my right oblique where my hipbone was, I jerked. I was ticklish and his actions caused me to want to pull away from him and to also remain where I was.

I moaned as he took joy in my squirming. Taking a break from torturing me, he tugged on the drawstring of the sweatpants I was wearing and pulled them down. Next he removed my panties and my white cotton socks. He moaned out in anticipation as he got a whiff of the juices that were making me moist. Diving in like his last meal was between my legs, he placed my manicured feet over his shoulders as he penetrated me with his tongue.

I gripped the comforter. There was something about the way he worked his tongue that left me writhing. He lapped and sucked until his tongue found my clitoris. This caused me to jump, but with my legs over his shoulders, there wasn't anywhere for me to run to. Continuing to explore the inner depths of me, he found my G-spot area. Now I was groaning, moaning, and whimpering as he pleased me. I was enjoying what he was doing as well as his company. Intimacy with someone where there was mutual chemistry always heightened things.

Moving his tongue in slow circular motions, then darting it in and out, and then slowly using it to tickle me, I was getting lightheaded. My breathing was labored and heavy. Moving his tongue from my vagina, he kissed my inner thighs, then my calves, and finally the heels of my feet. Placing my toes in his mouth, I felt his teeth gently grace my skin, causing my senses to jump. He kissed and sucked on each toe before moving back in the direction that he had originated from.

With his face once again between my legs, it didn't take much before I began squirming and moaning again. Pushing his head deeper and deeper, hearing him slurp up my juices, excited me.

"Oh my gosh…Ed...Ed...Edrian…please don't stop! I'm about to cum! Please don't stop!" My body began to convulse and I continued to grind my pelvis against his face. Pinning me down by wrapping his arms around my thighs, Edrian stayed with me as I rode the wave of ecstasy and climaxed.

As I came down from my moment of elation, Edrian went to

the bathroom to grab some towels. When he returned, he was completely nude. I could see the black condom that sheathed his engorged penis. He was so anxious to get inside me that he didn't even give me the chance to orally pleasure him.

Turning me on my left side, he raised my right leg in the air and sideways, he entered me from the back. Putting the head inside of me, he allowed me to adjust to his girth. I was lubricated from my climax and I began to gyrate and push back until I was completely impaled onto his dick. I loved how he didn't just shove it inside me, and allowed me to slowly take him in.

As I relaxed and he moved his hips in motion to match my thrusts, he suddenly pushed me completely over until I was face down and on my stomach. Edrian's thrusting increased in pace, his balls slapping against my ass, and his grip on my wrist tightened.

"Ugh…oh shit…oh shit! Take this dick! I wanna fill you with my babies."

I pushed back but, to my dismay, things weren't getting started. Things had just ended. Was he serious? What was that? It was only like thirty strokes? He got me halfway up the mountain and was now telling me that the journey was over.

Pulling out of me, he pulled the condom off and went to the bathroom to dispose of it. I lay motionless, still in a state of awe. When Edrian returned, he instructed me to get on all fours and to push my ass in the air. Placing a towel under me, he began to eat me out again.

Now that's what I'm talking about. I thought he was done, but he was capable of multiple nuts. He was taking a break so that he could get it back up. Pulling away from me, he reached to the nightstand and grabbed the bottle of Moscato wine. Tilting the bottle down, he let the wine drizzle between my buttocks and he slurped it up as it reached my vulva.

When the bottle was partially empty, he placed it on the floor and replaced his tongue with his fingers. I reached back until I found his penis. It was limp and shriveled like he had just gotten out of the pool. I was mistaken because there was no way that he was getting it back up.

Now I was irritated. His foreplay game was so on point, but when it came to serving the goods, he couldn't deliver. I realized what I had to do. I had to fake the funk so he would leave me alone and I could go to sleep.

Going into full actress mode, I gyrated my hips and began bucking back and forth. I let some groans escape from my throat and five minutes later, I was informing him that I was having an orgasm and, like most men, he was so self-absorbed thinking he had really put it down that he actually bought it. Good thing the wine had kept me wet.

I rested on my back as Edrian slept next to me. He was snoring lightly and I was counting the spackled dots on the ceiling, hoping that they'd help me to fall asleep. I couldn't go to sleep; I didn't know what to make of things. Edrian seemed like a great guy, the lead up to the sex was off the meters, but the sex I could do without. It wasn't that it was entirely horrible. It's just that as soon as it began it was over.

I convinced myself that it was a first-time fluke. Maybe he was really anxious, causing him to climax sooner than he wanted. This seemed plausible, I told myself. I hated to get rid of what seemed like such a great man because he couldn't lay the pipe like I needed. Persuading myself to believe that this was what happened, I managed to slip into a light sleep.

CHAPTER 43
Anjel

I entered the Havana Bistro Café located in the K-Mart shopping plaza on Orange Blossom Trail and Sand Lake Road. The girls and I were meeting to do a little catching up. I was dressed for the temperamental weather. It was currently in the mid-70s. So I was sporting a pair of capris, sandals with wooden soles, and a cotton short-sleeved shirt.

Waving to the staff, I headed toward the back. My girls were already seated. There was no need to order. I was a regular at the restaurant. The staff knew that I wanted roasted chicken, arroz con frijoles (rice with black beans), and plantains.

"Glad that you could make it," Alexandria said in between bites of her food.

"Always got to be fashionably late," Keri chimed in.

"Hey, what can I say? Traffic was hell. What did I miss?"

"Shit, a lot," Shawna informed me, licking her fingers. "Shauntè, tell her what you just informed us about."

"Lawd! You all act like it's a big deal." Shauntè was stalling.

"Someone tell me what's going on?" I demanded.

"It's nothing. It's just that I've been dating is all."

"Congratulations. Who is he?" The table erupted in laughter. The waitress placed my sweet tea in front of me and I took a sip.

"It isn't a he. Seems like Shauntè decided that she'd see what it was like to play on the other side of the fence and try her hand at a little licky licky," Shawna teased.

I started choking on my tea. Alexandria reached over to pat me on the back. "How? When did this happen?"

"It's nothing serious. At that Valentine's thing we went to, I met this dude. He and I messed around some and one day he asked if I'd participate in a threesome. After a little begging, I decided to give it a try. One thing led to another, and the guy and I called it quits but I continued messing with his homegirl."

"So Shauntè, are you two serious?" I inquired, taking a bite of my plantains.

"We're simply enjoying one another's company. I've done everything but I haven't done enough. I'm not giving up on men; I'm just experiencing all aspects of my sexuality."

The girls and I took turns trading stories about what was going on in our lives. Too bad Noeshi couldn't make it. Her presence was missed. "So, ladies, do any of you want to join me for some shopping?" I put out the invitation.

"I'll pass. I've had enough for the day. My head is still spinning from learning about Shauntè licking on va-jay-jays, Shawna dealing with Mr. One Minute, and you giving the ass up to Mason's old associate," Alexandria stated.

"Look at Miss Goody-Goody. What did you do on *your* date? Did he get the panties?" I asked.

"What? You went on a date and didn't tell us?" the ladies questioned her.

"A lady has to keep a secret to herself; she definitely doesn't kiss and tell." Alexandria tooted her nose in the air, feigning to be a diva.

Trading a few more jokes, we all gave each other hugs and kisses. With a promise to get up at the end of the month, we all left the restaurant to head our separate ways. It was good seeing the ladies and cutting loose without all the drama.

After departing from lunch with my girls, I decided that I needed to do a little relaxing, and the only thing that helped me to relax was to spend some time doing a little shopping. So I headed to The Mall at Millennia on Conroy Road. I was in the mood to go on an all-out shopping spree and to update my wardrobe for the summer months that were coming.

Pulling into the mall, my cell phone began ringing. I danced in my seat to the melodic ringtone of Keri Hilson's "Pretty Girl Rock." It was amazing how I could sound just like Beyoncé whenever I was alone in my car. I didn't need anyone to tell me that I couldn't carry a note to save my life, but that didn't stop me from trying.

Before the phone stopped ringing, I picked it up and took a glance at the display. It was only Inola. I didn't have time to deal with her idiotic rants or threats. I'd let her call roll into my voice mail. I couldn't believe that I'd allowed her to talk me into doing the things that I had done to Mason. There's no telling what the heart is capable of when it's in distress. I was above all the things that I had done, but I had to admit that while doing them I felt a temporary relief.

It made me feel good to know that I was inflicting some type of hurt and pain on Mason. Even if it was only in my head, it made me feel better to think that he'd be just as upset with me as I was with him. The fact that he didn't ever call me out or call the police on me, even when he suspected that it was me, only drove me to continue doing what I was doing. I had talked myself into thinking that his lack of action was a sign that he still had love for me.

The thought of Mason brought about glum feelings. I was still hurt about learning that it was true that he had gotten his fiancée pregnant. I needed to get my ass into the mall as soon as possible before I had a relapse and found myself showing up to his office and acting a straight-up fool. I didn't have the nerve to storm into his office like Angela Bassett did in the movie *Waiting to Exhale*.

That was the movies; if I tried that shit in real life, I'd more than likely find myself behind bars with a restraining order taken out against me. I was upset, but I was also relieved. It took Mason's admission to get me to realize that I needed to really move on with my life. I didn't know when I'd be prepared to give my heart to another, or when I'd be ready to get my ass back in the dating field, but my heart now was being forced to let go.

Like the saying goes: "it was truly his loss." I would've built him up when he felt weak. I would've been faithful and stood by him even when he was wrong—just like I had done so many times before when we were together. I would've been that ideal woman that men talk about with their boys. There wasn't anything that I wasn't willing to do for him, but I now saw that, no matter how hard I tried, or what I did, I couldn't make someone love me unconditionally if they didn't want to.

I owed him an apology for all the shit I was putting him through, but that he wasn't going to get. I'd never be able to forgive him for the bouts with STDs he exposed me to, the way he called it quits, or the way he casually used me to bust a nut after he had called it quits. He flagrantly played with my emotions knowing how much I still cared for him.

The blame didn't just lay with him; it was also on me. No one can make you do something that you don't want to do. I had plenty of opportunities to walk away myself, but I chose to stay because I felt that he'd eventually realize my love was undying. I could've easily stayed off my back and kept my legs closed whenever he came around for a random hookup, but I didn't. I never thought that my pussy was addictive, but I did hope he'd realize no matter how many other women he fucked, he'd never find another one to put it down like me.

Before climbing out of my car, I placed my cell in the center glove compartment and headed into the mall. I needed to pay a visit to my favorite jewelry store, Tiffany & Co. Since I didn't have a man in my life, I'd have to dote on myself and treat myself to some comfort jewelry. Entering the store, I declined any assistance from the floor clerk. I took my time looking through the glass displays. I stopped when a particular ring caught my attention.

I felt melancholy as I stopped in front of the engagement rings. Staring back at me was the engagement ring that Mason had given me. It was part of the Tiffany Legacy collection. The ring had a patented cushion-cut Tiffany diamond. The 2.7 carat diamond was surrounded by bead-set diamonds. I remembered when the sales clerk had told me that the ring was inspired by the Edwardian Period.

I'd half-listened to him telling me that the Edwardian Period was from 1901 to 1910 in the United Kingdom when King Edward VII led the fashionable affluent. The United Kingdom's fashion during this time was influenced by the fashions and arts of mainland Europe. None of this even mattered to me; I just knew that upon first look that I wanted the ring that cost over $12,000.

When the sales clerk revealed the price, Mason had feigned a look of shock. He was doing pretty well at work, but I wasn't sure if it was an expense that he could foot. I remembered leaving the store, feeling dejected. I was calculating how much money I'd be able to pull from my savings to contribute to the cost. The engagement ring was presumed to be the responsibility of the man, but I didn't want any ring. I wanted *that* ring.

Three months after that day, I remembered it like it had happened minutes ago, Mason proposed to me. He went all out for that night. We were celebrating our second-year anniversary as a couple. The whole night was very romantic. We spent the day at Universal Studios and Island of Adventures walking around hand-in-hand. As the sun began to set, we went to dinner and we dined on sushi and Thai food. I tasted an eel roll for the first time. He always took pleasure in getting me to try new things and if it weren't for him, I don't believe I would've thought twice about trying a piece of eel.

After dinner, he treated me to front row seats at the Maxwell BLACKsummers' Night tour. That night Jill Scott was opening up for him. I loved the both of them. When Jill began singing "The Way," Mason excused himself to the restroom. After Jill finished the song, she informed the packed arena that she had a friend that wanted to give a shout-out to his girlfriend. It was at the moment that Mason appeared from the side of the stage; with a mike in his hand, he professed his love for me in front of thousands and asked me to join him on the stage.

When I stepped onto the stage, Mason bent down on one knee—just like they do in all the chick flicks that I loved—and he pulled a Tiffany's blue ring box out of his pocket and asked me if I'd do him the honor of allowing him to love me forever by being his wife. When he opened the ring box, I saw the Tiffany's Legacy ring. The stage lights bounced off of the diamonds. I was so astonished that I almost forgot to tell him that I would marry him. I remember the tears falling from my eyes. Overjoyed was an understatement.

Thinking back to that night made me smile; that's why I couldn't understand why Mason even had the audacity to utter at the club that night that I had pressured him to propose to me. It was him that suggested we stop in the Tiffany's store that day, and it was him that asked me to allow him to plan what we did on our second anniversary.

I still had the ring. I kept it locked in a safe deposit box with my other valuables. Now there was no point in me holding on to a ring that I'd never get the chance to use. I'd have to look into selling it to someone who would be able to use it.

I moved past the ring display and I stopped in front of the necklace display. Twenty minutes later, I was leaving the jewelry store with a white gold necklace and pendant, a silver tennis bracelet, and rose gold 18-carat diamond earrings. I dreaded seeing my credit card statement with the charges, which totaled close to $6,000.

Deciding that I had done enough damage, I headed out of the mall before I saw a pair of stilettos that I had to have. My summer wardrobe would have to wait. As I exited the mall, I took a look up in the sky. It was darkening as the clouds blocked the sun. It looked and smelled like rain. That would've been the perfect weather to go home and curl up in bed with that special one. Nothing fancy, just a laid-back evening where we ordered some delivery Chinese food and sipped on wine.

The single life wasn't for me. As I climbed into my car, I reached into my glove compartment box and pulled out my cell phone to call Bryce. Maybe he'd be free to stop by and spend some time with me. I hated to use him, but I was in desperate need of a cuddle buddy tonight.

Looking at the phone display, I saw that I had seven missed calls and an urgent text. The text and calls were all from Inola. I hit my voicemail indicator and listened as my phone connected. I braced myself for whatever drama Inola was going to bring. Something inside me told me that she was about to ruin my plans of a peaceful and stress-free evening.

CHAPTER 44
Kenton

"So Anjel brought you up to speed on everything that has been happening?" I asked Shawna.

"Yeah, she did. I'm pissed that you had been keeping me out of the loop. We promised not to keep secrets."

"Now, I usually tell you everything, but I thought some stuff she needed to tell you when she was ready," I told my little cousin. "By the way, now that I have your ass on the phone, how did you do on your finals?"

"I actually did better than expected. I walked away with an A and three Bs. It was my worst semester by far, but I'm getting senioritis. I'm lucky if I can get my ass out of bed and make it to class."

"I know the feeling. You're almost done so just stick through it."

"I hear you. So, what's with the text that you sent me the other night?"

"Give me a minute. I need to run to the kitchen and get something to drink," I said as I placed the phone on the sofa.

I headed to the kitchen to fix me a glass of vodka chased with pineapple juice and a splash of cranberry juice. I wanted to make my little cousin wait. She'd hit the roof when I revealed that I had run into Trevor the other night.

As I headed back into the living room, Kai met me at the kitchen door. She wanted a snack. I went into the refrigerator and grabbed the Tupperware that had her sliced apples. Dropping two of them in front of her, I headed back into the living room.

"Hello, Shawna?"

"What the hell took you so long? Unless something has changed, they're now making phones cordless."

I laughed into the phone at Shawna's rant. "I wanted you to wait a little before I dropped this bombshell on you."

I told Shawna about running into Trevor the other night when I was out and about. I told her how he was now married to a woman, and about their open relationship. I closed with the actual events that transpired the night when I walked in on him in my bathroom.

"So how was that? That must've been awkward seeing him out of the blue, but I'm glad that you were able to get some much-needed closure. Maybe you'll be able to date again without the fear of giving your heart to another."

"Let's hope so, but I'm not making any promises. I'm still trying to get Marcel out of my system. It's funny how he and I were only together for such a short time and I'm missing him like he was the one."

"So why haven't you reached out to him?"

"I don't really know; I think I needed to make sure that before I stepped to him, I'm truly ready to give him what he wants. I need to make sure that I'm ready to give my heart to another." I was growing tired of everyone pressuring me to reach out to him. I'd make that leap when I was ready. I didn't need any persuading.

"Have you heard from that crazy guy, Demario?"

"Fuck no! If I see his ass again, I'll probably have to catch a case. I can't believe that fucking punk threw a brick through my window."

"Cuz, don't you think that he had a good reason to do so?"

"Hell no! What the fuck is this? A Jazmine Sullivan video? I'm not down with the breaking windows and shit."

"Then stop breaking these fellas' hearts. I remember there were times when I had to talk your ass out of trying to do the same thing to Trevor."

"I never did thank you for pulling me off Demario. But enough about that; when are you going to tell me about your date with that Edrian guy?"

"With who?"

"Oh, now you have amnesia? I'm talking about the guy you met at Starbucks. Did you break down and give it up the other night?"

"Yeah, I did. I didn't plan to. The vibe was there and we both were feeling it. Shit happens."

"I don't dispute that it does. I'm just puzzled as to why it took you two dates to give him some. Usually, you do a test drive by the end of the first date."

"I was trying something different."

"So, how was it?"

"What do you mean?"

"Don't play with me. I'm asking was it worth the second date."

Shawna let out a deep sigh. "The foreplay was off the chain. He had me pulling at the bed sheets and my toes curling, but the disappointment came when it was time to actually do it."

"What? He was too small?"

"No, he wasn't small at all. He was a good eight inches and as thick as my wrist."

"Okay. So, he didn't know what to do with it?"

"I can't really say. Before I knew it, it was over."

"Ah, I got you. He's a minute man."

"I don't really know. The foreplay was really hot. I'm thinking that he was overly excited."

"You don't sound too convinced. Keep telling yourself that so that you'll begin to believe it." I laughed at my own joke. "This must be karma paying your ass back for teasing me about breaking my dick."

"I'm going to give him another chance. Since that night, he's been sending me 'thinking of you' emails and texts."

"So, what if the second time is a dud, too?"

"I'll have to deal with it when we cross that bridge. I've never had to tell a man that he had a problem with pre-ejaculation. I'm not sure what to do. I'd hate to not give him a chance because of something like that."

"More power to you. I don't have the time or patience to deal with a grown-ass man who can't seal the deal in the bedroom."

"Well, I actually really like him. I think it was the excitement from it being the first time."

"Let me know how that turns out."

I finished catching up with Shawna for a few minutes more before finishing up the phone conversation. I was in the mood to get out in the streets tonight and have a little fun, but I needed to catch up on some projects for work if I wanted to keep my clientele.

Heading into my upstairs office, I felt a buzz on my cell phone. Looking down at the screen, I saw that it was Anjel. I'm sure she wanted to talk about the latest drama in her life and I decided to give her a call a little later when I was headed out to the club.

CHAPTER 45
Shawna

I was glad that Noeshi had invited me out for a night on the town. So much was going on and I needed some time, peace, and relaxation. I couldn't believe that Shauntè was now into bumping pussies, Kenton was having problems getting it up, Edrian was a bedroom disappointment, and now Mason had impregnated some heifer. Anjel was pretending that she was okay with everything, but I'm sure that her façade was only to save face.

I desperately needed this night to get my groove on before I had to help everyone to deal with their problems. When I had returned home from lunch with the girls, there was a notice left on my door for me to stop at the leasing office to pick up a package. I decided that I'd pick up the package before I got inside and settled in.

When I entered the office, the female leasing agents all started teasing me and making jokes. When the property manager emerged with twenty-four white roses in a crystal vase, I saw why I was getting all of this attention. I took the flowers and card back up to my apartment.

There was no need to wonder who I'd made such an impression on. I knew that it was Edrian. Opening the card, my speculation was confirmed.

Dear Shawna,

Thank you for inviting me into your home and spending the evening with me. It was one of the most romantic and intimate evenings that I've experienced in a long time.

I can't wait to see you again.

Sincerely,

Edrian

I was definitely taken aback by Edrian's effort, but I had to admit that I really wasn't looking forward to spending another night with him. My fear of disappointment was still present. No matter how much I tried to convince myself that the sex was something that could be worked on, another part of me was saying that he was too damn old to have to train how to fully pleasure a woman.

Plus, he had already texted me two times and left me three voicemails. Either I had really put it on him two nights ago, or he was a bug-a-boo. I hoped that he wasn't going to turn into one of those fatal attraction-like guys that forced a woman to take out a restraining order, change her number, and to relocate to simply find some security.

I'd leave it to chance. Maybe I'd slip up and give him another chance and maybe I'd put him in the friend zone. I had to admit that the two of us had chemistry out of the bedroom and it'd really be a waste to throw it away for a haphazard night of romance.

Placing the flowers on the kitchen's bar top, I kicked off my shoes and headed to my room. I immediately began undressing. Standing only in my bra and panties, I kicked the rest of my clothes in the corner. I'd pick them up later. One thing I didn't do was to leave my shoes where I left them. Picking them up, I went into my closet and put them back in their place. I was beginning to take immense pride in my growing shoe collection.

Glancing at the clock, I saw that it was only 4 p.m. and I had enough time to get in a good nap before I needed to get up and get ready to hit the streets with Noeshi. As I climbed into my bed, I heard the melodic tone that I had assigned to Anjel emanating from my cell phone. I didn't want to deal with her at the moment. I loved her to death, but a person could only deal with so much drama before you ran them away. If I had to hear her griping about Mason one more time, I'd probably break both my arms and jump off my balcony into the pool below to drown myself.

Settling in under the covers, I let the chill from the air conditioner help ease me into sleep.

I was awakened by someone snoring next to me. When I rolled over, Noeshi was in the bed beside me. She must've used the spare key I had given her to let herself in. I'm glad that she had come by because she had a tendency to take all damn night to get ready whenever we were going out.

Pulling myself out of the bed, I tiptoed in the darkness toward the direction of my kitchen. "Goddamit!" I yelled as the pain resonated through my toe. Noeshi had left a bag in the middle of the walkway.

"Watch your step," Noeshi muttered.

My outburst woke her up. Yawning, she stretched her hands out over her head before pulling herself from my bed.

"When did you get here and invite yourself into my bed?" I asked her, massaging my foot.

"About an hour ago; I knocked on the door and rang the bell, but your ass was in a deep sleep. I used my key to get in. You were doing so much mumbling that I had to put a pillow between us in case you got a little frisky in your sleep," she gibed.

"I know the difference between a clit and a dick. You don't ever have to worry about me doing a one-eighty turn like Shauntè."

"So, she told you, huh?"

"What; you already knew?"

Noeshi chuckled before admitting that she had known. Apparently, Shauntè needed some advice and had gone to Noeshi. No matter what Noeshi believed in or was into, she was the most open-minded and tolerant person that I knew. She could always listen and give a person some constructive and nonjudgmental feedback.

"So, what do you think about it?" I asked.

"It's just a phase. That's one thing about women; they can go back and forth between men and women and society doesn't really judge them. It has something to do with the fact that they aren't physically penetrating each other's orifices with an actual penis."

"But it's okay to penetrate one another with dildos and strap-ons?"

"Apparently, it is. I don't make the guidelines and, to be frank, I could not care less. I say that people should do whatever makes them happy. Plus, strap-ons and dildos are no different than a man pleasuring his woman with a vibrator and toys. There are always loopholes when it comes to lesbianism."

"Interesting," I commented, "So, do you want to shower first or do you mind if I go ahead?"

"You sure you don't want to shower together and conserve water? I can wash your back and you can wash *mine*," Noeshi teased.

"Funny. I'm going to go first and I'll lock the door behind me."

Twenty minutes later, I emerged from the bathroom. The smell of the pomegranate bath wash permeated the room. My head was still wrapped under a towel. I didn't want to risk getting it wet while I was in the shower. I had wrapped a towel around my body and was air-drying. I'd put some moisturizer on before I was completely dry.

"It's all yours," I informed Noeshi.

Noeshi headed toward the bathroom, but as she walked down the hall, she took off her panties and bra, tossed her head back, her hair falling over her shoulders; as she stood before me butt-naked, she blew me a kiss. In retaliation, I threw one of her shoes that she'd left in the middle of the floor, at her. I barely missed her as she escaped into the bathroom giggling. She was such a damn flirt.

There was one thing that I had to give to Noeshi. She was confident with her body and extremely confident in her sexuality. She knew that she liked men and that nothing or no one would change that. She respected all people of different races, backgrounds, and sexual orientations. In the past, she'd even dated a guy that she knew to be bisexual.

As Noeshi showered, I took the time to rub some cucumber and lime shea butter over my body, and then began to style my hair. I'd put the finishing touches on it when I was in my dress. Going to my dresser, I pulled out a crimson red thong and strapless bra set. I planned on wearing a cherry red single drape dress that stopped just shy of my knees. The wide-banded hem that made up the dress hugged my hips just right. I finished the outfit off with a pair of black leather mesh, cut-out, platform Christian Dior sandals. They were the last pair that Kyler had purchased for me. I had never had the opportunity to wear them until now.

As I put the finishing touches on my outfit by adorning it with some jewelry, Noeshi emerged from the bathroom and began to prep herself. She had already blown her hair dry. As she moisturized herself, I began combing out my shoulder-length tresses. I went into the bathroom to use the curling iron to tighten some of the curls and to apply some makeup.

Tonight, I was feeling a little extra. I added some fake eyelashes, some red lipstick that offered some contrast against my medium brown skin tone, and some light blush to bring out the structure of my cheekbones.

When I went back into my room, Noeshi was fully dressed. She was rocking a black mid-thigh dress that was definitely made for the club. The relaxed turtleneck design had a dual cross-over design with open shoulders, and long sleeves. I'm not sure who designed this revealing, but classy dress, but she was rocking the hell out of it. To top it off, she slipped into a pair of silver, open-toe stiletto sandals.

Grabbing clutches from my closet, we both headed downstairs for a night of much needed fun. We were driving separately, in case one of us found something that was worth bringing home for an evening of continued fun.

CHAPTER 46
Anjel

I listened to all of Inola's voicemails before pulling out of the mall's parking lot. In all of her messages, she was telling me to return her calls because it was an urgent matter that she needed to discuss with me.

Backing out of my parking space, I headed out of the mall's parking lot. Using the phone system of my car, I instructed my car's computer to call Inola. After two rings, she answered.

"Where the hell have you been?!" She scowled.

"Inola, I don't have to answer to you or give you an explanation of my whereabouts. What's so urgent that you've been blowing up my phone?"

"You're one disrespectful bitch! You probably were somewhere laying on your back with your legs in the air."

"Inola, I'm about to hang up," I informed her. The last thing I needed was to get into a shouting match with a woman close to her senior years. She wasn't going to continue calling me out of my name.

"You need to come over to Mason's place now!"

"I don't think so. I told you that he's moved on and there's no need for me to pursue him any longer."

"He was attacked last night. I brought him home from the hospital and that tramp of a fiancée is out of town and refuses to return home."

"What? Attacked? What are you talking about?"

"Oh, now I've got your attention, I see."

I was growing impatient with this senile old hag. "Inola, I don't have time for games. Tell me, what's going on, please?" I asked, softening my tone. I needed for her to tell me what exactly had happened and didn't want to risk angering her.

"Like I was saying, he went out last night and someone attacked him and knocked him unconscious. He called me this morning from the hospital, asking me to come and pick him up. The doctor said that he suffered from a mild concussion, a bruised rib, and some minor bruises."

"Inola, I'm sorry to hear that, but I don't think it's a good idea for me to come to his place. It's really not my place when he has a fiancée."

"He asked for you! Why do you think I'm calling? You can at least stop by for a few hours so that I can go home and put together an overnight bag. I've been here all day and he certainly can't be left alone all night by himself."

"Okay, okay. I'm on my way but, Inola, it's only for a few hours. If you don't come back by eight, he'll spend the night alone."

I hung up the phone and dialed Kenton. When he didn't answer, I hung up. I tried Shawna as well. I was hoping that she'd accompany me. I didn't want any drama if his fiancée decided to show up. Shawna didn't answer; I informed her where I was headed and when she got the message to meet me there. I gave her the address so that she could use her GPS system for the directions.

Merging on the ramp for I-4, I headed toward Maitland where Mason lived. It was going to be a forty-five-minute drive or more because of the traffic. Turning on my radio, I listened to the sensuous voice of Trey Songz serenading me. He reminded me of a younger version of R. Kelly in his early days. I couldn't help but to wonder if he'd be a fading trend and if he'd lose his popularity after a few albums. He had such a great voice, but singing about sex on almost every song got really boring. I wished he would stick to songs like "Your Side of the Bed." That song really highlighted his vocals and had a Prince-like vibe to it.

Just as I predicted, not more than ten minutes after I got on the interstate, I was sitting in standstill traffic. I had no patience for sitting in traffic. It was a waste of time that could be spent doing something productive.

I don't know what I expected; it was a Friday afternoon and people were trying to get home so that they could relax before heading out for a night on the town. Thinking about a night on the town brought back memories of Bryce. I really enjoyed spending time with him. He was really a good man; one that I wish I had met before Mason. Now, I was afraid I was too jilted by love to even entertain anything serious.

I was more than grateful that he had shown me what it was like to be wooed by a man. I had forgotten what it was like to feel wanted and desired. I had been so disillusioned by a broken heart that I hadn't entertained any advances from a man.

After an hour of stop-and-go traffic, I was pulling up in front of Mason's home. Hesitating, I slowly reached into the backseat to grab my Tiffany's bag. I wanted to place it in the trunk to ward off any attempts of a break-in. I had spent too much money and hadn't had the chance to call my insurance company to insure the new items.

Once my bag was secured in the trunk of my car, I headed to the front door. I rang the doorbell three times and no one answered. I could hear a car running in the garage. It smelled like exhaust fumes were coming from the closed door. Reasoning that it was probably Inola warming up her car to head to her place, I gave it no further thought. She had the nerve to call me a dumb blonde. Didn't she know that she needed to let the door up so that she wouldn't get carbon monoxide poisoning from the fumes. Pulling out my cell phone, I called Inola.

"Door is open," she softly spoke into the phone. She must've been upstairs with Mason and didn't want to wake him.

Entering the house, all the lights downstairs were off. The curtains were drawn, preventing any light from seeping through them. Walking inside, I turned to close the door, but was roughly pushed forward. I landed on the carpeted floor, burning my skin. The door slammed behind me and the lights were turned on.

"You're one ungrateful tramp. You have no respect for anyone else's time. You took your sweet time getting here, and let's not mention you haven't uttered one thank-you for all that I've done for you," Inola stoically spoke from behind me.

Turning around to address Inola, I scrambled to my knees but she kicked me from behind. I fell back to the floor. "Inola, what's wrong with you?" I shouted.

"Shut up! Shut up! And for the last fucking time, shut up! For months, I've had to listen to you whine and complain about how much you wanted Mason back. I threw you the ball and all you had to do was to run it, but you fumbled and allowed some bitch to sneak in and stop the play."

"What are you talking about?" I didn't know what she was referencing. It sounded like she was talking about playing some type of sport. I had no understanding of sports, or what they had to do with why she was attacking me.

Flipping over onto my back, I faced Inola. Instead of our eyes locking, I was staring into the barrel of a gun. I knew something was off with her crazy ass. I always described her as the evil twin of Annie from *Misery*. I was wrong. That comparison was too good for her. She was an extremely demented and sadistic old hag.

"Inola, what are…you…you…doing," I stammered. I was beginning to perspire and fear had overcome me.

"Get up!" she snarled. Her tone was menacing and full of anger. I don't know what I had done to push her over the edge, but I had to follow her directions if I didn't want her to pull the trigger on the gun in her hand.

Rising to my feet, I stood in front of Inola. I was looking her in the face and could see the coldness in her eyes. As she stared back, it was like I was looking into the eyes of another person. She didn't appear to be the same woman.

"Turn around and go into the kitchen."

I did as I was told. As I entered the kitchen, she turned on the lights behind me. I couldn't stop myself from rushing toward Mason who was seated at the table. His hands were bound behind him, a bandana was tied around his mouth, and his head was slumped down onto the table.

"He's all right. Now get away from him," Inola directed. "Don't you have any manners? Get him a glass of wine." She waved the gun in the direction of the cabinet that contained the wineglasses.

Doing as I was told, I went to the cabinet and opened the door to grab a wineglass. As I pulled the glass out of the cabinet, I felt a sharp pain in the back of my head. Inola had hit me with the butt of the gun. The cold steel was the last thing I felt before I stumbled backward and fell to my knees. My eyes closed and before I lost consciousness, I heard Inola snickering in the background. Then I was out like a burned-out light bulb.

CHAPTER 47
Kenton

I was cruising on the East-West Expressway. Pressing on the accelerator, the engine purred as I reached 75 mph. I had learned the streets and knew where the cops were hiding. Zooming in and out of traffic, I relaxed in my seat. With my left hand on the steering wheel and my right playing with the radio console, I searched for a station that was playing something aesthetically pleasing to my ears. Not finding anything, I steered my truck with my knees as I used my hands to connect my mp3 player to the radio.

With my eyes shifting back and forth between the road and my mp3 player, I scanned though my playlists. I was in the mood to cut loose and unwind. I didn't need to hear anyone singing about their ups and downs with love, their troubles with life, or any of the other depressing things that many singers subjected listeners to. Settling on my dance mix, I hit the play button and the reggae-inspired beats filled the cabin of my truck. Jamaican reggae rapper Sean Paul began rapping over the infectious, hard-hitting beat. Throughout the song, he would switch from English to Patois. I didn't understand half of the things he was saying, but that didn't stop me from bouncing along to the thumping of the bass-line and attempting to mimic the melody of the song.

Slowing my speed as I reached my exit, I fought my way to the far right to get off at the upcoming exit. I was lucky that the club was almost right off of the expressway. It'd be a snap to get back on so that I didn't have to worry about pesky cops bothering me with their random checkpoints. I didn't condone drunk driving, but what they considered to be legally drunk could be obtained after a drink and a half. I'm sure that I wouldn't have any problems. I always tried to wait thirty to forty-five minutes before getting in the car after having a drink. If I could, I'd also drink plenty of water to dilute some of the liquor and try eating something greasy. I wasn't sure if any of this actually worked, but it had kept me out of jail thus far.

Pulling up to the front of the club, I left the keys in the ignition. The club had hired a parking service to valet park patrons' cars. As the young attendant came to my door to hand me a ticket, I requested that he park my ride somewhere safe with a promise to take care of him before I left. With a nod of his head, the asshole jumped behind the wheel of my ride and sped off to the empty parking spaces. I winced at the sound of my tires screeching.

Smoothing out my shirt, I made my way to the small line to go through the security measures that the bouncers subjected everyone to. When it was my turn, the burly bouncer instructed me to hold my arms straight out to my sides and he proceeded to pat me down. For some reason, my pat-down lasted a little longer than everyone else's. When he was done, he looked me in my face and smiled.

Does this fat fuck really think I'll give him the time of the day? I thought to myself. I looked the bouncer up and down. His stomach extended well below his waistline; he had at least a thirty-eight-inch waist, which didn't look too well on a guy who stood 5'7". My standards sometimes could be high, if not outright unobtainable. I was constantly told that I'd never be able to find true love if I didn't learn to lower my standards, but I didn't see why I needed to when I felt that whomever I dated wasn't lowering theirs to be with me. Let's keep it real; they got to wake up with me next to them so why couldn't I wake up to someone that was on my level?

I could spend the entire evening talking about the things I required from someone that was trying to seriously date me. To me, everything wasn't about the physical. There were several qualities that I sought in a potential mate that had to do with their mentality, personality, education, and financial stability.

With time, experience, and age, I was learning that you couldn't spend life fucking everyone that was willing to let you stick your dick inside them. I'd been feeling this way for a long time, long before Marcel ever came into the picture, but the thought of the aftermaths of love gone wrong caused me to run away from commitment with the quickness. Trevor had immensely hurt me, but he wasn't the first and I was sure he wouldn't be the last.

I was getting lonely and needed to find true love. I realized that deep down inside love sometimes involved putting yourself out there and risking the chance of getting hurt. I didn't need a therapist to tell me that the reason why I couldn't maintain an erection was because sex was simply becoming an act for me. It was something to do to pass the time. I didn't need for anyone to tell me that sex for me lacked intimacy. It lacked meaning. It was a quick nut that left me unsatisfied and searching for the next cheap thrill.

Tonight, I wasn't here in the club to find a random piece of ass to bring home. I wanted to let go and have a good time. I could have called up a number of my associates to join me, but I didn't want to be burdened with anyone's issues with love or life. I believed that much of my hesitation about giving myself to another had to do with others sharing their failed love experiences with me. Many times I couldn't stop from wondering why Mason had done Anjel the way he had, why Shawna was going through much of the shit that she was, or why my boy, Roderick, had taken a chance on love to only be burned—literally.

All of them were good people. If they couldn't find love or escape the wraths of love, then how would I be able to do so? It's clear that I needed to surround myself with people who were in healthy relationships.

I made my way to the center of the club where the bar was located. I needed a stiff drink to ease my nerves. Catching the eye of the bartender by flashing a smile, I leaned over the bar and yelled over the music that I wanted Bacardi Select and Coke with a slice of lime. Nodding his head in acknowledgment, he turned his back to me so that he could get the ingredients to make my drink.

When he came back to me, I slapped a ten-dollar bill in his hand. As I turned to leave the bar, I felt a tug on my shirt sleeve. Turning back to the bartender, he reached out his hand and handed me a napkin before moving to assist the next person. Looking down at the napkin, I saw that he had scrawled his name and number on the napkin. He was cute. Actually he was cute as fuck! I'd think about calling him, but I had my reservations about dating someone that worked in a bar. To me, they had too much access to cheat. Their professions were no different than a flight attendant, or as I dubbed them "flight hoe." The opportunity and temptation to cheat was too high for my liking.

Taking a sip of my drink, the warm brown liquid slid down my throat. As was my norm whenever I was in a club alone, I moved to the back of the club. I liked to people watch and enjoy the eye candy. I found a vacant spot, settled in, and posted up against the wall. Taking another sip of my drink, I watched bodies of all shapes, sizes, and builds twisting, gyrating, and grinding along with the music. The speakers were banging out a hip-hop cut by Nicki Minaj.

As the next song blended in, the bodies adjusted to the change in beat. Looking into the crowd, I noticed a familiar face. As the face turned completely in my direction, there was no doubt that I had seen who I thought I'd seen. For the next ten minutes, I watched Marcel smiling and dancing with who appeared to be a new love interest. The two of them danced closely. Grinding their bodies against each other, they exchanged kisses.

I took in the look on Marcel's face. Part of me was a little disappointed that he had moved on and found someone that appeared to make him happy, and another part of me was elated to see that he had managed to elude the cycle of hurt. All I could do was to hope that his new beau realized that he had a good man and wouldn't do like I had done and push him away because of internal insecurities.

I thwarted off advances to dance as I watched Marcel. As I watched him, our eyes connected and he smiled at me. I nodded in his direction in acknowledgment. He momentarily turned his attention to his dance partner and whispered something in his ear. With his attention diverted, I took the opportunity to slip away into the crowd. He was happy and there was no need for us to bring up the past or for me to express that I'd been missing him and that I was sorry about how things had gone down. If he wanted to get in touch with me, my number and email information hadn't changed.

It was good to see him smile again. Tonight would replace the memory of him fighting back the tears as he left my place that dreaded morning. Before exiting the club, I discarded the remnants of my drink in the trashcan. Seeing a twenty-four-hour Krystal burger restaurant located at the next block, I walked down the street to get something to eat and to wait for my slight buzz from the alcohol to pass before I made the trek back to my place.

CHAPTER 48
Shawna

"So, is this the only way that I can get some love from you?" Kyler asked me.

Damn, out of all the places that Orlando had, how the fuck did I haphazardly run into him? Noeshi had ditched me about an hour ago, and I had opted to stay at the club to get my dance on. I didn't need a circle of girls with me to have a good time. I enjoyed my own company and that was exactly what I had done. When asked to dance, I'd dance with a few; when asked to buy me a drink, I'd allow them to spend a few dollars; but when they wanted my number, I'd tell them that I was in a long distance relationship. Of course, for the alpha males this only opened up the door for them to flex and to spit some tired-ass game in my ear.

I didn't want to hear anyone tell me that they could love me better, they could treat me better, or that I wouldn't have to worry about coming home alone to an empty bed. Sometimes men needed to understand that some women actually took commitment seriously. I wasn't some naïve little girl that got star-struck over some tired-ass lines. The only thing that most of these men wanted was to take me home and to bed me. If they had gotten me a week ago, they probably would've gotten the chance, but after spending time with Edrian, I'd come to realize what it was like to actually go out on a date.

Although the sex had been a big disappointment, that didn't overcome the way that I felt when I got the flowers he had delivered. The sex didn't counteract all of the attention that he'd been doting on me. Regardless of how I acted, I loved the text messages and voicemails—in moderation. I needed to sit down and have a serious talk with him. I needed him to understand that I wasn't trying to move into one of those overnight, whirlwind romances. I needed a friend—someone to hang out with and get to know.

I'd been thinking a lot about that night and his underperforming; I came to the conclusion that part of my disappointment might have been attributed to us still being strangers and there being no actual emotional attachment between the two of us. When a person loved another, they took time out to please their partner and to learn their partner. When two strangers got together, it could turn out one of two ways. It could be a hot night of passionate fucking, or it could be a night of passionless sex with each rushing to reach their climax before the other.

"How are you doing, Kyler?" I asked. I hoped he could sense my annoyance in the tone of my voice.

"Damn, after all the time and money I've spent on you, that's all I get? I don't get a hug or a smile?"

"Now why would I want to show you any type of love? You've made it plain that I was nothing but a lavish expense. There was no love between us. You have a fiancée and had no intention of upgrading me from a fuck to being your official woman."

"Shawna, why would I do that? I know you've heard the saying, 'you can't turn a hoe into a housewife.'"

Hoe? Was he really standing in my face and disrespecting me? I never could understand why most men thought that it was okay for them to be promiscuous but whenever a woman acted the same, they were beneath them, or they wanted to refer to them in a derogatory name.

Looking Kyler up and down, I sucked on my tongue and rolled my eyes as I turned my back to him to walk away. Before I could take two steps, I felt his hand tightly gripping my bicep. Standing behind me, he brought his face down to my ear and in a low, menacing tone, he snarled, "Don't you ever turn your fucking back on me when I'm talking to you! Your busted ass still owes me for all the money I've dished out!"

I took a deep breath. I could smell the liquor on his breath. I tried to count to ten to calm myself. I really didn't want to get all hood on his ass but he was making it hard for a woman to maintain her class.

"Hey, Kyler! How you doing, man?" a recognizable voice asked over my shoulder.

Kyler loosened his grip on my arm and turned around to face the voice. "W'sup, Edrian? It's been a long time. How ya been?"

"I'm good. When's the big day?" Edrian pressed, stepping around Kyler and standing to my side.

"It's this fall. We'll be sending out invitations soon."

"Looking forward to it. If you don't mind, I need to steal my girl away from you," Edrian informed him, placing his arm around my waist and leading me away.

Awkward couldn't express how I was feeling at the moment. I was relieved that Edrian had appeared when he had because I was certain to be sitting in the back of a police cruiser. I could only take a person calling me out of my name so many times before I reacted with a fist in their grill. Edrian led me to the patio of the club where the music wasn't as loud as it was indoors and where people were posted around conversing.

"I hope you didn't mind me addressing you as my girl. It looked like you needed a little rescuing."

I was actually relieved that Edrian had stepped in when he had. I felt a pang of guilt that I hadn't taken the time to return any of his calls or to even thank him for the flowers he had sent earlier.

He was turning out to be a good guy—something that I wasn't used to.

I was so used to guys pretending to be one thing, and when it all came down to it, they were no different than any other guy. "I owe you an apology," I began.

"Don't worry about it. I think I know what's going on."

"You do?" Could he know that I was a little standoffish about the sex? Did he know that I was a little worried that he had a problem with pre-ejaculation and wouldn't be able to put it down in the bedroom to my satisfaction?

"Yeah. I jumped the gun the other night. It wasn't my intention to have sex that night, and it didn't help that I was so excited that I didn't last as long. I hope you didn't feel that my intention was to sex you and leave you, or that I'm incapable of going the distance.

"I never told you that I've been celibate for the last two years; that night, all of that built-up sexual anxiety was a little too much for me. I guess all the self-love doesn't compare to the real thing." He raised his left hand to illustrate what he meant by self-love.

I was glad that he had addressed that night. It made things a lot easier. It also helped to explain his lack of stamina. As much as people liked to pretend that sex didn't mean that much, for a highly sexual woman like me, it meant a lot. A relationship where two individuals weren't sexually compatible only led to someone seeking what was missing from someone else. I was never one to step out on my partner and I wasn't going to start now.

Edrian and I parted ways after making plans to get together again, and to take it slow. Exiting the club, I climbed into the car. Retrieving my cell phone, I saw the message indicator blinking. I always left my phone in the car so I didn't have to worry about carrying it around, or like the ghetto broads, sticking it inside my bra. It simply wasn't that serious.

Dialing into my voicemail, I listened to Anjel asking me to meet her at Mason's house because he had been in some type of accident. I don't know why I even bothered putting up with her. She was like an alcoholic that couldn't let go of the bottle. Slamming my phone down in the passenger's seat, I turned the key in the ignition and headed home. I'd call Anjel in the morning to see how things turned out.

Frantically dialing Kenton's number, I waited for him to answer. I had been calling Anjel all morning and she hadn't answered. Her phone rang until it rolled into her voicemail. This wasn't like Anjel. She always had her phone with her, and she rarely missed a call. She conducted most of her business meetings with her phone. I even had stopped by her house.

"Hello..."

"Kenton, have you heard from Anjel?" I rambled, not allowing him to finish his greeting.

"Well, good morning to you, too. No, I haven't spoken to Anjel today. Why?"

I briefly explained to Kenton that she had gone over to Mason's place and was a little worried about his fiancée starting some drama.

"Kenton, can you call her on three-way to see if she'll answer your call?"

Kenton clicked over to dial Anjel's number. He clicked back and I could hear her phone ringing. Just when it appeared that it was going to roll over to her voicemail, someone picked up. The person on the other line didn't say anything, but you could hear them breathing deeply into the receiver.

"Anjel! Anjel, are you okay?" I hysterically yelled into the phone.

"Who the hell is this?" an unfamiliar female voice tenaciously snapped.

"Where's Anjel?" Kenton demanded.

"So, it's the faggot and his slutty cousin. The gates of hell are waiting for both you to enter. Now, stop fucking calling because we're busy!" Then the phone went silent. She had hung up.

Kenton tried to redial the number but it went straight into voicemail. Whoever had answered the phone had turned it off. He tried again with the same results.

"Shawna, are you home?"

"Yes. What do you think we should do?"

"I don't know. I have no idea where Mason lives. If we go to the police, there really isn't much we can say."

"Wait! She left Mason's address in the voicemail she left me. We can put it in the GPS system or MapQuest it."

"Okay, you get the directions and I'm headed over to scoop you up. I should be there in about twenty minutes."

"I'll have the directions by then." My voice wavered as the fear began to overcome me. Mason's fiancée had apparently run into Anjel during her visit and I was worried that something had gone down. Why else would she have answered Anjel's phone?

"Shawna?" Kenton called as I was about to disconnect the call.

"Yes?"

"Don't worry; everything will be okay."

"I hope so, Kent."

Disconnecting the call, I went into my bedroom. I had a bad feeling.

Entering my closet, I counted the number of shoeboxes on the top shelf. Reaching for the sixth box from the right, I pulled the top off of the box and removed the towel that concealed my gun. The steel felt cold to the touch and the automatic pistol felt like it weighed a ton. I had only used it a few times at the firing range. I hated holding it, and the loud bang that erupted whenever the trigger was pulled scared me. Even though I had taken several classes, I still was afraid to use it. But crime was on the rise, and I was a single female living alone. Many nights it had put me at ease just knowing that it was in the apartment.

I checked the barrel to see if it was still loaded. There were bullets in all of the chambers but the first. In order to shoot someone, a person would have to basically pull the trigger twice. This was also for my safety. A lot of people had accidentally shot themselves, and I wasn't trying to be put on that list.

Closing the barrel and putting the safety on, I placed the gun in the small of my back.

"Lord, I hope that Anjel is okay and that we're overreacting," I uttered aloud to the empty room. It had been awhile since I had talked to the Man above. Hopefully, this prayer would miraculously make it to Him.

I looked at the digital clock on my nightstand. I was growing impatient waiting for Kenton to arrive. I didn't know what the plan was, but for the first time in a long time, I felt fear. Not for myself, but for Anjel. I had a real uneasy feeling.

"Shawna," I heard Kenton call as he knocked on the door. He had made it. I rushed to open it and let him in.

"Are you okay?" he asked. He could see the worry etched on my face.

I nodded my head yes.

Turning his back on me, he confidently yelled over his shoulder, "Good. Let's go see who that bitch was that answered Anjel's phone."

CHAPTER 49
Anjel

I struggled to regain consciousness. I could hear Inola yelling in the background. Trying to bring my hand to my head, I realized that I couldn't move. I tried to scream, but there was something in my mouth preventing me. My head was throbbing and I slumped forward until my head hit the table.

Still attempting to come to terms with what had happened, I heard Inola snapping derogatory words from the other room. I wasn't coherent enough to catch her entire conversation. I did manage to hear her calling someone a "faggot" and shouting something about a "slut."

Managing to let out a moan, I forced myself to lift my upper body. While my eyes tried to gain focus, I saw Mason sitting across from me. His mouth was still gagged and his hands were still bound. I noticed that his eyes were glazed over. He looked as if he was trying to communicate something to me, but the sounds he made were inaudible and muffled.

Inola. "It's about time you awoke. I didn't think I hit you that hard."

She came to the table. Her eyes bore down at me. She wore a look of displeasure. Her lips tightened and her forehead had deep furrows. I wasn't sure what was going on. I was still trying to remember why I was in Mason's kitchen. Then I remembered the call I'd received from Inola telling me that Mason was hurt, and that I needed to come by. I recalled entering through the front door, and then everything else became unclear.

Pulling a chair out from the table, she sat down. She looked from me to Mason and then back to me. She seemed to be in deep thought, trying to figure out what her next move should be. Looking into her eyes, I noticed that something was different about her. Her look was menacing and her voice was icy. It was if she was someone else.

Placing the handgun on the table, she pushed away from the table and stood up. Coming toward me, she reached toward my face and I yanked away. I didn't want her anywhere near me, let alone touching me. With both of her hands, she forcibly pulled my head back toward her. Untying the towel from my mouth, she instructed me to keep quiet until she told me otherwise. Looking at the gun on the table, I realized that I had to do what I was told.

Moving toward Mason, she untied the bandanna around his mouth. The two of us remained silent. Inola was running the show; with our hands tied, there was little that the two of us could do. Glancing at the gun on the table, she made sure that we didn't forget that she was in charge. Going back to her chair, she took a seat.

Placing her hands on the table, she crossed them. With the gun within her reach, once again her eyes darted from me to Mason. The room was quiet. The only sound that was heard was our breathing. I was trying not to panic, but a crazed woman sitting less than a yard from me, with a gun inches away from her grasp, made it hard. My breathing quickened. The silence was killing me. I could feel my chest tightening and my breathing becoming labored. I was having a panic attack.

"Calm down! I'm not going to hurt you. Well, not unless you do something stupid. Take a few deep breaths." Inola's voice was now nurturing and calm. It was almost motherly.

"Come on now; control your breathing and try to relax."

Mason said, "Inola, why are we tied up?"

Inola replied, "This was the only way that I could get you guys' attention." The vengeance in her voice now returned. "For months, I've watched you play games with this poor girl. I heard you boasting around the office about your rendezvous with random tricks you met at the club."

She turned toward me. "And you, Anjel, I went out of my way to help you to win Mason back. I gave you all the ammunition you needed, and you failed to complete the job. Somehow, the two of you managed to make a complete mess of things." She looked back at Mason. "Mason, you couldn't keep your dick in your pants and winded up getting that bitch pregnant, but she isn't a problem anymore. I made sure to handle her and that little situation."

Turning toward me, Inola's lips tightened and she looked as if she wanted to strike me. She appeared to be struggling to get her thoughts together. Again, silence filled the room.

"At the moment, I don't really know what to say to you. I can tell you one thing, your mother was very misguided when she named you. There's nothing angelic about you. I can't believe you chose to throw your legs up for a set of pretty eyes and a big dick.

"Yeah, I know you let Bryce climb between your legs. I pray that you used protection. I don't want to have to do away with another bastard child. Now, what to do…what to do?"

Her fingers traced the gun. She seemed to be intrigued by the small piece of metal. "It's funny how something so small can be so powerful."

Mason tried to remain calm as he asked, "Inola, why don't you tell us what this is all about?"

Inola glared at him. "I could've sworn that I instructed the both of you to not speak until I told you to. But since we're all here, we can go ahead and bring things to an end."

"What do you mean, 'to an end'?" I managed to stammer. I didn't know what Inola was thinking or what had caused her to go off of the deep end. This clearly had to be much deeper than my situation with Mason.

"Aw, it looks like someone's found her voice. Where's that snotty tone you usually have? Could it be this?" She picked up the gun and pointed it at my chest. Smiling, she took pleasure in my fear. "See how much power it has?"

Deciding to stall her, I pushed my fear away and baited her. "So you brought us here to kill us?"

Inola glared at the gun and lowered it. "That I haven't decided yet. You see, I believe in the power of love and the two of you were destined to be with one another. I have a sixth sense about these things. That's why I helped you so much, Anjel. I went to great extremes to make sure that you had everything you needed to seal the deal; yet you fell victim to the power of the dick. It just happened to be the wrong dick!"

Mason asked, "Where's Janine?"

Inola. "You know I don't think the baby was yours? She was trying to trap you into marrying her. She's a sneaky one. I thought you were smarter than that, but I guess that's what I get for assuming." After a slight pause, she continued, "Let's just say, Janine's taking a long sleep."

Now I realized why I'd heard a car running and had smelled exhaust coming from the garage when I'd arrived. A tear slid from my eye as I thought about a helpless, pregnant woman breathing in the poisonous fumes. I couldn't stop thinking about the innocent child that didn't deserve any of this.

"Inola, tell me you didn't," I sobbed. "Please, tell me you didn't."

I noticed Mason's eyes misting up. He didn't know whether or not the baby was his or not. I don't know how much he knew, but it wasn't hard to surmise what Inola had meant when she said that Janine was taking a deep sleep.

Inola. "Oh, stop all that whining! She was a problem and I had the solution. I'm so tired of hearing about Janine. Janine this and Janine that. Baby this and baby that. Shut up! Shut up! Shut up! Soon, she'll be a thing of the past, and now we have to decide how to move forward. So, Anjel, I'm thinking we should go for an early winter wedding. What do you think?" Her tone softened.

I looked at Inola. She must've lost her common sense. She had alluded to killing a pregnant woman, and now she wanted to sit and plan a wedding while she held me hostage at gunpoint.

"Inola, Mason and I aren't getting married. We've come to terms and realized that we aren't meant to be together; maybe it's time you do the same."

"No! No! No!" she screamed. Pushing away from the table, the chair fell backward as she stood to her feet. "It isn't over! You two are meant to be together and if it's the last thing I do, I'll make sure that happens. Do you hear me?"

She lurched forward and grabbed the gun from the table. The look in her eyes was wild as she swayed the gun from left to right. She was indecisive about what to do. Whatever her plan was, it was falling apart. She must've thought that by eliminating Janine, Mason and I would rekindle our romance. No matter what we said, no matter how hard we tried to convince her, she couldn't come to terms with realizing that the love that he and I shared had dissipated.

"You're no better than Richard!" she yelled at Mason. Her voice was no longer controlled. Pain was intermixed with her anger.

I sensed her moment of weakness. "Who's Richard?"

She turned her attention and the gun to me. Her voice softened. "Richard was my husband. I gave him everything he asked for. I was the perfect wife to him, but when we found out I couldn't conceive due to medical problems, things changed. He told me that he was no longer in love with me. Doesn't that sound familiar?" she directed over her shoulder in Mason's direction.

"I never will understand why women continue to give and give for a chance of true love, and in a blink of an eye, a man can say they don't love you anymore or question whether they ever did love you. They move on so easily to the next unsuspecting heart to repeat the circle of hurt."

Inola began to sob. Lowering the gun, she paced the room. Something was troubling her, and what had happened between Mason and me had only triggered things. She somehow was reliving her own relationship with her deceased husband. It was if she was enduring the hurt all over again.

"Inola, did Richard die in a car accident like you told me?" I questioned. I needed to stall her while I collected my thoughts.

"He was in an accident and it was one that involved a car," she sneered. "He didn't even see it coming."

Mason made an attempt to placate her. "Inola, you know that what happened between Anjel and me had nothing to do with what Richard did to you."

"Don't try and pacify me. I realized that it's two different situations, but when someone makes a commitment, they must see it through; no matter what. I had to teach Richard that. Our vows stated that we were to be together until death did us part. He didn't realize that, so I made sure that he did."

Mason. "So you were behind the car accident?"

A sinister look appeared on Inola's face. "I did what had to be done. We made a commitment before the state and before the church. It was a lifelong commitment. I made sure that he honored his part.

"I tried to help you, too, Anjel. I tried to help you to have the happiness that I never had. I really tried to help you, but you cursed me. You told me that my efforts were wasted and that you wanted to allow *him* to renege on the promise he made to us!" she spat, jabbing the gun in Mason's direction.

"Us?"

Inola replied, "Don't play with me, girl. You know what I meant. Now, what to do? What to do?"

Mason said, "How about untying us so that we can all discuss this like civilized adults?"

Inola gazed at him with madness in her eyes. "Do I look like a fool? I know what has to be done. Until death do us part?" She raised the gun, her finger on the trigger, and then she hesitated.

I closed my eyes. I refused to witness this. Everyone always talked about how good it felt to be in love. How it made you feel like you were on Cloud Nine. But no one really prepared you about the downsides of being in love. Nobody spoke of the pain and lifetime of hurt that it brought. No one really talked about the damages it brought to the heart, body, and psyche.

Some people successfully were able to shake off the hurt and pain and move on. While others, like Inola, spent their lives being tormented by an empty promise.

I opened my eyes as a large crash came from the other room.

CHAPTER 50
Kenton

I didn't have a game plan, but that wasn't stopping me from speeding down the expressway. I had a feeling that something wasn't right when someone answered Anjel's phone. I wasn't quite sure why she felt compelled to stop by Mason's house. I would be happy when she found the strength to walk away from him for good.

There was no telling what a woman would do to defend what they felt was their own. In this case, I knew that Anjel still cared for Mason, and I'm sure his pregnant fiancée wasn't going to let him go without a fight. The two of them must've met face-to-face and some drama had gone down. This was the only explanation that I could come up with. How else would the woman who answered Anjel's phone know so much about Shawna and me?

There was a time when Shawna and I would hang out with Mason and Anjel. He and I weren't the closest, but we were cordial. Like many black men, he was afraid of being typecast as "gay by association." In casual conversation, he had probably discussed Shawna and me with his new love.

Shawna asked, "Kenton, can you slow the fuck down?"

I had been driving in a daze. My foot pressed down on the accelerator. Looking at the odometer, I was hitting 85 mph when the speed limit was only 65 mph. I was nervous and my adrenaline had me amped at the same time. I heeded Shawna's warning and eased up off of the gas pedal.

To ease the tension, I turned the volume up for the stereo

using the button situated on the steering wheel. The sweet soulful voice of the late Teena Marie serenaded us as she sang about being out on a limb. I hummed along to the tracks. I didn't really know the lyrics, except the chorus.

Shawna asked, "So what's the plan, cuz?"

"I don't have one."

"So, we're just going to drive up to his house and kick in the door?"

"Don't be so dramatic. I'm hoping that we won't need to even go that far. Something about the way that woman spoke to us on the phone and refused to let us speak to Anjel, rubbed me the wrong way."

"Yeah, that whole thing has me unedged."

"You nervous?"

Shawna shrugged. "Just a little bit. I hate going into things and not fully knowing what I'm getting myself into. Plus, I'm hoping that we're overreacting and that Anjel isn't even there."

I glanced down at the directions to ensure that my GPS system was taking me in the right direction. I had muted the sound and was using the map on the display to guide me. Exiting the interstate, I made a right off the exit and traveled for two miles before making another right at the 7-Eleven gas station. According to the printed directions Shawna had brought, we were less than five minutes away from Mason's residence.

I slowed my speed as we looked for Mason's subdivision. When we entered, we used the directions to guide us to his street. Stopping three houses away, I saw Anjel's car parked out front. I took out my cell phone and attempted to dial her number again. Like before, it went straight to her voicemail.

My stomach turned queasy. Her car was out front and some strange woman had answered her cell phone earlier.

"You have your cell phone on you?" I asked Shawna.

"Of course. I never go anywhere without it. Why?"

"Put it on vibrate so the ringer is muffled. I'm going to see if I can find out what's going on by looking into a window, or trying to find an open door. I'll have my Bluetooth on so we can talk. If I tell you to go, I want you to go and not hesitate," I instructed Shawna. My voice wavered and my jaw tightened from tension.

I climbed out of the car, and dialed Shawna's number so we would be connected. She climbed into the driver's seat and behind the wheel of my SUV. I crept down toward Mason's house. I could hear Shawna breathing in my ear through the Bluetooth.

As I approached the house, I could smell exhaust coming from the garage. I relayed this to Shawna. I circled the house, gently tugging at windowsills and turning doorknobs. The house was secured. As I headed back to the front of the house to complete my circle, I could hear voices coming from within. One voice seemed to be elevated and angry.

I stopped at the window where I'd heard the voices coming from and through a small slit in the drapery, I could see Anjel and Mason seated at a table. Hovering above them was an older woman waving a gun back and forth. She seemed upset. I whispered in the phone to Shawna what I was witnessing.

"Shit, Shawna, some bitch is waving a gun at Anjel and Mason. They both appear to be tied up or something; neither of them are moving or trying to get away from her."

Shawna asked, "Who is she?"

"I don't know. She looks too old to be his pregnant fiancée. It could be someone he was screwing around with."

Shawna said, "Kent, I think we should call the police."

"No time. We have to do something now. By the time the police arrive, someone will end up hurt. Oh shit! Shawna, we've got to get in. I think this bitch is about to pull the trigger."

"Shawna? Shawna?" I whispered loudly.

She didn't respond. I could hear her breathing.

Shawna finally spoke, "I'm going to get us inside. Meet me around front and don't be mad at me for what I'm about to do."

As she finished her statement, I heard the screeching of tires. Moments later, I heard the sound of metal crunching and glass breaking in my ear as the house shook. Simultaneously, a gunshot could be heard from inside the house.

I rounded the front of the house and saw that Shawna had driven my SUV through the front of the house. The airbag had deployed and she seemed to be woozy. I squeezed around the truck to make my way inside the house. I wasn't sure what I was going to find, but I had to get my ass inside.

I entered the house and made my way to the room where I had seen Anjel and Mason. Without thinking, I rushed to both of them and began untying Anjel's hands.

"I wouldn't do that if I were you," I heard a voice telling me from behind. I recognized it as the same voice that answered Anjel's phone earlier.

I stopped untying Anjel's hands and turned around to stare into the barrel of a gun. I raised my hands in surrender. I could see a devilish smirk on the strange woman's face. Her outstretched hand holding the gun tensed and I could see that she was pulling the trigger of the handgun.

I closed my eyes and said a quick prayer. A microsecond later, a gunshot interrupted the night. With my hands still in the air, both raised at my shoulders, I heard a body slump to the floor. I opened my eyes.

The strange woman was lying face down with blood spilling around her body. Behind her was Shawna holding an automatic pistol. From a distance, police sirens could be heard.

I raced toward Anjel and untied her. As I struggled with the rope that bound Mason's hands, I heard Shawna sobbing. She remained in the same place, still holding the gun. Tears fell from her eyes like rain falling from the sky. I went to her and embraced her. Easing the gun from her hand, I informed her that everything was going to be all right.

A police car pulled up in the driveway and the three of us rushed outside. I needed them to help untie Mason. As I tried to explain what had happened, another gunshot emanated from within the house.

With guns drawn, the officers entered the house. As they screamed at someone to put their gun down, I hauled Anjel and Shawna away to another police cruiser that had pulled up. With the help of a female officer, the two of them were placed in the back of the cruiser.

As it sped away to safety, I turned back to the house. I needed to know what had happened. I could hear an officer talking into his radio for an ambulance. As I tried to enter the house, an officer stopped me and informed me that it was a crime scene.

They pointed for me to go to the curb, where I waited. Minutes after an ambulance arrived, the strange woman was escorted out on a stretcher with her hands cuffed to the rails as the paramedics treated the gunshot Shawna had inflicted.

I wasn't sure what this meant. I'd heard the gunshot. Mason was still inside the house. No one would tell me what was going on. From bits and pieces of conversations, I heard there was a casualty and the medical examiner needed to be called.

A tear fell from my eye. Anjel was going to be devastated by the news. Turning around, I headed to a police officer and asked if they could arrange for me to be taken to the police station.

As I waited, I did my best to pull myself together. Both Anjel and Shawna were going to need me. It was going to be a long night.

ABOUT THE AUTHOR

Timothy Michael Carson is a Florida native, but currently resides in Atlanta, Georgia with his two German Boxers. *Love's Damage* is his second contribution to the literary world.

When not writing, Timothy is perfecting his skills at Georgia State University. He will complete his undergraduate degree in journalism, with a public relations concentration, and a minor in English in the fall of 2011.

Timothy is also a poet, freelance journalist, and the founder of Ready2Speak Books. He is presently working on his third novel, the follow-up to his literary debut, *When the Truth Lies* (2010), titled *After the Smoke Clears*. To stay current with Timothy, please visit his website at: www.ready2speakbooks.com. Timothy can also be found on Facebook: Timothy Michael Carson-Writer and Twitter: authortmcarson.